UNDER MY SKIN

LAURA DIAMOND

UNDER MY SKIN by Laura Diamond
All rights reserved. Published in the United States of America by Swoon Romance. Swoon Romance and its related logo are registered trademarks of Georgia McBride Media Group, LLC.
No part of this book may be used or reproduced in any manner whatsoever without written permission of the publisher, except in the case of brief quotations embodied in critical articles and reviews.

ISBN: 978-1-944816-98-8
Published by Swoon Romance, Raleigh, NC 27609
Cover design by Hunter Blue

This book is dedicated to those who dare to follow their heart.

"The heart has its reasons which reason knows not."
— Blaise Pascal

UNDER
MY
SKIN

PART ONE

LIFE AND DEATH

Chapter One

Adam

Waiting for someone to die so I can get their heart makes it hard to fake things like happiness, joy, and laughter. Anything my parents and I do—a spontaneous weekend trip to New York City (Mum says she needed a change of scenery), splurging on front row tickets for a concert (because I scored an A+ on the latest English essay), or celebrating yet another round of blood tests by clinking spoons over a hot fudge sundae (fudge is brilliant, there's nothing else to say)—amounts to killing time. The goal of so many seconds' and minutes' silent deaths? A phone call from my heart surgeon saying they've a heart for me.

Every moment I wait is another moment wasted, time lost to a life I shouldn't be living while wishing for a healthy one I'll probably never have.

Thump-thump. Thump-thump.

With a slow exhale, I press a palm to my chest.

"Keep beating," I whisper. "We'll get through this together."

My poor bum ticker is tired, too weakened by the marathon of keeping me alive to make it to the finish line. Unfortunately for me, I'm not sick enough to be prioritized on the transplant list, but I'm too ill to survive much longer on this cocktail of meds. I have to hover one beat away from a fatal arrhythmia before they'll grant me the coveted Level 1 status. Then it's a gamble if they'll find a matching donor.

Odds are I'll die before I graduate high school.

Thump-thump. Thump-thump.

A gust of wind slashes across my body, burrows up my nose, and yanks at my hair. I hook my fingers through the wire fence wrapped around the Empire State Building's observation deck and toggle my lip piercing—two black hoops side by side—with my tongue. Spires top the fencing, curving inward far above everybody's heads to prevent suicides. I wonder what it'd be like to leap off the building's edge. Death would be surprised that I found him before he called on me.

I close my eyes, imagining falling, flying, letting go. The initial rush of it collapses into near panic. My stomach plummets, shooting down fast, and my wobbly heart races, alarmed. I grip the fence links tighter, clenching my jaw.

"Easy now, we're okay," I murmur. How cruel of me to test my heart like this. He can't take it. I should know better.

I force my eyes open, reciting apologies in my head. Below, the city crowds its little island, holding millions of people within its streets, all oblivious to my suffering. Skyscrapers stab at the pale blue horizon and white clouds streak across the sky like scars.

NYC, Manhattan, The Big Apple … it's *so* different from my London. Mum and Dad insisted on coming to the US "for the best care possible for their only son." The little upstate New York town we three Brits invaded boasts having one of the most successful cardiothoracic surgeons in the world. It's also stuffed with quaint New England-y type homes, thick clusters of trees eager to assault me with their pollen, and more cows than people.

That was months ago. Along with my heart's steady decline, we'd crossed a bunch of things off ~~my~~ (my parents') bucket list (for me). Mum and Dad call it progress. I call it pretending. I do my homework, excel at classes, and say "thanks, Doctor" at the end of every check up. Isn't this all going swell?

Sometimes I wonder what I'm doing it for. Then I remind myself Mum and Dad gave up their whole world for me. Being The Good Son is the least I can do for them.

My heart, calmer than before, slows some, then pauses a little too long between beats. I count: one, one-thousand, two, one-thousand, thr—god, it's too long.

I hold my breath for a second, willing my boggy ventricles to contract. They don't.

Time slows. The edges of my vision darken. My chest tightens as if anticipating the stillness of death. A distinct pressure builds in my skull.

My legs weaken. Palm pressed to my breastbone, I drop to my knees and squeeze my eyes shut.

Ba-thump-rump!

A powerful beat explodes in my chest. I exhale sharply to force air out of my lungs. Dizziness swirls before settling into a frothy bubbling.

"Hang on. Don't pass out," I say, shuddering.

My heart rumbles in reply.

Clipped footsteps rush toward me.

"Adam! Are you okay?" Mum kneels next to me, digging her fingers into my shoulders. Her fear hides in the breathlessness of her question. We share the same terror that I'll slump over, dead, at any second. She'd never admit it though. Saying it out loud means it'll happen.

"Peachy." I nod, stuffing down the thought of Paramedics dragging my body to the lift and out of the building on a gurney. Mum would throw herself on top of me, sobbing and wailing. Dad would pry her off me. He'd tuck her in his arms and whisper soft words of encouragement. Things like, "he's not suffering anymore" and "he'll always be with us in spirit."

"What happened?" A naked intensity infuses her voice.

"Nothing. Retying my shoelace," I say, fingers fumbling at my trainers. I bite back the urge to fold into her arms.

Mum tucks a loose strand of hair behind my ear. She hates it this long, but I don't want to cut it. A minor rebellion, along with my lip ring. Her pupils almost entirely eclipse the dark blue of her irises. She manages a half-decent smile, but the line in the middle of her forehead deepens with worry. "Are you sure? Did you have an attack? Any chest pain, shortness of breath, dizziness?"

She whittles off the questions rapid-fire. The

standard rundown, like an automatic diagnostic system check. My cardiologist trained her well.

"*Adam?*" She presses two fingers to my neck, checking my pulse.

I shirk away. "Yes. I mean, no. I'm alright. It wasn't an attack."

She frowns, sitting next to me. We press our backs against the concrete half wall, sights of the city forgotten. She clasps her free hand with mine so tightly that her knuckles turn white. People circle us, some glancing down with annoyance, others simply walking past like it's a normal thing for two people to plop on their bottoms at the top of the Empire State Building.

"It was more of a flutter, really," I say. She deserves some honesty.

Mum nods like she understands, but she doesn't. She can't know what it's like to wonder which heartbeat will be your last or when it'll happen—while you're sleeping, taking a shower, walking to class, climbing a flight of stairs … All she can do is watch.

"I hate this." I tip my head back to stare at the cloudy sky.

"Oh, honey, I know. I hate it too. You're so brave, how you're handling this, you know that right?"

I snort. Standing up to a bully is brave. Bungee jumping is brave. Eating fried cockroaches is brave.

Wondering if today will be my last day is not.

I don't say any of those things to her.

Mum pats my knee and stands up, facing the city, face set with determination. She will be victorious over my failing heart, not because she believes it, but because she *wills* it. Whenever I have a "hiccup," she rushes in, quickly assesses my status, and, if things are okay, resumes life as normal ASAP. *Don't give the sickness too much attention or it'll become a reality,* she says.

Mum takes a cleansing breath, wiping the slate clean of my little scare. "Isn't the view beautiful?"

"It's great," I mumble, rising to my feet.

"Your father is on the other side. Let's go find him." She leads the way, weaving between couples and families. Giggles and excited screeches embrace us. Bleats of car horns, carried by the breeze, add question marks and exclamation points to the general chatter. Sharp stones of energy jostle inside me.

Dad stands at the barrier with his hands in his pockets. His back is to us, but I recognize the trifecta of contrast that is my father—bomber jacket, shaved head, and cowboy boots—something he embraced with abandon when we moved to the US, much to Mum's dismay.

Mum shimmies up to him and molds her body against his side, two halves reunited. The top of her head barely reaches his shoulder. He wraps his arm around her, easy and relaxed like a dangling scarf. They've been together so long that it's a reflex greeting.

This is how they'll be after I die. A solid team, joined by love and affection. High school sweethearts who attended the same university so they could be together.

They'll be fine after I'm gone.

My heart trembles at the thought, then sighs as if accepting the idea. If I die, it'll get a break from working so hard to keep me alive. Not sure if I'm ready for such a permanent solution, though.

I stuff my hands in my leather jacket pockets and

stare down at my trainers. One of the laces has come untied. For real, this time. I stoop over to tie it and while I'm down there, I recuff my dark wash jeans. One flip, two flips. Otherwise, I'd spend the whole time walking on the hems and I can't stand how it feels.

When I'm done, I join Mum and Dad at the fencing. Dad holds up two coins and says, "Want to look through the viewfinder, Lisa?"

"Why not?" Mum says, planting a hand on either side of the viewfinder.

Dad inserts the money. "Your turn after Mum's, alright Adam?"

Mum glances over her shoulder at me, hesitating. I wonder if she wants to turn the magnifier lens on me, into my brain to read my thoughts. I catch her staring at me that way a lot. The broken Rubik's cube she can't fix.

My throat tightens. "Yeah, sure."

Mum peers into the lens, scanning the sights from left to right while Dad narrates. She gasps and coos, all jolly-good-times. It clashes with the look she'd just given me.

I sigh. She wouldn't have to fake happy if she didn't have to worry about me all the time. I'm the weight wrapped around both of their necks, dragging them down.

Yet they carry on. Stiff Brit upper lips and all.

Dad turns around, flashing his own smile-mask at me. It's full of tension, held together by invisible strings running from his nose to his lips. Lines crease his forehead and tug at the corners of his eyes. They weren't there a year ago. "Son, come take a look at this."

I'm not the slightest bit interested in peering through the viewfinder, but I owe Mum and Dad the effort seeing as how they've sacrificed so much for me. The best I can manage is manage a half-smile, hoping Dad doesn't catch on.

Mum steps out of the way.

Dad gives me a geography lesson—there's New Jersey, and Ellis Island where all the immigrants used to be processed, and hey look, the Statue of Liberty, such a lovely gift from France. About thirty seconds into his lecture, the shutter drops with a click.

I straighten. "It shut off."

"That quick? Bollocks." Dad fishes his hand in his pocket. "Hang on a sec."

I shrug. "Nevermind. I hate looking through those things anyway."

He jiggles the coins. "Well maybe your mum wants to use it again. Lisa?"

"Sure, David," she says. The breeze tosses a piece of her tawny, shoulder-length hair into her face. A heavy cloud rolls overhead, casting us in shadow.

Mum catches my frown. Her smile fades.

I don't give her a chance to ask if I'm alright. "I'm going to head to the lobby. Take your time."

"Are you sure?" Mum asks.

I nod. "Yes. You guys have fun."

She narrows her eyes. "Are you alright?"

I drag my fingers through my hair. So much for avoiding the question. "Yes, Mum. I'm fine. It's … "

What is it? Is it that I totally hate how much I've wrecked everything for them, or is it that I'm getting tired of the faking, the bucket list that isn't mine, being away from home (and the friends I've refused to keep in touch with), the constant tension of waiting for the other shoe to drop …

I suck in a breath and shiver from the wind. Without the sun, the previously warm fall day has taken on the frigid chill of winter. "It's too cold up here."

Dad's gaze trips over us and volleys off toward the horizon. He probably thinks I'm a weakling.

Well, I am. Healthy people don't wilt in the cold. Strong, teenage males don't whine about the temperature. Loving sons don't ruin family bonding.

"We won't be long, honey." Mum does the diplomatic thing by honoring my request, but she won't tolerate being up here for long while I make my way downstairs alone. Can't spend too much time without my guardian.

"Don't rush. Really," I say.

On her tippy toes, she pecks my cheek with a quick kiss. "Love you."

"Love you, son," Dad parrots.

I'm not offended. It's a reflex, like how he wraps his arm around Mum whenever they're within reach of one another. I'm just glad he doesn't hug and kiss me like Mum does. "Ditto," I say.

Like a slip of fog, I slink inside and wait for the lift along with a crowd of windblown, ruddy-cheeked tourists. The doors open, spilling out a flood of eager sightseers. I tuck into the left front corner once the folks ahead of me board.

There's really nothing to do in the lobby except stand around awkwardly, trying to stay out of peoples' way, so I wander outside. I stuff my hands in my pockets to protect them from the chill. My knuckles scrape against my cell phone.

Dr. Shaw, my psychiatrist, wants me to check in with her whenever I think about death, even if it's the middle of the night. I don't go so far as to text her at three am, but lately it seems like I'm phoning her all the time. She reassures me that therapy is working. I feel it's making me more obsessive.

I pause next to a potted evergreen, out of the way of the foot traffic. I draw my mobile out of my pocket and select *Dr. Shaw* in the message app.

Thumb hovering over the keyboard, I stare at the blinking cursor. To text or not to text. That is the question. We'll end up discussing the trip during our next session anyway. She'll catch my lack of updating her in real time by pulling out my thoughts word by word. The conversation will invariably end with her asking, "Why didn't you text me when it happened, Adam?"

Best to get it over with now. I type: *I had the thought today.*

I click send.

For a few seconds, I watch the screen, waiting for her to reply. I can't expect her to be right there to answer me. She's probably in session with someone.

A group of students pass by, chattering and laughing, light as bubbles. They halt at the curb to wait for the light to change. They're all wearing NYU sweatshirts and carrying messenger bags or laptops with silkscreen logos about "being green" and "tolerant of diversity." Adventurers embarking on the quest known as Life. What it must be like to have a whole lifetime to look forward to, no dead end staring back at you.

My mobile buzzes.

It's Dr. Shaw. *Tell me the exact thought and context.*

I had a flutter. After, I saw Mum and Dad. Their backs were turned to me and I thought: They'd be happier without me. They'll be fine after I'm dead. I click send and try to ignore the gnawing pit in my stomach. My message seems dramatic now that I've sent it off for her to scrutinize. It was better left unsaid.

A bubble with three dots surfaces at the bottom of my screen. She's typing right now. I suck in a dry, exhaust laden breath.

She replies: *What evidence do you have that they'll be happy?*

That was simple. *They were laughing.*

Your death will be devastating to them.

My heart twinges a bit. Will be? Does she somehow know I won't make it until I find a donor? Maybe the surgeon told her I'm not a candidate. I blink and re-read her statement. No, I'm over-reacting. She's just countering my argument with logic. It's her style to challenge me with the opposite idea so I'll find the reality somewhere between. Still, I'm not ready to admit she's right. Mum and Dad don't need me dragging them down. I text, *Yes, but they'll be alright.*

Of course they will. Life goes on.

Dr. Shaw is unrelenting in her approach. So different from Mum who tries to comfort me with delusional happy thoughts.

Right. And I'm such a burden on them now.

Whatever you think they're sacrificing is nothing compared to how much you mean to them.

I'm tired of waiting for my heart to stop.

Do you want it to stop? You won't suffer anymore.

My chest tightens, trapping air in my lungs. Tears prick my eyes. She's supposed to be talking me off the ledge by convincing me that life is worth fighting for. I sniff and wipe my eyes.

I mutter, "Stop it, Adam. She's sparring with you, to make you think about things from another perspective and to assess if you're strong enough to go through this. It's her job. And it's your job to prove to her that you deserve a new heart and that you've got enough strength to handle it." I glance around, afraid I've made a spectacle of myself by yapping at the plant. No one pays any attention.

My mobile buzzes.

Adam, do you want your heart to stop?

I have to answer her. The truth is, I want out of this life … but I'm terrified of death. *NO. I don't. I want my heart to keep beating for another hundred years … or more.*

I'll see you at our next session and we'll talk more about this. We might need to adjust your meds.

Ugh. I'm sick of swallowing pills. I'm not even sure they're doing anything. Still, I don't want to argue via texting. I already sound irrational enough with all this death talk. *OK.*

Text me if you need to. ~S

The initial meant she'd signed off.

As usual, she's left me more confused than when I started. Here, in the middle of a crowded city sidewalk, I'm on my own, alone, sucked into the quicksand of my jumbled thoughts.

Shaw is always warm and open with Mum and Dad, but when we're alone, her tone trickles with ice and the lines of her slender face sharpen. Her questions become knifelike jabs—straight to my jugular—all under the guise of therapy.

I rake my hand through my hair. Shaw works on the transplant team. She wouldn't blunder or lead me astray and risk my depression worsening—too much is at stake.

Since my mind is spinning on hyper drive, my body trembles with the overflow. I drift toward a coffee shop, lured by the temptation of the bitter brew. As a Brit, I should be craving a nice, classic, *cliché* cup of Earl Gray or English Breakfast tea, but call me a traitor. I don't care. Coffee is better.

I yank open the café's door.

Inside, I take a sniff, savoring the aroma of earthy Arabica beans. A barista scuttles behind the counter working machines I've seen before but have no idea how to use. The abrasive swooshing of the cappuccino maker cuts through the echoing conversations around me.

Mum doesn't want me drinking coffee, soda, and, yes, her beloved tea (unless it's green or even better, white). She's afraid the caffeine will induce tachycardia or make my heart "irritable." It's a word she picked up from my cardiologist.

Irritable. Like my heart has feelings.

The line isn't too long. I could order a decaf, slurp it down, and return to the lobby before Mum and Dad. I need it to take off the chill from the day. Yes. That's it. Besides, it'll take them fifteen to thirty minutes to catch a ride on the lift because of the ridiculous amount of people waiting, so I have time.

I snag a ten dollar bill out of my pocket and file in line behind a guy wearing a tweed jacket. The smell of stale cigarette smoke mixed with cat pee wafts off him. When we get to the counter, the guy orders a small coffee while scrounging through his pockets. He ends up forty cents short.

The cashier recounts the coins in her palm. Her frown deepens. "Sorry, sir. If you can't afford it, you'll have to go."

Mr. Tweed smacks the counter. "Come on, can't you help me out? You overcharge anyway."

"I can't. I'm sorry." The cashier—her nametag reads *Monesha*—furrows her carefully crafted brow in that same sympathetic but helpless expression that Mum gives me. She can't help it that the guy can't pay for his drink.

Mr. Tweed groans. "I was in Vietnam, you know. I served this country. Fought for your freedom. And you can't look past *forty cents*?"

Monesha cups a hand around her mouth and calls, "Thomas? I need some help here."

A tall, skinny man cranes his long neck in her direction. He waves to indicate he's on his way, but three other workers are surrounding him with their own mini-crises.

Monesha is on her own.

Seizing the opportunity, Mr. Tweed leans over the counter. "How about a half a cup?"

Other patrons have caught on that there's a scene.

I step around Mr. Tweed, make eye contact with Monesha, and plop the money on the counter. "I'll pay for his and I'll take a medium decaf light and sweet, please."

Monesha launches into action, clearly relieved I've solved her problem for her. She picks up the money. "That'll be five dollars and thirty two cents."

Mr. Tweed slides his hands off the counter. His

rheumy eyes lock onto mine with gratitude.

I give him a nod. "Thank you for serving your country, sir."

A thick beard obscures his chin. "You British?"

"Yes, I am."

"Ain't it grand how a foreigner respects me more than my own countrymen?" He snags his hand around my wrist. "Bless you."

"No worries."

The loud chatter and whir of machines resumes as we make our way to the pick up area. When I reach for my drink, my sleeve climbs up my forearm a couple inches.

Mr. Tweed taps the medic alert bracelet dangling from my wrist. "What's that for?"

"My heart might stop at any moment." I grip the coffee cup tightly, letting the warmth seep into my fingers.

He chuckles and shows me the bracelet on his wrist. "Mine ain't too good, either. Doc says I'm not supposed to get upset. Sometimes I can't help myself."

"Aren't you worried your heart will stop?" I sip my coffee, wincing as it burns my tongue.

He chugs his, smacks his lips, and shrugs. "I lived my life, son. Besides, not knowing if the Viet Cong's gonna ambush your squad and slit your throat in the middle of the night kind of cures you of the fear of death, you know?"

"Sure," I say, like I understand.

My mobile buzzes. I yank it out of my back pocket. Crap. It's Mum.

Where are you?!

I can picture her stomping around the lobby in

her heels frantically calling my name. She's probably running down a list of scenarios. I've collapsed in the bathroom. I went outside for a breath of fresh air and collapsed on the sidewalk. I collapsed in the middle of the lobby and the ambulance has already hauled me away to the closest hospital.

"Um, I have to leave." I offer my coffee to Mr. Tweed—he accepts it with a grin—and text back: *Outside. On my way*.

"Take it easy, kid." Mr. Tweed raises both coffees at me in a toast.

"Thanks."

I rush—if you could call a slightly fast walk rushing—to the lobby.

Mum's expression when she spots me washes me in a layer of squishy, lung-crushing guilt. She envelops me in a bear hug. "I was worried."

I catch Dad's scowl and lower my gaze. "I'm alright."

"Don't ever do that again." She lets me go to straighten her button down shirt and tuck a flyaway strand of hair behind her ear. Dad settles beside her.

"I'm sorry."

Mum checks her watch. "Well, what an afternoon. So, are my boys hungry?"

Dad hooks his arm through hers. "I'm a bit peckish."

We head outside, Mum and Dad ahead, me in the middle, and all the words we haven't said following behind, shackled to my feet and slowing me down. I screwed up. Mum should've yelled. I'd feel better if she yelled. That would be normal.

Chapter Two

Darby

The party throbs around me, pulsing with the head-crunching beat. Arms flail, hair whirls, and bodies thrash. I ride the wave and let the collective energy take me over. I don't know the Asian kid dancing in front of me, but I like him from the top of his spiked black hair to the tips of his neon green sneakers. The guyliner and painted black nails are the perfect icing to this sweet piece of cake.

He smiles at me. My stomach squirms, screaming with a bad case of the go-for-its. I wrap my arms around his neck and slide my fingers through his hair.

The guy responds by grabbing my waist. Yanking me close, he kills the space between us.

I meld to his lean body, stretching my neck so our mouths are even. His spicy cologne circles me as tight as his arms. It feels like the room has warmed by at least ten degrees. I inhale another breath of him. The room, music, and lights all fade away until it's just him and me, a fire pit ready to ignite.

I lick my lips. His hands slip to my butt as his mouth closes over mine. He tastes like beer, chaos, and good times. I rise to my tip-toes, digging my fingernails into his neck.

He slithers his tongue past my lips. Me-to-the-*ow* he's got a tongue piercing!

I duel with him for the title of Most Passionate Kisser until a strong hand clamps around my shoulder to haul me backward.

I whirl. "Hey!"

It's my twin brother, Daniel. Thinks he's my body guard with his face all hard angles in a scowl. His dark eyes fume. "What are you doing?"

I shrug. "What? I'm having fun."

Guyliner hooks a thumb through his studded belt. "Hey, dude, we were dancing." His voice is gravelly and rough, like his kiss.

Daniel squares off with him. "More like groping."

Guyliner frowns. "What's your problem?"

"You're molesting my sister, that's my problem." He shoves Guyliner.

Guyliner stumbles back a step, cocking a fist. "Hands off."

Daniel matches him. "I should say the same to you."

I wedge between them, plant a palm in each of their chests, and pry them apart a few inches. "Guys, *guys*. Stop it." I throw eye-daggers at Daniel. "I wanted to dance with him."

"He's a scumbag. Treated Mads like crap."

Mads. Madeline. Daniel's secret crush. Ugh. Yuck.

Disgusting. If they ever hooked up, I'd have to disown him. She's way too cheerlead-y bubbly pop-tarty sweet for me. Her bedroom is probably decorated with lace, glitter, sparkly crowns, and pink teddy bears. "So? We're just dancing."

"You were sucking on his tongue like it was a lollipop."

I purse my mouth. "I can handle myself."

He sighs. It's the first crack in his resolve. Oh yeah, he'll go down in a ball of flames by the time this is done. He just doesn't know it yet. "He was all over you."

"And I was all over him." I arch an eyebrow at him.

"Yeah, she was." Guyliner wheezes a laugh. His hand finds my rear end again. His other arm winds around my waist like he owns me.

Uh, I don't think so buddy. I pry myself away from him. "I'm so over this." I storm away from them both, wading through the sweaty crowd toward the door.

"Bitch," Guyliner calls out.

I show him how long my middle finger is.

Outside, crisp air smacks me in the face. It's such a contrast from the sweltering heat inside. I suck in a dry breath. The layer of sweat coating my skin combined with the steady breeze makes me shiver. Jack Frost has moved in early this year.

I prop my back against the brick wall and jam my hands in my jeans pockets. Good old Daniel, always ruining everything. I just wanted to dance. And play tongue war.

The door flies open, hinges screeching in protest. Daniel bursts through and zeroes in on me immediately. The light from the neon sign above the door stains his face a pale red.

"What the hell is wrong with you?" Strands of his dark hair fall into his eyes. He shoves them away with his hand, topping off his frustration with a heavy sigh.

"Excuse me?" I cross my arms and watch a rusted out sedan *a la* 1980 crawl past.

He blocks my line of sight to get my attention. "You don't want to be seen with that guy. People talk, Darbs."

I start walking down the block. "I don't care what people think. Besides, we were only kissing."

"I'm looking out for you."

"Why?"

Daniel matches my pace. "Because you're my sister and I care about you."

"You don't want my reputation to make you look bad." Poor, perfect Daniel. Basketball star, debate team captain, and straight A student with a smile every dentist would envy, Daniel lives in a world of popularity I'll never hope to visit. Must be so hard for him to have a slacker, loser sister like me. I get it. Really, I do. He's afraid people will call me a slut for making out with a stranger on the dance floor. I'm the pimple on his otherwise flawless face.

He exhales as if I've slugged him in the gut. "That's what you think?"

I snort.

He nudges me with his shoulder. "Come on, drop the tough guy act, okay?"

At the corner, I pause, not because he's gotten to me but because I've realized I should've turned left rather than right. The car is parked two blocks in the opposite direction.

I can't deny everybody likes Daniel better and

it's because he's a genuine person. A good guy. Responsible. We're two different people. A fact that gets forgotten because we shared Mom's uterus at the same time. "I can take care of myself."

"You say that, but who picks up the pieces when you come home, crying and wailing because the latest Mr. Guyliner has broken up with you?"

"Did the phrase Guyliner actually fall out of your mouth?"

"Isn't that what you call it?"

"Yeah, but it's funny coming from you." I smirk, trying to suppress a giggle. "I never asked you to 'pick up the pieces.'"

"No, but I always do." He drags a hand through his hair. "The car is the other way, you know."

"I figured that out. That's why I stopped." I grin at him.

He chuckles. "You're an idiot when you get mad."

"Thanks." I punch his bicep. My hand bounces off, ineffective. He's a wall of muscle. "Seriously, though, you could have a lot more fun if you stopped worrying about me all the time."

He tips his head to the sky to stare at the stars. "Hmmm, I'd have so much free time I could pick up another hobby."

"Ha-ha."

We walk toward the car, argument left behind at the corner.

* * *

Mondays suck. Well, pretty much every morning does, but Mondays are the worst. They're the start of the week, the five day marathon filled by a gauntlet of challenges, each one harder than the last. A pop quiz in math, then an essay in history, followed by a science lab—I'm paired with a kid who smells worse than a dumpster in summer—and a finale of reading aloud in English lit. Nothing strikes fear in my heart more than staring at a page of wobbly letters scrambled across a page … unless you ask me to make sense of them all while standing in front of a class of my peers.

I hit the snooze button so many times that I don't have time to shower. After yanking on a pair of paint-stained jeans with holes in the knees and a black cable knit sweater two sizes too big (also with paint stains), I pull my black and blue striped hair in a ponytail, brush my teeth, slap on some mascara and lip gloss, and fly out the door.

Daniel's waiting in his car—a cherry red 1967 Mustang Coupe Dad and he had restored. Dad spends extra time with Daniel on projects like this one. He doesn't do the same with me, but really, how awkward would it be sharing paintbrushes and palettes with Dad?

The answer is very. Extremely. Beyond the ability to imagine awkward.

I heave open the door and slide into the black leather seat, suppressing a shudder at the thought of painting with Dad.

"Thanks for waiting," I mumble, pulling the door shut with a solid *thud*.

"I was about to leave." He turns over the engine. The metal beast grumbles to life.

I click on the seat belt, chipping my neon yellow nail polish on the buckle. "You could've avoided this by waking me up." I have to shout over the horrid sound grumbling from under the car's hood.

He shifts into reverse, laughing. "I thought you could take care of yourself."

I roll my eyes.

"I have double practice after school today, so you might want to take the bus. Unless you occupy yourself with something else." He grabs the travel mug from between his legs and takes a long drink.

"And miss a ride in this pile of bolts? No way." I snatch the mug out of his hand and suck down two gulps before the super sweet taste hits me. I grimace. "Ick, can you say *diabeetus*?"

"Don't hate on the Mustang. She's a classic." He swirls the mug. "And light and sweet is the only way to go."

"Black is better. It's simple."

"It's bitter."

We banter for the rest of the drive, then part ways at the school's main entrance. Our schedules couldn't be more different—I'm in some regular classes with extra breakout sessions with smaller groups during the day because of my special ed-ness—and I'm okay with that. Daniel's pity-stare is hard enough to deal with as it is. Plus, I don't need exhibit A sitting next to me when the teachers compare me to him. I get enough of all that at home. Things like, "Daniel doesn't struggle with this. Why can't you do your homework like Daniel? Why don't you ask for Daniel to help you?"

I stop at my locker to grab my books and notebooks. Six paintbrushes fall out onto the floor as soon as I pull the door open. Of course.

History is my first class and it's with the "regular" kids. Thanks to Daniel, I'm not facing a tardy.

I slip into my seat, mentally preparing to become a vegetable for the next forty-five minutes.

Mr. Watkins sits at his desk in front of the room. He's already scribbled all over the whiteboard. The mess of letters blur together into nonsense. It's too much for my dyslexic brain to unscramble. No matter how much money my parents spend on tutors and gimmick programs, I can't seem to figure out what everyone else sees so easily.

Instead of copying the factoids, I continue the doodle I'd started yesterday in my notebook. My new series is Fire and Ice and want to capture jagged fracture lines in a random, but meaningful way. That's where things get interesting—in the contrast.

Zig-zags cascade along top half of the paper, some thick, some thin, all shooting off from the starting point. Along the bottom are rows of lapping flames. They'd look better with my colored pencils, but they're sitting abandoned in my locker, so I have to highlight and lowlight with shading.

Stephanie Veene bumps into my arm as she brushes past me. My pencil streaks across the page. A dark gray line cuts the flames in half, ruining the whole thing.

"Slut," she says in a fake whisper.

In the next seat over, Madeline Frank, yes, *Mads*, smirks and nods, "Yeah, *slut*." Stephanie's echo. I don't feel bad that Guyliner treated her like crap. I do feel bad that Daniel likes her. He's way better than her.

Stephanie settles in the seat directly behind me, snickering. She's a Varsity Cheerleader and has all the blonde hair and lack of brains to go with it. It would be so satisfying to take a pair of scissors to her French braid.

"Excuse me?" I say.

She purses her perfectly plump lips. "Did you have a good time giving a blow job to that guy at the party?"

"*What?*" I wheeze the question, shock stabbing my chest.

A satisfied smile slithers across her face. "Everyone's talking about how you hooked up with him."

Mads laughs like a hyena. Too bad her red, puffy eyes give away the fact she's cried recently.

I shoot to my feet. "I didn't hook up with anybody you gossip-addicted bitch!"

The entire room freezes. The only sound comes from the ventilation system's mechanical hum. Stephanie stares at me with her eyes wide. Mads clamps her hand over her mouth.

"Miss Fox." Mr. Watkins voice slices the heavy silence. "Starting your nonsense early, I see. Well I'm not tolerating it today. Please report to the Principal's Office."

"She started it," I say, pointing at Stephanie's smug face.

"Miss *Fox*. Don't make me repeat myself."

I gather my stuff, tears stinging my eyes. I clench my jaw. There's no way I'll let myself cry here. Not in front of everyone, especially Stephanie.

Watkins stands. The scrape of his chair grates on my nerves. "Apologize to Miss Veene before you go."

I grip my History book so tight that the binding creaks. "She's a liar."

"I am not," Stephanie sputters.

Mr. Watkins raises a hand to silence us. "I believe you, Miss Veene."

I gape at him. "That's so unfair. You just don't want to piss her off so you don't have to deal with her rich daddy."

His puffy cheeks redden. "Miss Fox. Apologize and go to the office. *Now*."

Ding-dong-ding.

The three tones mark the final bell. For me, it's a death knell.

"Fine." I turn to Stephanie and stare down my nose at her. "I'm sorry you're so pathetic that you get off on bullying people." Then I turn to Watkins. "And I'm sorry you're too thick to see the truth. I'm *not* sorry for standing up for myself." I keep my chin up until I get to the hallway, then nearly collapse to my knees in the hallway.

I really screwed up this time.

Chapter Three

Adam

Mum drives me to school. No school buses for me. Her excuse is that it's on the way to work, but the real reason is she doesn't trust that I'll be okay out of her sight. Quality time has turned into every waking moment time and the pretense of making every moment last has turned into Cardiac Arrhythmia Watch 24/7.

I clutch my well-worn paperback of Mary Shelley's *Frankenstein* close to my heart. The doctor robbed graves, stealing body parts to create his monster. I suppress a shiver. In a way, the transplant surgeon does the same thing by harvesting a donor's organs when they're on the brink of death. If I get prioritized on the list, I'll be waiting for that poor victim to arrive. Then I'll steal his or her heart and with it, their life.

Then I'll be the monster.

Fingers tight around the book, I stare out the window. Light flurries skitter across the windshield, chasing one another in a ceaseless dance. Frankenstein's creation pursued him across Europe, tormenting him. The monster couldn't handle his existence; he resented Frankenstein's gift of resurrection. I wonder, will I resent my new life? Will having another person's heart locked inside my ribcage change who I am?

I release a shaky breath.

The car jerks to a stop at the stoplight.

"Are you alright?" Mum asks.

Reality crashes around me. The car gently vibrates as it idles. Suffocating heat blasts out of the vents. I'm not alright. I haven't been alright for a long time. But if I say so, Mum will have me at the doctor's office in a heartbeat. Or in the very least, she'll call Shaw for an emergency session.

I shove the dial closed to shut off the dry air blowing on my face. "Yes, I'm fine. I was just thinking."

"About what?"

I'm afraid I'll become a monster. "Um, nothing."

"As long as you're feeling okay." The statement hangs in the air between us like a cloud of Sarin gas.

"I'd tell you if something was wrong."

"I trust you."

I nod. She means it, but I don't believe her. She wouldn't have to keep tabs on me all the time otherwise.

She reaches over to brush back my shaggy hair. "You need a haircut. I'll make an appointment for this weekend. We can catch a movie after, and maybe get some fish and chips."

"I don't want a haircut." I turn away, cringing at how whiny I sound.

There's a long pause, then a soft, "Oh."

My stomach twists. "Sorry. I just … I feel smothered sometimes."

She pinches her lips into a thin line. "Smothered. Because I want to take you to a movie?"

"That didn't come out right. What I mean is—"

"No, that's what you meant."

"*Mum.*"

She grips the steering wheel so tight that her knuckles turn white. "I hope you know that I love you very much and if something happens when I'm not watching, I could never forgive myself."

"I know. But whatever will happen will happen—"

"Not on my watch."

"You can't stop my heart from giving out."

"You bloody well better believe I can."

The light turns green. Mum slams her foot onto the accelerator. The car jerks forward.

Five minutes later, we arrive at the high school, both of us fuming like the exhaust pipes on the school buses stuffing the driveway. Students scurry about, a mindless colony of ants scrambling to prepare for the day.

I tuck *Frankenstein* away and grab the strap of my backpack.

"Wait a minute." Mum grabs her purse from the back seat. She frets with a loose string on the strap.

My fingers grip the door handle. "Mum?"

After sucking in a deep breath, she opens the clasp. Slowly, she pulls out a pill bottle.

"What's that?"

She reads the label. "Ziprasidone. Doctor Shaw prescribed this for you last week. She said I'd know the right time to talk to you about it."

My throat goes dry. Changing meds had been part of Shaw's plan all along. She must think I'm getting worse. "Why didn't she say anything to me?"

"She doesn't want to give the impression of being a pill pusher. You are doing therapy and she doesn't want you to associate medication as the go-to solution for everything. She said it clouded the therapeutic relationship."

My eyes cross at the psychobabble. "Hiding things from me isn't okay."

Mum tips her head to the side. "She said you might challenge this."

"She gave *you* control over medications I put in *my* body." Inside, I'm shaking. I clench my fists.

Mum uncaps the bottle and shakes a tablet into her palm. "We're all on the same team, Adam. This is supposed to work with your anti-depressant to make it more effective. Doctor Shaw said it will also help keep you calm so your heart won't be as stressed. You've been acting more upset lately and after what happened in the city … "

"More upset?" My voice cracks, something it hasn't done since I hit puberty.

"Adam, you don't do anything, talk to anyone, or have any fun. You've cut off everyone from home, and—"

"My heart is dying," I interrupt.

"You're still alive."

"For how long?" I mumble.

Mum's eye twitches. "This isn't the time to give up."

I cross my arms and squint at the dashboard. "I'm not taking any more pills."

Mum plucks her water bottle from the center console. "And I'm not taking no for an answer."

I close my eyes, trying desperately to control the bubbling frustration threatening to burst out. "I don't need it. I'm calm." I say it slowly.

"I can tell you're upset. Your hands are shaking and your ears and face are red."

I open my eyes.

She extends her arm so her hand is practically under my nose. The tiny white pill in her palm sits there, waiting.

My stomach gurgles, churning as if I'd already swallowed the tablet. "A pill won't fix me ... or my heart."

"I think it's a good idea." Mum's hand trembles, like her voice.

I suck on my lip ring.

"Just try it."

"If I say no?"

"Doctor Shaw can fit us in anytime."

In other words, I have no choice. I plop it on my tongue, then wash it down with two swigs of water.

"Thank you, Adam," Mum says softly. She insists on giving me a kiss and makes me go through two rounds of, "I love you."

"I'm going to be late." I open the door, letting in an arctic draft.

"Go on, then. See you after school. Oh, and make sure you eat some breakfast—the medicine works better if you've eaten."

"Alright."

I make my way inside as fast as the slogging crowd and my heart will let me. A part of the group, but also alone. There's ten minutes left of breakfast, so I grab a bagel from the cafeteria. Like Mum wanted, I'm fortified with food and psychiatric medication. Ready to face the day.

My homeroom is across the building on the second level. At the lift, I press the up button and wait. The usual wheelchair kids—a grand total of two—aren't around. Good. No awkward stares and waves and hellos. They know my heart won't tolerate exercise, but it's still weird since I've got two working legs and all and they, well, don't.

The janitor pops out of the nearby maintenance room. He props a sign against the lift's door, then jerks his head in my direction. "Elevator's out of service."

Bollocks. I scuff my heels to the staircase. All I have to do is go slow. I hover at the handrail as precious seconds tick by.

The football team streams past me, dressed in their jerseys. One player—I think his name is Daniel—smacks into my shoulder. "Hey, sorry man."

"No worries," I say.

He pauses long enough to clap my back with a warm palm, then continues on. He jogs up the stairs so easily. My heart whines at me in the form of jerky beats. Flashes of New York blink at me.

The first warning bell rings. I slide along the wall away from the stairs, hanging onto the handrail. I'll wait for everyone else to get to class so I can take my time climbing the stairs without anyone watching. If I'm late, I'll tell the teacher about the lift. A legit excuse.

The hallway clears. I'm alone.

My palm sweats from holding the railing. *Come on, Adam, buck up. One step at a time.*

"Well, heart, let's do this." I take a couple breaths

and march up the stairs. I count each step, one through ten, pausing at each one. At the landing, I take a break. When my heart has managed some semblance of regularity, I ascend the final ten.

I'm panting at the top, victorious, despite my slow motion climb. It seems I've scaled the equivalent of Mt. Everest with the way my legs wobble and my head bobs like a helium balloon. A sharp tightness jabs my breastbone. A barb streaks toward my shoulder and another toward my jaw. My heart is wielding a sword and is attacking me. I drop to my knees. A layer of sweat slicks my hot skin.

I press my forehead to the wall. It's cool, soothing. "Don't stop beating, now. It's okay, really. I won't make you go up any more stairs."

My stomach churns the pill I swallowed. The medicine is supposed to keep me calmer. What if it's doing the opposite?

I shake my head. It's just a pill and it can't possibly affect me that quickly.

The second warning bell rings. I'm officially late. A funny thing to worry about, considering my heart is killing me.

Mercifully, the tightness in my chest begins to lessen.

My heart has forgiven me.

I sigh with relief. Soon enough, I can stand relatively straight. Using the wall for support, I stumble to Ms. Engel's classroom. I wipe the bits of sweat off my forehead, turn the knob, and slip inside as quietly as possible. Of course, the entire class turns to stare at me.

I halt, caught in the threshold. Anxiety ping-pongs between my sternum and backbone. A fresh layer of sweat pickles my face and body. The edges of my vision start to darken. Oh bloody hell.

I dash to my seat—thankfully, it's directly in front of me—and sit down, lowering my head to the desk. If I keep my head and heart level, maybe the swirling will go away.

"Adam, you're late. Please explain yourself," Ms. Engels asks.

Without lifting my head, I say, "The lift was out of service."

Snickers ripple through the room.

"Quiet, class." Ms. Engels' tone carries a warning. "Adam, do you need to go to the nurse?" It's the follow up question of doom.

More snerks and giggles cascade through the students.

I lift my head. The swirling worsens. "N-no."

"Alright." Ms. Engels starts roll call.

My pulse rushes in my ears, almost drowning out her voice, and the darkness at the edges of my vision spreads. That awful slipperiness of a wonky beat slithers in my chest. It's followed by the dreadful pause.

I count. One-one thousand, two-one thousand, three—

When Ms. Engels says my name, I slump to the floor.

* * *

Someone's calling to me. It sounds distant at first, but seems closer each time as I claw my way out of the freezing pit of unconsciousness. "Wake up, Adam. Can you hear me? *Adam*."

I try to answer, but a mumbled groan comes out instead.

"He's awake." Whoever it is has a masculine voice. He presses a palm on my shoulder. "Look at me, Adam."

I open my eyes to slits. "Whaflumblemed?"

The guy leans closer, turning his ear to my mouth. "Say that again."

I clear my throat and wince. It's like sandpaper is rubbing against my vocal cords. "What … happened … to … me?"

"Looks like your heart tripped out on you. How often does that happen?"

I don't answer.

The guy draws my eyelid open and shines a light in my eye.

I turn my face away. "Ow."

He gently directs my head straight. "Gotta check your pupils."

While he's assaulting me with a penlight, I wiggle my fingers and bend my knees to see if I still have control over my body. Someone else grabs my ankles. They ease my legs down.

"Lay still. We're here to help you." It's a woman's voice this time. She must be holding my legs.

"I'm fine." It's true. My heart doesn't hurt anymore. I clumsily swat at whatever's in my nose.

Principal Shepherd stands behind Ms. Engels, astute and somber as always. Ms. Engels cups my hand in hers. They're sweaty, like mine. "You're okay, Adam."

I pull away, stomach twisting. I can't handle her pity.

"Keep the oxygen on until we get you to the hospital." The male EMT gives me the I'm-a-professional-so-you-have-nothing-to-worry-about smile. I've seen it a million times. It's not to be trusted. People smile to hide the truth. I'm going to die. I'm just waiting for it to happen. Every second of every day.

Ms. Engels wipes her hands on her skirt.

Principal Shepherd says, "I had the secretary call your Mom. She'll meet you at the ER."

"She's going to freak out." Especially after our non-argument argument about me being fine. She'll never believe me when I say I'm okay again.

The EMT says, "Let's get him on the gurney, then we can load him on the ambulance."

"The lift is out," I say.

"Lift?"

"Elevator."

He cocks an eyebrow.

"I'm English."

He chuckles. "No problem. We'll get you out. Roll on your side." He places a backboard next to me and angles it, ready to wedge it under me.

"I can get on the gurney myself."

"Stubborn one, eh?"

With a resigned sigh, I roll to my side so he can put the backboard in place. Then I cross my arms and rest my hands on my stomach so the team can scoot me on the gurney.

"You're a pro," the EMT says.

"I've done this before." I scan the room while he

and his partner connect the safety straps. It's empty. Ms. Engels must've cleared the students out while I was unconscious. What a sight I must've been, sprawled on the floor, pale and sweaty.

Now that the EMTs are jostling me around, a dull throbbing in my head escalates to a sharp drumming in time with my heartbeat.

"My head hurts," I grumble.

"Bet it does. You whacked your skull on the ground when you passed out." Ms. Engels tucks a loose strand into her bun. Her hands shake. "I've never seen anyone go down that fast. I wished you'd have said something." She glances at Principal Shepherd, then gives me a small smile. *Chin up, you'll be fine*, it says. Too bad the wideness of her eyes says something else.

The entire class crowds the hallway. Despite Ms. Engels and Principal Shepherd urging them to move toward the opposite end of the hall, they linger, gazes locked on me. I want to scream at them to stop staring, but I'd just look like a lunatic.

The EMTs load me on the ambulance. We arrive at the hospital ten minutes later. Inside, a nurse is waiting to direct us to an exam room. A perk about having heart condition: you get to jump to the front of the line, no waiting.

Mum's at the nurse's station. I'd like to ask her how she beat an ambulance. She's bundled up in a thick, puffy coat, gloves, and a scarf. She bounces from one foot to the other, her knee-high boots clicking with each step. "*Adam.*"

"Mum." I sound weaker than I like.

She rushes to my side and clamps a hand over mine. "What happened? Tell me everything."

I give her the run down while the nurse wraps a blood pressure cuff around my arm and an aide fixes an ID bracelet around my wrist—the broken lift, taking the stairs, and passing out in class. Mum's face collapses with every word.

"You shouldn't have taken the stairs, especially after what happened this weekend." She brushes my hair with her fingers like she did this morning. With each swipe, layers of stress peeled off her face until she returns to the serene, Buddha-esque complacency she wears during a crisis.

"I had to get to class."

"You should've gone to the main office and explained the situation to the Principal, or even the school nurse. They'd have excused you."

It's a rational, logical solution. I retreat into silence while the nurse interviews Mum for my medical history and again for the ER doctor. The doctor tries to talk to me, but Mum interrupts if I don't answer quickly or thoroughly enough. The phlebotomist takes blood work, a tech hooks me up to an EKG machine, and even a neurologist does her thing checking reflexes and whatever, all thanks to me hitting my noggin.

After they're all done, Mum says, "I'm going to step outside and call your father to let him know what's going on."

"Tell him not to come."

Her brow furrows. "Why not?"

"There's nothing for him to do here."

She sighs. "Oh, alright. I'll talk him into staying at work. For now."

An hour later, the surgeon, Dr. Jervis, shows up. He wouldn't be here if this was some routine, unimportant jerkiness of my heart. Jervis carries a clipboard all official-like and clears his throat. His bald head shines in the fluorescent light.

Mum rises from the plastic chair in the corner—about two feet away—and grips my hand. I just stare at my feet.

Dr. Jervis walks to the opposite side of my bed and says, "Your heart is in an unstable rhythm and your cardiac enzymes are elevated. It may have been from the extra stress this morning or it could be a continued deterioration of your condition. At this point, you're not stable enough to go home so I'm recommending you be admitted for continuous cardiac monitoring. We'll connect you to telemetry and have you moved to the cardiac floor."

The words tunnel into my ears, down my throat, and knot around my heart. I can't stay here, tethered to wires and IVs, surrounded by sterile walls and the bitter antiseptic smell. Nope. Nada. No way. I breathe faster, shaking my head. "I'm going home."

He scratches his cheek with the end of his pen. "I'm sorry, but that's not an option right now."

"I can wear the monitor thingy at home."

Dr. Jervis scribbles something on his papers. "The cardiac nurses are better trained in managing your condition, and I think you're ill enough now to be prioritized on the list."

"You say it like it's a good thing."

"It is. It's one step closer to getting better."

One step closer to death, more like. "How long am I going to be here?" I ask.

He clicks his pen. "It's hard to say."

"That's not an answer."

"*Adam*." Mom clamps a hand over my wrist.

"It depends on when a donor comes up. I know it's hard. With any luck, it'll be over soon." Dr. Jervis gives a quick nod.

A steady ringing grows in my ears. Dr. Shaw has been so diligent in assessing my thoughts about death and ensuring I'm not suicidal. Little did she know, my heart was making the decision on its own, regardless of anyone's input—not Mum's, not Dr. Shaw's, and not mine.

"The good news is, with you in the hospital we'll be able to get you directly to the OR when a heart is available." Dr. Jervis's upbeat tone frays my nerves. Slicing and dicing is what a surgeon lives for. Dr. Frankenstein had the same optimism ... until he created his demise in the form of a reanimated corpse.

Mum shakes the doctor's hand with both of hers. "Oh, that is good news. Thank you, doctor."

I grit my teeth. Being at the top of the list means two things: 1) There's no going back from here, and 2) I get first dibs on a heart, but that's only if I stay alive long enough for a matching donor to come along.

Chapter Four

Darby

The secretary frowns when I walk into the office. She has the phone pressed to her ear. Her lipstick travels well past the edges of her lips. "An ambulance? For what?" she says to the caller. Her voice is rough from years of smoking. Her face looks like used tissue paper—thin, wrinkled, and ready to tear at the slightest touch. White dots of spit cling to both corners of her mouth. If I painted a picture of her face, I'd use a black Sharpie for the lines and mix sand in taupe paint to create texture for her skin.

A high-pitched yelling spurts out of the receiver.

The secretary holds the phone away from her ear. "Ms. Engels, calm down. I'll call 911." She switches phone lines, fingers flying over the buttons in a blur. Her eyes dart to me while the line rings.

"Mr. Watkins sent me here." I keep it short and sweet.

She points to a bench. "Sit there."

I sit and drop my backpack to the floor. "How long do I have to wait?"

Ignoring me, she rattles off information into the phone. Some kid collapsed in his homeroom class. As soon as she finishes giving the school's address, she calls Principal Shepherd. "I called an ambulance for a student … and Darby Fox is here."

Shepherd pops out of the hallway before the secretary has time to set the phone down. She catches sight of me and says, "Oh, Darby. There's an emergency. You'll have to wait."

I stand. "I can come back later."

"Don't you dare go anywhere." She points a finger at me.

"If someone's dying, you don't need to worry about me."

"Sit. Down."

Half an hour and a bustle of EMTs, gurneys, and gawkers later, I follow Shepherd into her office. I know this monotone room well. It's all order and ninety degree angles. Like her tan suit, the Oriental rug has boring muted colors. Two streamlined leather chairs face the desk squarely. The informational pamphlets about drugs and safe sex are organized just so on the table between the chairs.

On her spotless desk sits my school file centered perfectly on her ink blotter. It's thick and frayed at the edges from so much use.

Shepherd sits in a high-backed leather chair, her spine as straight as the rest of the room. Her hair is a bit out of place. It's the only sign she's been ruffled by what happened.

She rests her gaze on me. "Miss Fox. What brings you here today?"

"Is that kid all right?"

"He's fine. No need to worry. Please answer my question."

The woman is impossible to distract, even when one of her students gets hauled off in an ambulance.

I shrug. "Stephanie Veene called me a slut."

Principal Shepherd tents her fingers. "And … ?"

"If Mr. Watkins would've listened, she'd be sitting in this seat right now." I slouch to offset her stiffness and focus on the window behind her head. The blinds are open. Sunlight glints off the windshields of the parked cars outside, creating a halo around Principal Shepherd's head. Someone as goody-goody, follow-all-the-rules as her would never understand a screw up like me.

"Perhaps I should call them both in."

"Stephanie will just talk her way out of it like usual and Watkins will back her up."

"There are two sides to every story." She swivels in her chair a couple inches, reaches for the blind wand and twists it, shutting out the glare. "And Mr. Watkins had to make a judgment call."

"His *judgment* is wrong."

"How so?"

I bite my tongue, kicking myself for blabbing. Daniel would say I have to pick my battles. I do. Every single one.

"Hmm?" Shepherd doesn't let her question slide.

"He completely ignored what Stephanie did."

"You're the one who ended up here and she didn't."

"Exactly! Totally unfair."

She nods, but her lips purse a bit. "I still haven't heard your role in the incident."

"I defended myself."

"What did you do?"

"I called her a bitch."

"And ... ?"

"There's no *and*."

She purses her lips. "You can't fight back."

My leg jitters, like my thoughts. "Am I just supposed to let her get away with it?"

"The reality of your situation, Darby, is that you keep getting into altercations with other students and—"

"*She* started it."

"*And* this behavior cannot be tolerated." Shepherd opens my file and fingers through the layers of pages, each one neatly cataloguing every misstep I've made since I set foot in this school. A three inch stack of evidence proving I'm a liar.

I pick some paint on my jeans with a fingernail. "All I did was call her on her crap."

She arches a brow. I wonder if she's ever had a wild side. It's doubtful. "You can't keep doing this, Darby."

"I had no other choice."

"There's always another choice."

"You don't understand."

"Explain it so I can." She continues to flip through my file, shuffling detention slips, letters to my parents, suspension orders.

"She wouldn't have stopped."

"Stephanie has a less than desirable habit of provoking others."

I'm stunned into silence. My jaw drops and everything.

"Wouldn't you agree?" Her dark eyes spark with what I guess is curiosity. Maybe she really wants to know what I'm thinking.

Or she could be baiting me.

I twist a lock of hair around my finger until I can feel my pulse. "Dunno."

She sighs. I bet she's tired from the sheer magnitude of how many times we've had this conversation, whether it's about a shouting match I've had with another student, or the number of classes I've skipped during the week, or the one time I egged a teacher's car. Repeat: One. Time. "Regardless, the actions of others should not dictate our own."

I can't suppress rolling my eyes. "How would you handle someone calling you a slut?"

"I'm sure it was hurtful, but returning hurt for hurt doesn't help."

I stuff my hands in my pockets. "Whatever."

She props her elbows on the desk. "I'll let you off with a warning today, but I will be sending an email to your parents."

I stand. "Fine."

She rises from her chair. "Darby, I wish you'd give up this attitude. You're a bright girl and have a lot of potential. If you put as much energy into your art as you do getting into trouble, you'd go far."

"Uh-huh." I head toward to the door. She has no idea how much energy I put into painting. I give my whole soul to it. Mostly every waking moment is taken up with it. People have no idea. They just see bad-girl Darby who's too stupid to get over her dyslexia.

"I'll be keeping an eye on you."

She's not the only one.

* * *

After school, I take Daniel's advice and ride the bus home. I don't want to take the chance he's heard about my trip to the Principal's office. Sometimes his lectures are worse than Mom and Dad's.

As soon as I arrive home, I set up a study session on the kitchen island, creating an altar made up of a notebook, my English textbook, a couple of pens, and a dictionary. All so Mom can see that I really am trying. I need to earn brownie points any way I can to buffer against Shepherd's email.

At first, I pretend the words have some meaning that I can understand. Unfortunately, the letters scramble almost immediately and I'm left staring blankly at the page, mind looping the crap day like a *gif* from Hell.

My eyes bug out at the tumbling letters and words. I blink a few times, then rake my gaze across the room to clear my mind. Pale late afternoon light filters in through the breakfast nook's bay window. It matches the dove gray cabinets and stainless steel appliances. I imagine what paints I'd need to create the exact same colors onto a canvas.

The front door creaks open. It slams shut a second later. Mom's measured steps make their way from the foyer to the kitchen. She drops her purse on the counter next to me and shrugs out of her pea coat. "Oh, wasn't expecting anyone to be home."

"I didn't feel like watching Daniel and his friends play with a ball."

"You could be working with the tutor on your reading. Principal Shepherd says he's willing to stay after school to work with you." Mom fills a pot with water and sets it to boil.

"It doesn't matter how many tutors I have, words will never make sense."

"I don't buy that, Darby. You're just not trying hard enough."

"How do you know? You don't have a dyslexic brain."

"It's not an excuse you can use for your entire life. Better to master it now before—"

"Just drop it, okay?"

"You'll have to figure it out sometime." Mom adds spaghetti to the pot.

"Whatever." I dismantle my study altar.

"Darby." She tucks a lock of her long, gray hair behind her ear and sets her dark brown eyes on me.

"*What*?" I steel myself, waiting for her to question me about Shepherd's email. There's a zero percent chance Shepherd didn't send one and I've totally blown any chance of impressing Mom with my "studying."

Mom stares me for a long time. "I don't know what to say to you anymore."

"Don't say anything."

"Fine." Mom pours a jar of marinara into a saucepan.

My mind fuzzes. That's it? We're not going to keep arguing? Either she hasn't read Shepherd's email, or she's waiting for Dad. My stomach tightens.

I hide in my room until dinner. Daniel arrives at five thirty. Dad comes in at five forty-five. My heart threatens to jump out of my throat at five fifty-five. We all sit at the dining table promptly at six.

It's all I can do not to barf on the polished oak table.

I sit across from Daniel, quiet. The seconds tick by, measured by the antique Grandfather clock behind me. I suck down half a glass of water, but can't manage a single bite of spaghetti.

After gracing Daniel with a few "atta boys" for being awesome at everything, Dad settles into serious mode and says, "Did you check your email, Annette?"

Mom shakes her head. "No."

He tips his head toward me, his dark blue eyes honing in on me like a heat-seeking missile. "Principal Shepherd sent one. Darby called another student a bitch."

Mom lowers her fork. "Why?"

Heat creeps up from my neck to my ears. "It wasn't my fau—"

"You say that every time. I don't want to hear your excuses. You need to take responsibility for your actions." Dad clenches his jaw. His cheeks redden, probably like mine. It's his blood pressure skyrocketing. One of these days he's going to get so mad at me that he'll stroke out.

Quick, hot tears blur my vision. "I'm sorry I can't be perfect like Daniel."

Mom clears her throat. "This is about you, Darby."

"Yeah, don't drag me into this." Daniel raises his hands.

"It was all about Daniel five minutes ago." Waves of anger crash over me. This is so unfair. I swallow a hard mouthful of fury and almost choke on it.

"If you did something praise-worthy, I'd praise you," Dad says.

"All I am is a big giant mistake, right?" I stare at the chandelier, letting the light burn into my eyes to sear away the swelling tears. "You don't even want to hear my side, do you?"

"I'm tired of your lies, Darby. You're grounded until further notice." Dad sighs, exhausted from the burden that is Darby.

I wipe my wet face with my fists. "I'm not lying. If you'd give me a chance to explain."

"I don't need your explanation. Principal Shepherd did a good enough job." Dad tosses his fork onto his plate with a tinny clatter. "Why can't you be more like Daniel?"

His words crush me under a ton of disappointment. It's out in the open now. There's no denying it. I'm the parasite twin, the reject.

I'm out of my seat and in my room before my napkin hits the floor.

Chapter Five

Adam

The room I'm assigned to is supposed to hold two patients, but since I'm considered a minor on an adult floor, I won't get a roommate. It's well enough, considering Mum and Dad will take turns staying with me. A day watchman and a night watchman.

Mum watches from her perch on the window ledge that's at least two feet deep while a nurse's aide finishes setting up a cot for her. Dad's settled into the recliner in the opposite corner holding a pile of linens on his lap. They'll go on the cot once it's ready. Mum called him after Dr. Jervis' announcement to let him know what happened. He dashed over after wrapping a few essential things up at work, despite my request not to.

"I'll stay here tonight, Dave, and I'll call in at work tomorrow," Mum says, her tone efficient and direct.

Dad nods, crossing his feet at the ankles. "Sounds good. I'll come right after work. Want me to bring take out?"

"Sushi, please, dear. Let's keep it healthy."

God, I hate sushi. Guess I'll have to suffer with whatever the hospital kitchen offers.

All because of a little wonky beat of my heart, I'm here, chained to a monitor, Mum's going to sleep on a crappy cot and miss work—plus her weekly reading group—and Dad will be spending his evenings in the hospital instead of at home where he could be managing overseas projects when other researchers are still active.

Camping out in a hospital room for an unknown amount of time isn't on their bucket list for me. Suppose I can scribble it in pencil at the bottom.

I sit in the middle of the hospital bed, with my legs folded. The nurse had insisted I change into a gown, but at least she'd also brought pajama bottoms so I don't flash anyone. I pick at the silicone dotting the bottom of my hospital-issued gripper socks.

"You guys don't have to stay. I've got an entire team here and they won't let anything happen." I speak with my most authoritative voice, though I'm reassuring myself as much as them.

"Of course I'm staying, Adam." Mum slides off the window ledge. She tidies her cot to prove her point, making the tightest hospital corners I've ever seen.

"Mum."

"I'm not leaving my son here," she says. It's a decree, binding, final.

Dad stands. The leather of his jacket creaks with his movements. He's been here for hours, but hasn't bothered taking off his coat. "I can stop by early in the morning to drop off some fresh clothes."

Mum glances at the duffle bag Dad had brought

for me, fluffing her pillow obsessively. I can pick her thoughts out of the air. Dad forgot to bring her bag, the brown leather satchel carrying a change of clothes and travel-sized toiletries housed permanently in her closet for emergencies.

I stare at the ceiling. My gaze trails from the antennae picking up my telemetry signal to a metal track cutting the room in half. The curtain affixed to it is tucked between two bedside stands, an unnecessary divider.

"Bring my bag too, dear." Mum speaks with a jovial tone, but the smacks she gives the pillow are anything but light.

I clear my throat. "Please, Dad, take Mum home. I'll be fine."

Mum tips her chin down. "You're anything but fine."

Dad rubs the top of his head.

I dodge her jab and counter. "Wouldn't you rather sleep in your own bed? I know I would."

Mum shrugs. "I'd rather be here with you."

She probably won't let me have a moment to myself from now on, with what happened at school. I hope she won't follow me into the bathroom.

"What's going to happen? I'll be sleeping all night. I think." I fuss with the wires connected to stickers spattered across my chest. They plug into a small device tucked into my gown's pocket that transmits a wireless signal to the antennae above. An EKG tracing comes out on a monitor at the nurses' station. The wires get in the way more than anything.

Dad smirks. "You know nobody gets sleep in the hospital."

Mum sits on the cot, stubborn as ever.

I play my final, most desperate, card. "I'll sign myself out against medical advice." Technically, I can't really refuse treatment because I'm under age, but I give it a shot anyway.

Mum doesn't bother justifying my lame move with an answer.

"Nice try, son, but you're not going anywhere." Dad pinches Mum's cheek. "I'm sorry about forgetting your bag, love."

She picks at a fingernail, then lifts her face to him. A smile softens her lips. "No worries, David. I'm not mad." She gives him a forgiving peck on the cheek.

Dad kisses her forehead. "See you in the morning."

And just like that, they're back to their lovey-dovey selves.

"Goodnight, Dad."

"Love you, Adam."

The overnight nurse enters as Dad leaves. He's wearing black scrubs and Hipster-style glasses that clash with his pudgy, middle-aged physique and way too mainstream crew cut.

He checks my blood pressure and makes sure the stickers are still sticking. "I'll do my best to leave you alone, unless your heart decides to jump into an unstable rhythm, of course. The best thing you can do now is sleep. I'll be watching on the monitor. Try not to toss and turn. The leads might come off and I'll have to wake you up to reattach them."

After he leaves, Mum tucks me in like I'm a five year old. "Are you comfortable? Do you need another pillow? Are you warm enough?"

"I'm okay." I use the call button remote to turn off the overhead lights and then turn on the TV. I click through the channels, not really paying attention to the shows.

She leans over me, blocking my view of a CGI-green screen-actor battle-scene mash-up of a SyFy super awesome train wreck of a movie. "That's a horrible reflex you've developed."

I frown. "Huh?"

"Whenever I ask a question you say, 'I'm alright' or 'I'm fine.' It's hard to know what you're really thinking." The brightness from the TV illuminates her hair from behind, a holy glow. The way she's sacrificing her happiness for me should earn her sainthood. I should write a letter to the Pope.

Then again, if she'd ease up and drop the inquisition for a minute, maybe I wouldn't have a "reflex" response.

She peers into my eyes. "Adam. Are you in there?"

I twist the call bell cord around my fingers. "Yes. It's just … this sucks. I don't want to be here."

She caresses my cheek with her warm hand. "You're prioritized on the transplant list now. With any luck, we won't have to wait long. But we have to be patient."

"You think everything will be fixed when I get a new heart."

She straightens. "It will."

I chew on my lip. A new heart isn't the end of this. It's the beginning. I'll have to get used to taking a fistful of anti-rejection meds, wearing masks during cold and flu seasons, and a rigorous (for me) exercise routine. Plus, it doesn't guarantee I'll have a normal life span. "I don't know."

"You're just nervous. We all are." She tucks into bed … um, cot. It doesn't look comfortable at all. My mattress is a thousand times cushier in comparison, and it's not that great either.

"Don't stay up watching TV all night," she says.

I should turn it off now, but I'm not tired. Well, my body is fatigued, but my brain gallops onward. How long will I be in the hospital? If my heart recovers some, do I have to stay until the heart comes, or will I be bumped down the list again? What if my heart gets worse before a donor comes along? Dr. Jervis had also mentioned things like LVADs—left ventricular assist devices—machines attached to my heart via tubes running into my chest and external pumps designed to keep my blood flowing.

I suppress a full body tremor. I really will become Frankenstein's monster.

It's unnatural to cheat death this way. How far can things go? Can I depend on a machine? Can I handle knowing someone else must die so I can live?

I close my eyes. It's clear to me now. I don't deserve life if I'm stealing it from someone else. I don't.

It would be kinder, more humane, if I were to die.

I take in a shaky breath. A tear slides from my eye. I let it trickle down my cheek unchecked.

I should text Dr. Shaw, but it's too late. Maybe I shouldn't tell her. We'll have enough to talk about when we meet. She'll probably come to the hospital to see me. She's done it before.

At midnight, I shut off the TV and lay flat in bed, afraid to move lest I jostle the leads and telemetry pack.

At three AM, I'm still awake, listening to my pulse rushing in my ears. When—no, *if*—I get a transplant, it'll be another person's heart pushing blood through my body. I wonder if it will sound the same, feel the same. I wonder if I'll know it's not mine.

I squeeze my eyes shut to push the questions and blinding fear from my mind. For a moment, it works and I float in blissful, quiet darkness.

In the depths of infinite blackness, a vile idea claws its way to the surface. Blood drips from its fangs and its yellow eyes ooze contempt.

It snarls, mocking me.

I might die on the operating table.

I shake my head, rattling the idea. Of course I'm going to die on the table. The surgeon will be removing my heart and replacing it with someone else's. I'll be dead in those minutes between. I'll only come back to life if the surgeon has magic in his hands.

Mary Shelley was decades ahead of her time.

I slide my gaze around the darkened room, abandoning any hope of sleep. My phone rests on the bedside stand, neatly tucked next to *Frankenstein*. Perhaps that wasn't the best choice of reading material. I stick my tongue out at the book for good measure, then pick up my phone.

Selecting the web browser app, I wrack my brain trying to remember the ridiculous name of the newest drug Shaw prescribed. I doubt Mum would've given it to me if the risk was too high.

I type Z-I-P-R and Google does the rest.

Ziprasidone pops up. I select it and get a list of links. Clicking on the second one, I gulp.

Ziprasidone: For the treatment of Schizophrenia, Bipolar Disorder, and hallucinations.

What the hell? I'm not schizophrenic.

I scan the rest of the article, skimming over phrases like *take twice daily* and *take with food for better absorption* and halt at the words:

Although rare, ziprasidone can cause significant QT prolongation, leading to a potentially serious unstable rhythm of the heart.

I sit up in bed, clutching a palm to my chest. My raspy breaths fill the room. I don't know what the bloody hell a QT is, but I do know Shaw had given me a drug that could affect my heart.

Surely, she knows about this side effect, especially since she works with heart transplant patients.

The question then is: Why did she prescribe it for me?

* * *

Dr. Shaw stops in after lunch.

I chew on the questions I want to ask her, grinding down each word into a finely polished accusation. The temptation to speak first settles in the back of my throat, hot and coarse, but I want to see what she has to say first.

Mum pops out of the Barco lounger parked next to the foot of my bed. She sets her Kindle on the windowsill. "Hello, Doctor. I'm so glad you're here."

Dr. Shaw smiles at Mum. Her dark eyes simply glow with warmth for her. "I wish I could've gotten here sooner, but I had other clients scheduled this morning."

Mum eats it up like chocolate pudding. My stomach churns on the stale sandwich I'd choked down. "Oh, it's not a problem, really."

Dr. Shaw extends a hand. "What happened yesterday must have been quite a shock."

Were you expecting it? I wonder.

Mum clasps both hands around hers. "You have no idea. It was so sudden. He was fine when I dropped him off at school and then the teacher called. I've never driven so fast in my life. Blasted through a couple of red lights, even."

Dr. Shaw nods in sympathy, gesturing for Mum to sit back in the lounger. "I can't imagine how frightened you were."

"I'm still terrified," Mum confesses.

"Of course." Dr. Shaw lowers her brows. "I hear Adam's heart isn't functioning as well as it was, but at least he's been prioritized on the list."

Mum sucks in a shaky breath. "Silver lining, I suppose."

I love how they talk about me like I'm not here. I dog-ear the page I'm on in *Frankenstein* and lay the book next to me. I wasn't reading it anyway, what with all my stewing on Shaw's choice of medication for me.

Dr. Shaw turns her attention to me. The brightness in her eyes dims. The lines of her face, earlier fragile and soft, morph into stern angles as her brows arch and lips thin. A sign of guilt? "Good afternoon, Adam. How are you?"

I pick at a snag in the blue blanket covering my legs, dissecting the fibers like I want to dissect her expression. "Fine."

Mum clucks her tongue. "It's so frustrating, doctor. He just doesn't tell us how he really is. I don't know what to do anymore." She wrings her hands. The vertical line in the middle of her forehead deepens.

I curl my fingers into fists. "Maybe if you hadn't made me take the new pill, this wouldn't have happened."

Mum withers, stepping away from me as if I'd spewed poison at her. "I … I don't believe that."

My sickly heart plummets into my stomach. I didn't mean to hurt Mum. This is Shaw's fault.

"It was the stairs. The added stress weakened your heart." Mum sniffs, shaking her head. She wipes wetness from her eyes with a tissue snaked from her pocket.

"Ziprasidone causes unstable heart rhythms. I should think a doctor would know that." I give Shaw a death stare.

Dr. Shaw frowns at me like a Catholic nun judging a misbehaving child. "I don't think it's the medicine, Adam. It was designed to help you stay calm."

"Did you forget about me having heart failure, oh, and the fact that I'm not schizophrenic? Minor details, I guess."

Mum huffs. "Adam! How could you doubt Doctor Shaw's expertise?"

"Look it up. Everything I've just said is written down, in black and white." My voice echoes in the room.

Mum glances at the open doorway. Chatter from the nurse's station drifts in. "Shh, lower your voice."

Dr. Shaw purses her lips. "Perhaps Adam and I should speak in private for a bit."

"Sounds like a good idea. I need some fresh air anyway." Mum snatches her coat from the cot and rushes out, shutting the door behind her.

Mum left me. She left, never second guessing Shaw's intentions. Unbelievable.

I toss the blanket aside to draw my knees up.

Dr. Shaw's direct attention is sort of like throwing yourself on a fire. My skin feels like it's burning.

"I discussed the side effects with your mother. I told her it was safe, especially at the dose I prescribed."

"Thanks for talking to *me* about it."

She places her red bag on the plastic chair for visitors and strides to my bed, heels clicking on the tile floor. Her tight bun, crisp white shirt, and black skirt contrast starkly with the mint green walls and pastel flower wall border. "We've got a lot to talk about."

Dread scrapes its dirty nails down my back. I glance at the door. My legs twitch, ready to launch me out of the room.

"Have you had more suicidal thoughts since you texted?"

"No." I curl my fingers around my toes.

Shaw eases onto the bed so close that her hip touches my arm. I drag my gaze up to meet her dark eyes. She arches a brow. "Uh-hmm. Considering what your mom said about you minimizing things and your uneducated assumption that I purposefully prescribed you a medication that will make you sicker, how can I trust you?"

Anger burns through my entire body. "Trust *me*? How can I trust *you*? That medicine could've killed me."

"I thought you wanted to die."

My whole body tenses. I can't even blink. Inside, my heart withers, as unsettled as I am about what she's said.

"It's hard to have a conversation when only one person is talking." She shifts closer.

"Adam, are you in there?" There's a silvery tinkle to her voice. She's playing with me. This whole thing, it's all a game. Mum is duped, Dad is oblivious, and I'm stuck in a room alone with a viper. I'm just not sure if she wants to poison me with her venom or simply mess with my head.

"Um ... " I'm disarmed. The argument I was so prepared for before her arrival demolished. My trippy heart leaps into a faster—and wobblier—pitter-patter. I try to keep my breathing steady. The room is so stifling that my throat screams for water.

She taps a finger against my temple. "You're such a bright, insightful, and pensive boy with so much potential. Don't shut me out. I can help you."

I pinch my eyes shut. "No."

Her fingers press lightly on the inside of my wrist.

I hold my breath.

After a few seconds, she sighs. "Your heart isn't regular now and the medicine isn't in your system anymore. Do you need more proof that it wasn't the ziprasidone, or are you satisfied?" Her weight leaves the mattress. After a few clicks of her heels on the floor, the plastic chair creaks.

I chance taking a breath and open my eyes.

"Shall we start our session?" Shaw sits with her hands laced in her lap.

"I don't have anything to say," I whisper.

"Your mother is terrified you'll die before you get a transplant."

"I might."

"Do you want that to happen?" Her voice is smooth like her serene expression, as if I'd never accused her of anything. As if she hadn't just played with my emotions.

I shake my head, hoping it'll clear the confusion from my mind. It doesn't. "No."

"Then why do you spend so much time thinking about suicide?"

"I don't want to kill myself."

"But you're thinking about death. Fantasizing about it. Desiring it." The quicksilver in her tone cuts me.

It also severs the noose she's tied around my neck. "That's not true."

"But it is. Would you like to review the texts you sent me?" She unclips her phone from her belt and holds it up. A new rope binds itself around my psyche.

"You're twisting things around."

"I'm challenging your thoughts so you can see how illogical they are." She tightens her hold.

I struggle against her. "What happened to insightful?"

Her eyes spark with friction. "You seem more agitated today. I understand you're angry with me, but really, would you have even tried the medicine had you known about the *very rare and unlikely* effect it has on cardiac conduction?"

"No."

"Exactly. So let's move beyond this … hiccup … and focus on you. What's been on your mind?"

I'd known for a long time my life expectancy is a fraction of everyone else's. I'm a faulty model. It's the hand I was dealt. I should accept it for what it is. Instead, I'm gripping hope around the throat, strangling it, forcing it to change the natural order of things to extend my time on the planet. And it comes at a cost.

"Talk to me, Adam. Let's not disappoint your mother any further. She worries about you so much, and, with your being tight-lipped, she has good reason."

I'm a fly trapped in Shaw's spider web. There's no escape, so I give myself over to her. "Someone has to die so I can live. It's not fair. And say they find a heart and the surgery goes well, will I be the same … after?"

"You're carrying around a heavy burden, facing existential questions decades ahead of when you're supposed to." The sweet and spicy layers in her voice are gone. It's just her now. She's dropped whatever technique she was using to challenge me.

Relieved, I relax my shoulders and stretch out my legs. "It's weird, is all. I want a new heart so I can move on, past this *nightmare*. I look forward to it, dream about it, but it also means I'm wishing for someone's funeral. That's kind of sick."

"It's the survival instinct. We all have it."

"So you believe me when I say I'm not suicidal?"

She tips her head to the side. "There's a difference between actively planning your death and passively letting it happen. On the other hand, they're opposite sides of the same coin."

"What do you mean?"

"Death is scary."

My stomach twinges. She's laying a new gauntlet for me to navigate.

"And you face it every day."

I hold my breath, waiting for the next mental hurdle.

"Must be exhausting. Perhaps your fantasy of me prescribing ziprasidone as a method to hasten your death allowed you to reconcile your passive suicidal thoughts as logic. It allows you to kill yourself without actually having to do it."

A dull throbbing beats at my temple. I rub a finger on the spot. What is she saying? That I really do want to die and I'm not aware of it?

She points a finger in the air, the Socrates to my

Plato. "Furthermore, perhaps you tell your mother that you're fine because you don't want her to intervene to save you. Perhaps you want fate to make the decision for you."

I dodge her hypothesis with a lame block. "I *am* fine. My heart's still beating."

"Not for long."

The blow strikes me across the ribs. I can't breathe. She's won.

"I'm not saying that to hurt you. I'm saying it to remind you of reality."

"I don't need reminding." My voice barely passes my lips.

"The idea that everything is okay has taken such a deep hold that it's reached delusional proportions, which is a sort of psychosis. Delusions can become so deeply entrenched in a patient's mind that they disrupt therapy and I couldn't risk that ruining the progress we've made. It was one of the reasons I selected ziprasidone for you."

"I'm not crazy."

She stands. "You're in a hospital, connected to a bunch of wires, you need twenty four hour monitoring in case your heart goes into a lethal rhythm, and you've been prioritized on the heart transplant list. I'm not sure what more evidence you need to prove your imminent mortality."

I peer up at her. "Why are you trying to scare me?"

She leans so close our noses almost touch. "To show you how much you want to live and that you're willing to suffer the mental torment of having another person die for you to survive."

Chapter Six

Darby

Daniel parks his vintage prize in an empty spot at the back of the high school's parking lot. He closes his eyes and lets the engine rumble for a minute. A smile warms his face. God, he's in love with a car.

"Should I leave you two alone?" I ask, unclicking the seatbelt.

"Today's V-8 engines don't sound the same."

"Whatever, lover boy. A car is for transportation."

"Lover boy? I'm your brother. Isn't that, like, gross somehow?" He scrunches his nose and cuts the engine, halting the vibrations slowly turning my insides to Jell-o.

"Ugh." I open the door, yanking my backpack from the floor as I stand.

Daniel leans over and gives me a dimply smile that makes most the girls in our class swoon. Thankfully, my sibling powers have made me immune. "Love you too, sis."

"Shut. Up." I slide the bag's straps over my shoulders after slamming the door in his face.

His jock buddies swarm around the car, an Axe body spray army that instantly dwarfs me. As the smaller fraternal twin, I got the short end of the stick on so many levels and my small size is one of them.

They're all wearing their red and white letterman jackets. Pride oozes from them in the form of toothy grins and fist-pumping yelps. The Argyle Angels are anything but. More like devils with pitchforks, horns, and slippery tongues.

Tyrell, the basketball team's center, breaks free from the horde and pounds on Daniel's window. "Hey, Big D!"

Lamest nickname ever.

I tip my head back to take in the giants invading my personal space. Redwoods have nothing on these solid trunks of muscle. "Excuse me," I say.

No one moves.

"Get out of my way!" I chop my arm against rows of beefcake like an explorer hacking through jungle vines with a machete.

Several whacks later, I've made a dent in the meaty forest. The sun is brighter here, and the air clearer … even if it is heavy with exhaust fumes and teenage hormonal drama. Emo kids drape themselves on benches, geeks bow to their new tech, popular kids' gossip, and romantics hide between cars for a quick game of show me yours and I'll show you mine.

It's not a real love connection until someone gets slapped.

I smooth my hair—it's still wet from my shower— and tug on a blue strand. By the water fountain, I make a pit stop to catch what a pair of sophomores are saying about the kid who collapsed in class yesterday. The hallway noise is so loud I can only catch, "exchange student," and "heart condition." I move on to travel the high school highway alone, stomping my black army boots every step. It makes people move out of my way.

The second floor bathroom is down its own hallway and is rarely used, so I can dip in there to take a break before class. Unfortunately, a couple other kids have the same idea. They huddle just outside the door. Fantastic. I frown, ready to bark at them to get out of the way, when I recognize who it is.

Stephanie Veene.

And she's wrapped around Eric Thorton, the bad-assiest of bad-asses. Okay, so I get the appeal of danger, but Eric is a bad boy and not in a good way. He's one write-up shy of getting kicked out of school for good. Plus, he got arrested for drug possession. The idiot blabbed all about it in detention last week.

Stephanie giggles softly and gives him a sly smile with her lip-glossed mouth. His hands are all over her, and then his lips are too. I try not to vomit at the sight of it. This whole thing makes less sense than the essay I tried to write last night. Popular cheerleaders don't hang with outcasts.

They're so into each other that they haven't noticed me. I hang back, avoiding sudden movements.

My mouth salivates at the idea of shouting, "Who's the slut now?" With my luck, I'll end up in Principal Shepherd's office again.

More giggles ripple out of her, curdling my stomach. She's making out with a dude building his career for a jail cell and thinks nothing of it. I kiss a guy at a club and get crap for it. I clench my jaw.

"Are you coming to the game tonight?" Stephanie's voice reminds me of a cat's meow.

"Yeah, I'll be there. I just won't be in the bleachers," Eric says.

"You'll miss my half-time dance routine." Stephanie sticks out her lower lip.

Eric brushes it with his tattooed thumb. "Find me after. I have something to show you."

I bet he does. Ew. Yuck. Gross.

He breaks free from her and turns toward me. Our eyes lock. "The hell you doing here?"

"Duh, I'm going to the bathroom," I say.

He bumps into me on his way past. On purpose. "Whatever."

"Asshole." I rub my shoulder.

Stephanie locks her hip to the side and crosses her arms. "So you like to watch, huh?"

I grab the bathroom door's handle, flipping my hair back with a twist of my head. "You should be careful. People will talk."

"About what?"

"Sucking on Eric's face. He's one arrest away from spending ten to twenty behind bars."

She rolls her eyes. "That's ridiculous. You shouldn't spread nasty rumors about people. And what I do with Eric is none of your business."

"They're not rumors. He told me—"

"Blah, blah, blah. Why are you still talking?" She pops her gum. Her pleated skirt swishes around her legs and her curled hair bounces as she struts away.

Stupid blonde bitch.

I enter the bathroom and lean against the door,

locking it so no one else can come in. Heat flares in my face. I dig my fingernails into my palms. Since Shepherd says I can't fight back, I'll have to use a different strategy. And what's the best way to get back at someone? Give them a taste of their own medicine.

In Stephanie's case, it has to be humiliation.

I smile at myself. Principal Shepherd is right. I don't have to react to Stephanie when she provokes me. I can act first.

Oh, this bitch is going down.

* * *

The real reason I stay at school for basketball games is to work on my art. I paint better alone, away from home, away from Mom and Dad and Daniel. Tonight I have a different plan. Stephanie Veene is meeting a baddy after her halftime glory show and I want to know exactly what they're going to do. So I sit in the far corner of the bleachers closest to the doors and watch the beauty squad jump and twist around the basketball court while the two teams take a break on opposite benches.

After shaking their pompoms, boobs, and butts, the cheerleaders skip off court to a bleacher shaking round of cat calls and clapping. I circle to the locker room's back entrance and tuck myself behind an alcove. Only the main hallway light is on, so plenty of shadows cover me.

Eric hasn't shown up yet.

Who knows what he has in mind for pretty girl

Stephanie, but I'm gonna be there to see it.

And record it.

I pull out my phone, open the camera app, and switch it to record. I make sure it's silenced and the flash is off and hold my finger over the start button, waiting, waiting …

… waiting.

Twenty minutes go by and no one shows up. The game will be over before Stephanie and Eric arrive. Cheers from the gym echo down the hallway and the floor vibrates when the audience stomps on the bleachers. Must be a thrilling game.

Giving up, I stuff my phone into my back pocket. What a waste of time. I scuff my boots a bit as I walk toward the main hallway. At the corner, I spot a rush of blonde hair and red pompoms. I retreat a step, then peek around the wall.

Sure enough, Stephanie is doing her girly run toward the school's main entrance. Eric stands just inside the doors. He's wearing a black leather biker jacket, black jeans, and has a chain hooked to his wallet and belt loop. His dark hair is spiked with gel and a cigarette is tucked in his ear.

Cliché central.

I refrain from rolling my eyes because if I did, they'd probably get stuck.

Stephanie throws herself into his arms. "Hey, baby," she croons.

Eric twirls her around in a circle. "Missed you."

Their lips lock like they're trying to eat each others' faces.

Bile rises in my throat. Since when does the perfect princess fall for the scumbag? Does anybody know about it? Isn't Stephanie worried about her reputation like Daniel worried about mine? It's not like they're trying too hard to keep it secret.

I scan the hallway. Still empty. Not even one person wandering to the bathroom or outside to sneak a smoke.

Wouldn't it be disastrously beautiful to expose the tramp for what she is?

I pull out my phone to snap a few pics.

Shudders of revenge ripple down my spine with every click. Later, I'll decide how to share the news with the entire student body. Then Stephanie will get what she deserves.

* * *

Sleet pings against the windshield as Daniel drives us home. The Mustang's engine thunders and the heaters burp out stale hot air. I hold my palms to the vents. Should've worn more than a hoodie.

Daniel's thumbs tap against the steering wheel. His head bobs with the rhythm he's beating out. "Man, that was an awesome shot," he murmurs to himself. Well, I assume he's talking to himself. He knows I have zero interest in his mad basketball skills. "Three points," he follows up, as if I've responded to him.

"You lost the game," I say.

He slows the car to a gentle stop at the light. "I had the most baskets. Makes me high point player."

"There's no 'I' in team."

"Did you see me play? I saw you on the bleachers

at half time." The light turns green. Daniel snorts and presses the gas. The car fishtails a bit before steadying out.

"Are you sure you know how to drive in this?" I glare at him.

He totally misses it since he's staring at the slick road ahead. "No worries, sis. What were you up to, anyway?"

"It's none of your business."

He gives a low whistle—the universal what's-pissed-*you*-off signal. "Sorry for asking."

"Not that I have to tell you, but something very interesting happened tonight while you and your buddies were sweating all over each other."

He taps the brakes as we head around a curve in the road. The car weaves some more. "Oh yeah? What?"

I grit my teeth, partly at him, partly at how much the car is struggling. "Don't sound surprised that your three point shot wasn't the most fantastic event of the evening."

He chuckles. "Oh yeah? Come on, then. Spill it."

"I saw Stephanie Veene kissing Eric Thorton." I grin at the ice-slicked windshield.

"Uhh, so?"

My pride deflates like a torn balloon. "*So*? Stephanie called me a slut and she's the one hooking up with a known jerk."

"Why do you care what she does?"

"You care what I do."

"Of course I do. You're my sister." Daniel hits the brake as the car slides into another bend. He turns up the speed on the wipers. "Can't see a thing."

I huff. "You don't get it. I caught the perfect princess

sullying herself with a pig *and* I have the evidence to prove it."

"*Sullying?* You haven't actually been reading the Shakespeare assignment, have you?"

I whack his arm. "Stop being such an ass and listen to me."

He raises his shoulder in a mock dodge. "Okay, okay. What 'evidence' do you have?"

"Pictures."

Daniel glances at me. "Pictures?"

"Yeah, of them making out."

"You took pictures of people kissing? Why?"

I want to smack my forehead, or better yet bash it against the dashboard. "I can bring down the queen. All I have to do is post the pictures somewhere—"

"And what? It's not like you can put them on Facebook. When she sees you're the one who posted them, won't she do something about it? Like try to get back at you or something?"

"I'm not afraid of her."

"Darby, you don't need to get in any more trouble." His tone carries a warning I don't particularly like. I don't need a third parent.

"I can print them and hang them on the bulletin boards."

"She'll know it was you."

"Whatever. Her friends are your friends and you don't want me to get back at her because they'll get mad at you too."

"That's so not true. You know this little revenge plot of yours will backfire on you. Mom and Dad will go ballistic when they find out."

"They're already mad. What difference will it make?"

"If you stop doing stupid things, they won't be mad."

"What happened yesterday wasn't my fault!" I wave my hand for emphasis.

"You shouldn't let Stephanie get to you." He sounds like Principal Shepherd.

"You're just as bad as they are. This is a total double standard."

He shifts to a lower gear after cresting a hill. It's pure ice. I tuck my hands under my thighs. "I don't know why you're mad at me. You're the one who screwed up."

"Why didn't you stick up for me last night? I could've used your help then."

"There was nothing to stick up for. I warned you at the party and you ignored me."

"Wow, thanks for throwing that in my face. And newsflash, Mom and Dad listen to you, not me."

"What could I say about you ending up in the Principal's office?"

"Forget it." I cross my arms over my chest.

The car skids a bit. Daniel taps the brake. "I hope you drop this whole revenge thing."

"I said forget it, okay?"

"Okay. Geez." He hits the brake a little stronger.

The slope dips. We speed up, despite Daniel's shifting to first gear. The Mustang's back end swings left. Daniel counter-steers into it, but overcorrects. We spin to face a drop off bordered by a guardrail.

My heart races as my breath catches in my throat. I press my palms against the dashboard. "Daniel!"

"Shit!" Daniel works the steering wheel some more. The car whips in the opposite direction. We cross the double lines, right in front of a truck climbing the hill. Bright headlights wash us in yellow light.

We're going to die. Oh god, oh god, oh god.

"Hang on." He yanks the wheel right. The car slides on an angle, but doesn't entirely return to our lane. I scream, covering my face with my hands.

Air brakes squeal. Time slows until I can see individual shards of ice falling from the sky and feel the reverberations of my heart pumping blood through my body.

I suck in a breath.

In a click of infinity, the clock rushes forward and the truck barrels toward us, lethal and inescapable.

The truck slams into Daniel's door. *Boom!* Glass shatters as metal smacks metal, letting out a screeching cry. I jerk left into my seatbelt then crash into the door. My skull bounces off the window and I bite my tongue.

Like a hockey puck, the car slides across the road, aimed for the drop off.

"Daniel!" My voice cracks.

We smash into the guardrail. The impact launches me forward. The seatbelt holds tight but my head bobs so fast something pops in my neck. Searing pain streaks down my shoulders and arms, leaving my fingers an instant mess of numbness and tingling. Air shoots out of my lungs. Hungry blackness chews at the edges of my vision as an obnoxious blaring stabs my ears.

I turn my head toward Daniel, wincing at the crunching agony ripping down my spine.

He's slumped over the steering wheel. His eyes are closed. Blood streaks down his face. Something glittery peppers his hair. His hands lay limp in his lap. I slide my gaze to the spider web pattern marking the windshield.

No, it's not a spider web. The glass is shattered and bits of it sprinkle across the dashboard and, oh my god, it's glass in his hair, not glitter.

Warning bells drone in my head. His head must've hit the windshield! Wasn't he wearing his seatbelt? Why isn't he moving? Is he breathing?

Tears sear my eyes. "Daniel? Wake up, please. Daniel!"

I reach out to him. Pain spikes in my neck and swallows me whole until I'm consumed by darkness.

Chapter Seven

Adam

The next night, I'm still chewing on Dr. Shaw's words. I don't repeat them to Mum or Dad. There's no point to. My parents are eating out of her hand like tame deer and I don't have the energy to explain my side of the story.

Dad tosses our take-out containers in the trash. "I should head out. I have some work to catch up on."

Mum rushes to give him a hug and kiss. "Drive carefully. Looks icy out there." She gestures to the window.

Sleet attacks the glass like an orc army beating the walls of Helm's Deep. I nestle deeper under the covers. Nothing can touch me here. Not Dad's denial of my worsening illness or Dr. Shaw's challenges or Mum's flitting over me every two seconds. Not even Death, even though it resides deep in the chambers of my heart, waiting to draw the scythe across my arteries and veins.

I don't expect the Grim Reaper to stalk into my room in the darkness of night to steal my soul. My murderer is within and I can't run from myself.

Dad zips his coat. "I'll call when I get home."

Mum smiles. "Thanks, honey. Goodnight."

Dad waves at me. "See you tomorrow, son."

"Bye, Dad."

Mum busies herself with fixing her pillow and straightening her blanket. "What do you want to do tonight? Watch a movie, play a game … ?"

I click off the bedside lamp and face the window. The blinds are open, letting in light from the street. It's softened to a rosy glow from the fog and precipitation. The urge to confess what happened with Shaw coats my tongue, but I can't risk letting it past my lips. Mum would talk to Shaw about it and Shaw would deny it, or twist my words around, or maybe say I'm delusional. Maybe they've already talked about it. Shaw probably armed Mum with an argument should I bring up the subject. "I'm tired."

There's a long pause, followed by a soft, "Oh, alright. Guess I'll read for a bit."

Shutting her out makes me an ass, but I have no other option. Like I said to Shaw, she's infused my every waking moment, drowned any private thoughts, and snuffed out each glimpse of freedom I have left. Yes, it's better if I don't say anything.

Mum's shoes squeak slightly on the tile floor. Rustling of sheets blossom in the silence, then the soft pops of the cot stretching to bear her weight echo throughout the room. The bluish glow of her Kindle reflects off the ceiling, competing with the orangey blush of the streetlights outside.

Several agonizing minutes pass where I argue with myself. I should turn around, face her, and *talk*. About my thoughts, my fears, and what I think about the transplant.

Mum would proudly declare it a breakthrough to Shaw.

Shaw. She's supposed to be helping me through this, but all she does is play with my mind and confuse me. The woman really thinks I want to die.

Do I?

Air stagnates in my lungs as I trip on the question. I grab a fistful of blanket. My heart stumbles into a faster beat.

Enough! I can't afford to trigger another attack.

I take a few slow, deep breaths to steady myself.

Mum clears her throat. A reminder that she's there. Or an invitation.

I could roll over and say, "Mum, we need to talk."

Five little words. It'd make her so happy. Yet it's so hard to do.

I swallow the lump blocking my throat. *Sit up. Open your mouth. Come on. Do it.*

I shut my eyes and hold my breath. My heart flutters, anticipating my leap into openness. I clench my jaw. There's nothing beneath me to catch my fall. No safety net. I can't do it. I'm too much of a coward.

"I love you, Adam," Mum says, tossing me a feeble lifeline. I'm not sure if it's for her or me.

The plea in her voice settles over me like a layer of ice. It's sharp, biting, and suffocating.

"Adam?"

"I'm not shutting you out, Mum." I open my eyes and stare at the blinds slats. They start to ripple, an optical illusion. Acid rolls in my stomach at the lie.

"Yes, you are. I just don't understand why. What did I do to push you away?"

I turn my face into the pillow. "Nothing."

"Doctor Shaw says withdrawing is a sign of worsening depression. She's worried about you and so am I."

"I'm not depressed."

"You've been here two days and you've barely said anything. You hardly respond to the surgeon's questions. Shaw says you're clamming up in therapy." She sucks in a shaky breath. "We're so close to getting you a new heart and I'm terrified you'll give up before we do."

"It's not as easy peasy as ordering one from Amazon."

"*Adam.*" I hear a swish of blankets. Her weight dips into the mattress behind me. "How can you joke about such a thing?"

"You know someone has to die for me to get a heart, right?" My voice is muffled, what with me talking into the pillow and all.

She rests a hand on my shoulder. "I know, sweetheart. I know."

"I'm not sure you do. I mean, you seem happy about the idea."

"What I'm happy about is you getting well. That can happen with a new heart." She tightens her grip. "You have to focus on the positives. Doctor Shaw says if you keep thinking negative things the depression will linger and you won't heal as quickly."

I snort.

"You should trust her. She knows what she's talking about."

"Doctor Shaw isn't who you think she is."

She removes her hand from my shoulder. "Oh, Adam, really."

I grab a fistful of blanket. "I wish you'd believe me about her."

Her weight leaves the bed. A moment later, the cot creaks.

I lift my head from the pillow. "Well?"

Mum flicks off her Kindle. "Go to sleep, Adam."

Now who's withdrawing from who?

Doubt seeps into my skin like sticky tar. Shaw wants me to trust her but I can't trust what she's telling Mum.

I suck on my lip ring.

Mum says she doesn't know what I'm thinking. Then why do I feel so exposed and vulnerable, splayed open by Shaw's wit and calculating words?

* * *

The nurse, Tim, rushes in dragging a blood pressure machine at around six in the morning. He flips the light on without asking and announces, "We have a heart. Let's get you down to the OR."

I sit up, rubbing my eyes at the shock of fluorescent light.

Mum gapes at him, hair sticking up on one side and flattened on the other. "Wh-what?"

Tim rips open the cuff. The Velcro hisses at being torn from its clingy counterpart. He checks my vital signs. "You haven't eaten anything since midnight, right?"

"Before that," I say. "Where did the heart come from?"

He chuckles. "A donor, of course."

Glad he thinks I'm an idiot. I rub my eyes with my free hand while Tim jots down the numbers flashing on the machine.

A nurse's aide comes in, pushing a gurney.

"Here's your ride," Tim says.

"Where's the surgeon?" Mum asks, stuffing her feet into her sensible loafers. Her eyes are bloodshot as if she's been crying.

"He's harvesting the donor heart. They should be wrapping up soon. We need to get Adam prepped and ready to go for him."

I stare at Tim, frozen. "The donor is here?"

"You lucked out. The closer the heart, the less down time it has and the easier it is to reboot, so to speak." Tim smiles.

Icy tentacles slither through my belly. I shiver. "B-but … I'm not ready."

"Ready or not, it's time to go." Tim tosses my blanket aside. "Hop on the gurney, son."

I shake my head. My legs won't move. "I c-can't."

"We'll help you." Tim motions for the aide. They each hook an arm under my arms and pivot me to the gurney.

Nausea swells in my gut. Terror burns up my chest and explodes in my throat. This is it. My new heart is here. Someone's dying and I'm going to take their life. "I'm going to be sick."

Tim pats my shoulder. His gaze says, *man-up-buddy*. "Take a deep breath. It's going to be okay."

Mum is tapping on her phone. "I'm calling your

father." She glances at Tim. "How far can I come along?"

"You can ride in the elevator and down the hall, but once we pass through the doors of the OR, you have to hang back," Tim says.

Tim steers us down the hall from the head of the gurney while the aide guides the foot. At the lift, he peers down at me. "When you wake up, you'll have a new ticker."

I stare up his nostrils. "If I wake up," I mumble.

He pushes me onto the lift then sidesteps to face me head on. "You'll wake up. You're in good hands. Doctor Jervis is the best."

"And someone else will be dead," I say.

Tim straightens the blanket draped over my lower body. "The donor is already brain dead, son. His family has gifted his organs to recipients like you. It's a second chance at life."

Mum clasps hands with me. Her fingers are cold. "This is a good thing, Adam." A hardness creeps into her gaze, similar to Dr. Shaw's when she's working her psychological magic on me.

"Yeah." I rest my head on the pillow and count the ceiling tiles until we reach the OR entrance.

"Mrs. Gibson, you can say bye here." Tim nudges the aide to give us some space.

Mum places her palm against my forehead. "I love you, Adam."

"Love you too, Mum."

A tear slips free and trails down her face. "Be strong."

Thoughts crowd my mind—mostly fears about what comes after death—but I refuse to free them. It'll only scare her more. Instead, I grab her wrist and hold tight.

"Tell me what you're thinking," she pleads.

I've reached the point of no return. Once the doctor starts cutting, he'll crack open my chest, stop my heart, cut it out, and … I'll be dead. *Dead*. A heart and lung machine will pump blood through my vessels. What happens to my spirit in the between time? Will it stay attached to my body? Will it try to escape and fly to Heaven … or Hell? Will I float above myself and watch as the surgeon mutilates me? Will my soul accept a new heart? Will I become that monster?

Tim opens the door. "Time to go."

Mum's shoulders shake with sobs. "I'll see you soon."

"Bye, Mum." I release her wrist and her hands fall away from me as Tim wheels me into the OR.

Once I'm settled on the operating table, the anesthesiologist puts an oxygen mask on my face. She's wearing a hot pink bonnet. Her gaze latches onto me. The skin around her green eyes crinkles with a smile. She moves to my side and preps my arm for an IV. "I'm doctor Hillborn. Just try to relax and breathe slowly. The oxygen will help."

The two large, adjustable lights hang above me. They're focused directly on my chest. My heart's own personal spotlight. "What room is the donor in?"

"Don't worry about him." Dr. Hillborn glances at me, then refocuses on taping the IV tubing to my arm. She unsnaps my gown, exposing my chest. "These are old leads. You'll need fresh ones." Quickly, she removes the telemetry wires and adds new stickies to my chest.

Goosebumps cover my skin. "Did you see him?"

"Cold in here, isn't it?" She drapes a blanket over me after she finishes attaching the new wires.

I lift my head. "Don't ignore my questions. Please."

She pauses with her fingers still wrapped around the blanket's edge. "I don't know anything about the donor and even if I did, I couldn't tell you."

"But—"

"You have to focus on yourself right now, Adam." Her brow arches in that don't-bother-arguing-stance.

I lower my head. "What happens now?"

"Relax. Doctor Jervis will be here soon." She moves to a nearby monitor and presses a couple buttons on the screen. An orange tracing of my heart rhythm scrolls in a horizontal line.

I follow the jagged bumps and spikes. It's the last note my heart will write before it's removed from my ribcage.

Agonizing minutes pass until the surgeon arrives. A nurse helps him put on a blue gown and gloves. His thick-framed black glasses clash with his skull and flames patterned surgical cap. There's a light on the center of his glasses, like he's going spelunking. All the better to see my anatomy, I gather.

He walks up to the table with his head lifted high and says, "Ready?" His voice is filled with the power of his determination.

It's done then. The donor is officially dead and his heart is waiting to be implanted in my chest. I nod.

"Good. We'll get started then. I don't anticipate any complications. Before you know it, you'll be in the PACU." He turns to the anesthesiologist. "Let's get him sedated and intubated."

Dr. Hillborn walks me through counting backward from ten.

I make it to seven before falling into nothingness.

Chapter Eight

Darby

Images blur on a merry-go-round from Hell that spins faster with each turn. Sleet pounding the windshield. Daniel fighting with the clutch and brake. The truck's headlights impaling us. Crunching steel. Daniel's bloody face.

Pain stretches from my head, dragging its dirty talons down my neck and across my shoulders, ending in cold numbness at my chest. Something presses my body down. I can't move. I can't escape it.

A soft voice filters through the haze. "Darby? Can you hear me?"

My eyelid is pried open. An intense light shines in. I groan, but no sound comes out except for a rush of air.

"She's awake." The light is moved. A woman's face comes into focus. Straight black hair frames her soft cheeks and almond-shaped eyes. "I'm Doctor Wong. You're in the ICU. You're neck was injured in the accident and you needed surgery. We kept the breathing tube in to help you breath. Don't fight it."

Thoughts spark, so fast I can't catch them, like my mind is a net full of holes. I'm alive. Where's Daniel?

My stomach tightens. *Daniel.*

I try to say his name, but the tube in my mouth makes it impossible. I lift my arm. Something tugs on my wrist.

The doctor pats my hand. "We restrained you because you were agitated and I didn't want your neck injury to worsen."

I scream at her, but there's no sound except for more whooshing noises.

She presses two fingers against my palm. "Give a squeeze."

No, I want Daniel. I need to find him!

"Come on. I know you can do it," she says.

I bite the tube. Tears slide across my cheeks.

"Try, Darby."

My fingers twitch, then curl around hers. I grip her as tight as I can, until my arm trembles from the effort.

Finally, she nods. "Okay, relax. Good job. You're stronger than I expected." She smiles like I've just swum the English Channel. "Once you're able to breathe on your own we'll extubate you."

Extub—what?

She turns and walks away.

Wait, she can't leave! I try to sit up again. Pain immediately explodes down my neck and back. Little electric shocks zap my hands. I choke on the stiff tube stuffed down my throat.

A machine next to me starts beeping.

I roll my eyes to the right—a collar around my

neck holds my head straight. God, I'm suffocating. More tears bubble from my eyes. My lungs burn.

I kick and scream and flail and cry, but all it amounts to is a few lame jerks and a long whoosh from the tube.

I'm alone.

I'm going to die.

Three people rush in. The doctor follows them, shouting, "Sedate her, quickly before she injures herself more."

A woman in green scrubs holds me down by the shoulders. "You're okay, Darby. The machine is breathing for you. Try to relax, hon. It's alright." She talks in soothing tones, but she doesn't know *there's no air in my lungs. I can't breathe. I can't move. I'm trapped. Let me go*.

The nurse injects a needle of milky white stuff into my IV.

A raw burn crawls up my arm, blends with the fire in my chest, and pulls me under.

* * *

I'm floating, alone, in darkness. No sound, no light, no touch. Nothing. I'm nothing. Just random thoughts bobbing along, attached by silky threads dipped in dew. I don't know how long I've been here, or where here is, but I know it's peaceful. There's no fear, no pain, no anger, no sadness, just quiet. I could stay here forever.

"Darby?" A familiar voice calls to me. It's bright and sharp.

My soft thoughts jitter, disturbed by the intrusion.

The threads holding me together stiffen. Soon, I feel the weight of pressure, squeezing around me, pushing me down.

"Darby, please, open your eyes."

Mom.

"How is she, doctor?" Panic cuts through her question, tight and itchy.

"She's coming along. Woke up on her own earlier today. She fought the breathing tube, so we sedated her again, but she might come around soon."

I exhale, dragged back into my body, away from the soft comfort of where I was. *No. I don't want to leave this place. Leave me alone.*

"Will she be able to move, walk … ?" Mom sounds so worried. It brings me closer to being awake.

I huff against the tube blocking my throat.

"She just breathed again on her own," the doctor says. "Darby, take another breath for us."

I try to swallow but the tube is so thick I gag and cough.

"Good. Try again."

This time, I focus on moving air in and out of my lungs. *Whoosh. Sigh.*

"Excellent!"

I'm fully back in my body and I *hate. Every. Moment.* A scream pushes through me, but it comes out as: "Whooshhhhsighhhh."

Dr. Wong shines a penlight into my pupils, then says, "Follow my finger with your eyes."

I fist my hands and shake my head no.

"Don't try to move your neck. Just your eyes."

Mom rests her palm on my arm. "You can do it, hon."

She stands next to the doctor smiling, all encouraging and supportive. Her smiles are usually saved for Daniel while I get the narrow-eyed, thin-lipped disappointed face. She must be totally freaked out.

"Darby. Follow my fingers. I need to see if you can follow directions." The doctor barks.

I clench my jaw and follow the doctor's finger left to right, up and down, side to side.

"Good," she says. "I think we can wean you off the vent pretty quickly." All business, she flips a couple of switches on the machine next to me, and the rhythmic rush of air being pushed into my lungs pauses.

Nothing happens. I'm gonna suffocate again. *Shit.* A scratchy heat grows in my chest and pressure builds in my skull. *Why are they torturing me?*

Mom clamps her hands on either side of my face and stares into my eyes. The vertical line in the middle of her forehead deepens. This is the Mom I know. "Darby Fox. Breathe. In and out, like me." She shows me. In through her nose and out through her mouth.

I inhale. Air flows into my lungs. The machine assists me, but a lot less than before.

The doctor and nurse watch me for the next half hour, turning knobs and dials every few minutes.

When I'm completely breathing on my own, she shuts off the machine and says, "Alright. Let's get this tube out."

They sit me up, tear off the tape from around my mouth, and the doctor grabs hold of the tube while the nurse says, "Breathe out, hard."

Dr. Wong pulls the tube out and I start coughing.

The nurse rubs my back. "It's okay, keep breathing.

Slowly, in and out, yes, just like that. Good job!"

"Y-yeah, I got it." My voice is gravelly.

The doctor places her stethoscope on my back and moves it around. "Lungs sound clear," she announces.

The nurse fits an oxygen tube to my nose. "We'll keep this on for a while and observe you closely. You're doing great."

Dr. Wong says, "Ellison, keep an eye on her."

"Yes, doctor." Ellison raises the head of my bed. She fusses with my blanket. "How are you feeling?"

I wiggle my fingers. "Take these off?"

"Now that you're calm, we can remove them. No jumping out of bed though, okay?"

"Scout's honor."

She unties my restraints while Mom watches, hovering at the foot of the bed.

"Where's Daniel?" I ask.

Ellison glances at me, then to Mom. Her smile is sweet, but I catch the hint of worry in her gaze.

Mom circles to my side. She brushes my hair away from my eyes, a painfully tender gesture that I'm not used to. My first instinct is to jerk away, but for some reason I don't. For once, I'm comforted by her touch. "I'm so glad you're okay, honey."

"What happened to him?" I take in a shaky breath, grinding my teeth against the new tears blurring my vision. Seems I can't stop crying.

She tips her chin down, casting shadows on her face. Her brow twitches. "Let's talk about it when your father gets here. I'll call him."

"Is he in the hospital too? I want to see him."

"You just woke up. You need to focus on you now."

"*Tell me.*"

"Later, sweetheart." She goes back to fussing with my hair.

"Mom?" My chest tightens. If he was fine, she'd tell me. "He's okay, right? *Mom?*"

Tears pool in her eyes. She curls her fingers around my fist. "Daniel didn't make it."

Shock crashes into me, white hot. My insides melt. "What do you mean 'didn't make it?'"

"H-he survived the crash, but by the time he arrived at the hospital, he was brain dead." The tears stuck to her lashes fall down her face.

A wail grows in my chest, uncontrollable, powerful, and jagged. It rips out of me, exploding in a sob. "No! That's not true!"

The muscles in Mom's throat tighten. "His seatbelt was defective. It broke." Her voice is stringy and taut.

Fragments of the drive home whizz through my mind. Daniel struggled to keep control of the car while I argued with him. I distracted him. We'd probably be fine if I hadn't bitched at him for looking out for me like always. Selfish Darby strikes again. This time, my brother paid the price.

I shudder.

Daniel's dead.

Gone forever.

An ember of guilt flares deep in my belly. Heat spreads through my veins, singes my lungs, and engulfs my mind in a blaze.

It's. My. Fault.

I scream. The sound streaks across the room, down the hall, and returns to me to burrow deep into my soul.

Mum grabs hold of me. Her flowery perfume cocoons me in unfamiliar comfort. I sit rigid in her arms, struck by the truth that Daniel should be in this hospital bed instead of me.

I should be dead. He should have the second chance, not me.

But I can't take his place.

So I'll suffer here, wrapped in my mother's displaced love.

PART TWO

TÊTE-À-TÊTE

Chapter Nine

Adam

I'm surrounded by darkness and cold. It encases me in a coffin of ice, heavy, leaden, and unforgiving, as if concrete has been poured down my throat in the hopes of turning me into a statue. I am my own sarcophagus.

A steady beeping rings in a pulsing rhythm, a death knell meant for me.

This is the afterlife, and I will spend eternity here, alone, immobile, unfeeling.

More weight is added to me, shoving me deeper underground. I'm being sent to Hell. The agonized scream of another damned soul sounds in the distance. It turns the air to ice. I shiver, uncontrollably. Who knew Hell would be so frigid?

My eyelids are shut. I try opening them, ripping through the glue that gums them together. Distant light blurs above me, a glimpse of Heaven. Why is it so far? Why am I being punished?

I moan.

A shadow flits over me, an angel in white. Shimmery wings brush past, tickling my skin with warmth.

Take me with you. I reach up, but oh, my arm is too heavy to lift. The angel leaves, and with it, her peace.

"Don't go," I rasp. My throat burns as if I've already tasted hellfire.

Two familiar faces take shape before me. I blink a few times to focus.

"Mum … Dad … "

They erupt into toothy smiles, then descend upon me, all teeth and claws.

I jerk back, yelling, hoarse. "No! Stop! Don't hurt me!"

They retreat, startled. Mum covers her mouth with a shaky hand while Dad holds her by the shoulders. Frown lines warp their foreheads.

"What's wrong honey? It's Mum and Dad," Mum says, her voice shaky with a sob.

"Stay away, demons," I hiss.

The angel flies back in. Her wings have been replaced by a long white coat. Her halo is covered by a pink bonnet. "Adam, it's Doctor Hillborn. Remember me? Your surgery went well. How do you feel?"

"S-surgery? I'm not dead?" I ask, searching her face for an otherworldly glow.

"Of course not. You're in the PACU. We'll monitor you here for a while, then send you to the post-cardiac surgery floor." She straightens a gadget on my finger. "Your vitals look good."

"You're an angel," I say.

She laughs. "Aw, that's sweet."

"He thinks we're demons," Dad says.

I tear my gaze away from the angel calling herself Dr. Hillborn to Mum and Dad, or rather, the creatures who look like them. "This isn't real. I'm dead and in Hell."

Mum's face collapses deeper into anguish. "You don't know what you're saying. We need Doctor Shaw."

The Devil herself.

"NO, not her," I say, eyes wide.

The beeping that was so steady moments ago, quickens.

Dr. Hillborn places a warm hand on my shoulder. "Easy now, Adam, try to relax. It's common for folks to be a bit disoriented after surgery. You're not dead. This isn't Hell. You're okay. Things are oh-kay." She speaks slowly, looking directly in my eyes.

"But … "

"We're in the hospital. You just had heart surgery. This is your mom and dad. See?"

I scan the room, searching for any hint of falseness. It all looks normal. Except for the horror on Mum and Dad's faces.

They aren't demons. They're the same as they ever have been. Dr. Hillborn isn't an angel.

The only thing different here is me.

I lift a tentative hand to my chest. It's covered by a thick bandage. "God," I say.

Dr. Hillborn asks, "Are you in pain?"

I swallow. My throat hurts, like I've eaten a gallon of sand. The center of my chest aches as if it's been stuffed full with rocks. "Some."

"We'll help you manage it the best we can. It will get better, okay?"

I extend my hand. "Mum? Dad?"

Mum takes a tentative step closer. Dad follows.

I splay my fingers. "*Mum?*"

She nods, biting her lip, and clasps her hand around mine.

Dad moves to my shoulder and plants a kiss on my head. "We love you, son."

"I thought I had … "

"Shhh, it's okay, Adam," Mum says. "You made it. Things will be better now."

I smile at them. Because I'm supposed to, not because I feel it.

* * *

I sit on the windowsill, watching the flurries in their silent assault on the city below. The clouds have consumed the sun's rays, leaving the world to suffer in shades of blue and gray.

My butt is sore and I'm shivering from leaning against the cold windowpane, but I don't want to move and risk losing the sensation, my only anchor holding me to reality. I'm out of phase with the rest of the world, a half step behind, removed from everything and everyone.

Something changed in me when I was in surgery, other than the obvious heart-swapping. I came back different, un-whole somehow, wraithlike, a shadow of my former self. Not that who I was sat firmly planted, fully realized, to begin with. Illness had robbed that from me, uprooting my life, sapping the soil I tried to grow from. It left my limbs brittle and my mind starved.

On his ridiculously early morning rounds, Doctor Jervis reassured me everything went well. After claiming success he paused, staring at me with his brows lifted and hands spread apart. I guess he expected me to give him endless praise and thanks, like Mum. I didn't. Chance and fate wouldn't dare interfere with his confidence, and yet I dared to spoil his success with my crap attitude. He shrugged it off and turned to glow in Mum's gushing.

I should be grateful. Part of me is. The man saved my life, after all. Another part—the one that's sealed, separate from everything else—still wanders, indecisive, lost, convinced I didn't have much of a life worth saving.

Mum and Dad are ecstatic. They have no idea, of course, what's going through my mind. Neither does Dr. Shaw. She hasn't pried much from me since the surgery, not that she's had much chance to, given my post-op foray into hallucination. Once the anesthesia cleared—thanks to a good night's sleep from Dr. Shaw's prescribed dose of olanzapine—I got over thinking Mum and Dad were demons set on torturing me for eternity in Hell. Cheers to me. That being said, I still don't feel solid. I'm sure Shaw will catch on soon enough and we'll begin Round Two of our mental boxing match, with Mum and Dad standing by sidelines to cheer Dr. Shaw on.

I glance at the calendar posted on the wall across from my bed. Day two of a New Me. I've just got to figure out who this Me is.

I suppress another shiver. Ice huddles in the window's corners and spreads its feathery tentacles across the surface. It'll dominate the entire area in frost if the temperature keeps dropping.

With my teeth clenched, I trace my fingers along the advancing edge. Such a small distance keeps me from the raw element. Yet I'm here, exposed, frozen from the inside out. Nothing is as chilled as my heart. The new one beating in my chest.

The one I've stolen to survive.

I rest my forehead on the window.

A small voice, whispered from the back of my mind says, *I shouldn't be here*.

Someone knocks on the door. I pull my gaze away from the mess of snow. It's like tearing myself out of a trance.

Mum hovers in the doorway. She's wearing a surgical mask. A Doozy's Doughnuts bag rests in her palms. She swings it back and forth as she sweeps into the room. "Brought a treat."

I lower my legs to the floor. "Thanks."

She hands me a chocolate glazed doughnut. "There's peanut butter crème inside."

I take a bite. It's not on my diet, but I don't bother saying so.

"Yummy, right?" Mum hands me a napkin.

I wipe glaze from my mouth. "Yes."

She leans against the sill. "You seem so glum today. I thought … I hoped that things would be different now that you've had the surgery."

I plop the doughnut on a napkin and return to bed. "Mum, don't start. Please."

She shrugs. "Start what? I'm just trying to understand what's happening with you."

"Nothing's happening." Nothing she'd comprehend

anyway.

She tosses the treats into the trash with a heavy sigh. Clearly they were a ploy. One that didn't work as she'd intended. "There most certainly *is* something happening. I'm scared for you, Adam."

I draw up my knees. "You don't have to worry about me."

"Doctor Shaw says post-op depression is common. And on top of you were feeling before the surgery, well, it seems you're getting worse."

"Shaw says that?" So much for fooling everyone. I flip through TV channels. Pictures flit on the screen, barely having enough time to focus before I click onto the next program.

"She's trying to help you."

I snort.

"She can't do her job if you don't talk to her."

I drop the remote onto the bed. "I talk to her."

"That's not what she said."

I glare at Mum. "You're going to believe her over me?"

"You're holding something back and I can't trust that you're being totally honest, so, yes, I'm believing her over you."

I drag my hands through my shaggy hair. "Is it so wrong that I don't trust her?"

Mum throws her arms up in frustration. "What possible reason do you have not to trust her? She's a doctor. She cares about you."

My stomach roils. It wouldn't be the mental gymnastics she puts me through or how she twists my words or how she scowls at me when we're alone. Or how she simultaneously says she wants to help me live while convincing me I want to die.

Outside, a mess of snowflakes tumbles down, spinning a whirling dervish. Quiet chaos. Opposite to the cacophony in my mind.

"Adam?" Mum sits on the bed. She rests her palm on my hand.

"Why are you wearing a mask?"

"I woke up with the sniffles. Didn't want to risk you catching anything."

"You don't have to stay if you're sick."

She moves her hand away. "Your father will be spending the night with you. I need to run some errands, clean the house … "

I face her. "You need a break from me."

Her cheek twitches with the accusation. She's paler than normal and deep, purple circles color the skin under her eyes. "This is hard on all of us. You're not the only one going through it."

"Never said I was."

"Why are you so angry? This isn't like you."

"It *is* me. You don't want to see it. Just because you want me to better, doesn't mean it's going to happen."

Something breaks in her eyes. "If you look at the world—"

"*Mum.*"

"Let me finish." Her tone cuts me deeper than a surgeon's scalpel. "This pessimist viewpoint you've adopted won't get you anywhere. In fact, it'll interfere with your healing and I won't tolerate it anymore. We've come too far—we crossed the *bloody ocean* for god's sake—and we've waited too long for a donor heart to give up now."

"I'm not giving up."

"Could've fooled me." She crosses her arms. "You really think no one notices how you're acting? It's obvious you're not telling the truth and you're doing a piss poor job at pretending."

"I'm not the only one pretending."

Her mouth drops.

"You want honesty? Well, the *truth* is that I can't take any more of your 'Don't Worry, Be Happy' philosophy. You need to stop pretending we've got the happy ending, because we haven't." My chest tightens in progressive notches with each jab I throw at her, twisting like the wires holding my sternum together.

Her lips thin. She grabs her coat and shrugs it on, fighting with the collar a bit before it folds the right way. "I think Doctor Shaw needs to adjust your medications again. No matter what you say, I know this isn't you and I want my old son back." She turns on her heel and stalks out of the room.

I'm left alone to suck on the chalky bitterness of our conversation. Mum will be on the mobile with Dr. Shaw before she reaches the lift. Should be an interesting meeting when I see her next.

I move back to my windowsill perch to watch night fall. The snow has stopped, but dark clouds obscure the sky, blocking out the stars.

There's no light for me.

* * *

After snoring all night, Dad leaves at five AM. I pretend to be asleep. True to form, he doesn't bother me, not even to press a hand against my shoulder or whisper a goodbye. He didn't say much last evening either. Except for three little sentences that have run through my mind all night, shocking me awake when I teetered on the edge of sleep.

"You should be more grateful. Not everybody finds a donor. And you should give your mum a break." He said it between bites of his chicken salad sandwich.

I'd barely eaten half of mine. The taste of it had instantly shifted to sawdust in my mouth, so I'd abandoned the idea of finishing it. Dad either hadn't noticed or decided not to comment on it. He'd spent the rest of the evening working on his computer.

I toss back the covers, tense from spending several hours in a small room with him. I don't intend to be a disappointing son, but it's what I am. What I've been. New heart or not, I'm still broken. Ruined. Useless.

The window faces southeast, so the sunrise greets me, unashamed in its nakedness. I boldly stare at the pale yellow orb as it crests the horizon, daring it to blind me. A veil of haze diffuses its power so I end up with a couple darkened spots in my vision that fade in a few seconds.

When Dr. Shaw arrives late morning, I've accomplished five laps around the unit, a bath (no showers because of all the bandages and wires and things), and half of my History reading assignment. The gist of it is that Brits are bad and Americans are brave and relentless in their righteous quest for freedom. Good for them, dumping a bunch of tea in a harbor. Mum calls it a bloody waste. I'd say the same, if it was coffee.

A quick knock comes on the door. Shaw prances in

with a bright smile on her face. "It's good to see you out of bed." She plops her coat and purse on the cot. "Looks like you're working on some homework?"

I stick a pen in the book and shut it. "Yes."

"What subject?"

"History."

"What part?"

"Um ... " I shrug. "You really want to talk about my reading assignment?"

"Ah, don't like your studies?" She joins me on the windowsill and crosses her legs. Her pencil skirt stretches taught around her slight hips and her black leather knee-high boots cover her calves. She clutches something small in her hand, but I don't ask what it is.

"I don't really like the subject. Makes us Brits looks bad."

She chuckles. "Fair enough. We can talk about something else. How are things going?"

I scrunch into a ball, wincing at the pulling sensation across my chest that any movement makes. "Fine."

The corners of her mouth turn down like she smells something rancid. "We've discussed not using words like 'fine.' Describe how you're really feeling."

Thoughts bubble and churn, but none emerge fully formed or coherent.

"Come on. Spit it out. It doesn't matter how stupid you think it sounds." She nudges my toe with a manicured fingernail. Blood-red polish. "We have to break you out of this. You're parents are worried and frankly, I am too."

I chew on my lip ring. Cars congest the street below, along with a steady stream of pedestrians, filing in and out of a corner café. "I feel ... caged, like I'm locked away in a tower. I don't remember what fresh air is like. Food tastes bland. If I'm supposed to start acting normal, I need to get out of here."

She hops to the floor. "All right, then. Let's go outside."

I turn my gaze to her, wide-eyed. Hadn't expected that twist. "Yeah?"

"I'll get you a mask. You have a coat and shoes?"

I nod.

"Get dressed."

Five minutes later—and with the permission of the nursing staff—I walk through the main doors of the hospital with Dr. Shaw by my side.

She slides on a pair of designer sunglasses while I adjust the surgical mask that I have to wear in public. At least it provides a small barrier against the biting November cold. My pajama pants, on the other hand, don't.

Since the transplant, I've started a new regimen of immunosuppressant drugs that prevent my body from rejecting my new heart. Wearing the mask blocks airborne germs. Touching things is potentially dangerous too. Microscopic bugs are everywhere. Hell, the common cold could kill me. Maybe I should wear a biohazard bodysuit or spend the rest of my life in a bubble.

I press the mask's bendable nose piece tighter over the bridge of my nose, stuffing the idea of how unnatural it is to have someone else's heart pumping inside and how taking a handful of pills twice a day confirms it.

It's hard to believe my ribcage was splayed open and someone rifled their hands through my internal organs. It's also hard to believe how much stronger I feel. I have a heart that can adequately pump blood through my system. Despite the soreness in my breastbone from the wires and stitches, I can take a breath and be refreshed from it.

I don't have to worry about the lift being broken or passing out in class or dropping dead in the shower anymore.

We descend the front stairs and step off the curb to cross the street. At the corner, we turn left, heading downhill past the same café I'd watched from my window. I'm tempted to slip inside for a cup of coffee but I'm still not supposed to have caffeine. If my heart is so strong, I'm not sure why I can't, but I don't have money so the point is moot.

Shaw must sense my hesitation by the door. "Want to go in?"

"Nah." I stuff my hands in my jacket pockets and speed up, wishing I'd worn a hat. My ears are prickling from the cold.

She keeps pace with me—it's not like I'm rocketing down the street, but I'm definitely walking faster than I have in months. Her boot heels click with each step, confident and self-assured. "You sure? I can feel your temptation from here."

"I'm not supposed to."

"What about decaf?"

I huff into my mask, scrunching my nose at the moisture collecting along my upper lip. "I don't have any money."

"My treat." She flashes that bright smile again. The one she usually reserves for Mum. Must be some new tactic.

My stomach coils. "No, thanks."

She hooks her arm through mine, resting her hand against my forearm. "Come on. I think you need to loosen up a bit. It'll help you relax. Feel alive. You want to live, right?" She drags me to the café and we walk inside, arm in arm.

I fidget with my mask while she orders a skinny half-caff latte for herself and a decaf for me.

She pauses mid-order, turns to me with her coy eyes, and says, "How do you like it?"

This must be a new game. Dunno what it is or why, but I'm sure I'll find out soon enough.

"Sir?" The cashier raises her eyebrows.

Shaw nudges me. "You haven't chickened out have you?"

Her dare hangs in the air between us. I swallow the doubts churning up my esophagus. Mum says Shaw is a doctor and it's her job to help people. She wouldn't be in the profession if she had any other intentions. Besides, if I'm going to get better, I need to let go of my mistrust, for Mum's and Dad's sakes and my own. "Light and sweet, please."

The cashier doesn't flinch at my mask. She must see a lot of patients come through here along with hospital staff. She punches in the order with a winning customer service smile.

Shaw rests her purse on the counter. "Pick a table. I'll wait for the drinks."

Most of the morning crowd has left so most of the tables are empty. I select one by a window.

Shaw sits across from me and hands over my drink. She daintily sips her coffee while I tease the cardboard sleeve apart on mine. It frays beneath my fingernail like my nerves. I begin to wonder if we're waiting each other out.

Finally, she says, "I'm afraid we're backsliding here."

I tug my mask off to take a sip. There's a strange grittiness to it. The sugar must not have dissolved completely. "Why?"

Shaw eyes me lowering the cup. "Well, going for coffee is a big step, but you're quieter than ever. You usually open up a bit once we've broken the ice."

"I don't have much to say."

"Like I've said, you're one of the most pensive boys I know. So, when you tell me you don't have much to say, I can only assume your mind is clogged and you're struggling with how to unplug it. Therapy can be your plunger."

"And you're like Liquid Plumber." I take another sip, my ears ringing with the word, 'boy.' The grit doesn't taste like sugar. It's probably a synthetic substitute.

She catches the tremble of my hand. "You're anxious. Good thing we ordered the decaf."

How uncharacteristic of her to ignore my plumber comment. It might yet cycle around and make an encore appearance later. I slide my hands under the table. "I'm not nervous."

She gives me a half-smile. "We've been working together for months, now, Adam. I can tell when something is bothering you. It's better if you go along with the process and comply with therapy."

I gesture to the almost empty café. "If we're doing real therapy, shouldn't we meet in private, like in your office?" I can't believe I suggested being alone with her, but her office is a few blocks away, far enough where we wouldn't have time to walk there.

"Depends on the type. When reintegrating post-transplant patients with their new life, it's often beneficial to do every day activities with them to gauge their response and tolerance. It's sort of like systematic desensitization."

"How am I doing?" I glance out the window at the hospital, less than half a block away, regretting my question.

"You've barely drunk your coffee and your leg is jittering so bad I can feel the floor shaking."

I freeze. Bollocks, I hadn't even noticed my leg jumping up and down.

"What's making you anxious?"

I chew on my lip ring, studying the silver flecks in the fake granite tabletop while I mull over my options. I could tell her the truth—she freaks me out. Or I could play the game and offer some excuse about not adjusting to having a new heart. I lived with the defective one for so long. It's like upgrading a crappy four-cylinder engine to a supercharged V8. A nice idea, except my chassis is still the same economy car model. With rust. And bald tires.

"Adam?"

I drag my gaze up to meet hers.

She lowers her eyebrows to a straight line. "Where do you go when you retreat in your mind?"

"You know what I think about this whole thing. I don't have to repeat myself."

"What whole thing?"

I sigh. "The transplant. Having a new heart."

"What's it like?"

"I … don't know."

"Yes, you do."

I prop my elbows on the table and rest my forehead in my laced hands. A burst of cold air buffets me as a group of customers enters the café. Their chatter is bright, but it soon fades into the background. I focus on taking even breaths.

"Did you expect things to be different?" she asks.

"What do you mean?" My leg starts to jackhammer again. I drop my hands to the table.

She runs her finger along the rim of her coffee cup. "In a lot of ways, the surgery is the first step and the waiting before is, well, waiting."

"Right. This is my second chance. One door has closed and another opened." I leave off the yada-yada. I chug the rest of my coffee.

Her mouth tugs up in a half-smile. Wry. Challenging. "Which brings me back to the question. Did you expect things to be this way?"

I lean back in the chair and suppress a wince from stretching my chest. "What way are they?"

She narrows her eyes as if she's deciding how much to yield. "You've got a new heart, but also new responsibility. There are more things to worry about, like infections, rejection of the donor heart, and the need to constantly be vigilant."

"Vigilant?"

"If you get sick, your body can't fight it off like healthy people."

There it is. I'm not healthy. I've got a fresh start, I'm heart disease free, and I'm still weak. "What's the point?" I mumble.

Shaw drags her chair closer until our knees almost

touch. I fight the instinct to retreat. "Say that again? I didn't hear you."

I sigh. Once the words tumble out, I can't reel them back in. She'll hound me until I repeat them. "I'm wondering what the point of all of this is. I have a new heart, but now I have to take all these pills to prevent rejection and if I don't, my body will attack it. It's not a part of me. It's foreign. But it's also inside me, waiting to turn against me."

"That's the vigilant part I'm talking about." She spreads her palm on the table. Delicate blue veins tangle between the tendons of her hand.

"My parents think I should be fixed, but I'm not. I couldn't trust my old heart and I can't trust this one."

She retreats to the other side of the table. "Your father called me early this morning. He wonders why you're not more grateful for the gift you've been given."

I choke on a breath. It's like a lance has impaled my chest. So far, Mum has been the one to communicate with Dr. Shaw and Dad's taken a hand's off approach. Now they've all ganged up on me. None of them care to listen. They think they know what's going on, but they don't and trying to explain things only makes it worse. I give up. Forfeit. Surrender.

"To tell you the truth, I have to wonder the same thing." Steel glints in her eyes.

"I'm not talking about this anymore with you or anyone else." I stand and walk away from her.

The light-hearted-hey-let's-play-hospital-hooky outing is over.

Chapter Ten

Darby

Since I proved how well my lungs worked by screaming my head off, I was immediately moved to the pediatric wing. That was yesterday. Twenty four hours have passed since I woke up and my brother didn't.

He'd survived the crash. Or his body had. But his brain had been damaged so badly he'd never come out of the coma. Mom and Dad had decided to stop life support. They gave up on him.

And here I sit, empty, sometimes quiet and numb and other times crying uncontrollably. Mom and Dad don't know what to do with me. Nurses try to help me with games and treats and smiles. The doctor says my broken bone in my neck should heal and I'll be able to start physical therapy soon, but she worries about willingness to go along with it.

I sit in middle of my bed, wrapped in three blankets,

each pale pink. I rock back and forth, staring at the pastel safari animal decals plastered on the mint green walls. Baby giraffes, elephants, and gazelles jump across the painted grass under the lemon yellow ceiling. Their pale colors contrast with the plaid curtains that are bright red, green, and blue. The designer must've gotten confused. Are we in Kindergarten Scotland or Baby Zoo Africa?

I'm confused too. It doesn't make sense why I lived while Daniel, the perfect son, brother, athlete, friend, and student, died.

Mom and Dad should forget about me, but they keep trying to fix me.

I don't deserve it.

Mom went so far as to bring in my art supplies this morning. Says I should try painting to work through my grief. It can help me regain strength too. The canvases and supplies she brought lay abandoned in the corner, alone.

I have no desire to touch them. No desire to remember my old life.

Through it all, I keep breathing and my heart keeps beating while everything else inside me shrivels and dies.

Mom and Dad arrive after dinner. They hang their coats neatly in the locker-sized closet and drag two chairs to my bed.

Yay, broken family quality time.

Dad breaks the silence first. "Did you eat supper?"

I chew on a ragged fingernail.

Mom reaches for a can of Boost with a sigh. She pulls the tab and drops a straw into the hole. She holds the can under my nose. "Drink up. Strawberry is your favorite."

I glare at her with my best leave-me-alone face.

"Open your mouth," she says, like she's talking to a toddler.

I suck on the straw until it's all gone. I might as well chew on ash.

Mom sets the empty can on the table and sits next to me. She wraps her arm around my shoulder. "Darby, honey, please tell us what's going on. I know you're sad about Daniel. We all are. But we need to communicate in order to get through it. Sitting here, doing nothing, it's not healthy."

I pick at a scab on my hand. The pain distracts me from her comfort.

A tiny dot of blood pools in the groove. I wipe the droplet away with my thumb and then suck on it. The taste of bitter metal steeps on my tongue.

Dad unbuttons the top button of his shirt and tugs his tie loose. "Darbs, you need to snap out of this."

I rip my fingers through my greasy hair.

Mom rests her forehead against my temple. Her tears stick to my skin. "We've already lost one child. Don't make us lose another."

So they're holding onto me like a life raft, hoping I can stop the sinking Titanic that is our lives. They know I'm defective. They shouldn't waste their time.

"Leave me alone," I say. I want to add, "Forget about me. Pretend I'm dead. Move on."

"That's not going to happen." Mom pulls me closer.

"We love you, Darbs." Dad moves to the other side of my bed. He wraps his arms around both of us, sandwiching me in affection they'd ordinarily pour over Daniel.

Sweat breaks out across my forehead. My palms are clammy.

What they don't say is they loved him more. The strawberry drink sloshes in my stomach. It's sick that my brother has to die for my parents to pay me any attention. It's worse that I want to sink into it. But I can't. I don't deserve it. I'm the booby prize when what they should have is the grand prize—their perfect son.

I choke out a sob. "Why didn't I die?" The question comes out in a wail.

Dad hugs us tighter.

The pit of lava in my gut bubbles up.

"The accident was my fault." I wait for their arms to retreat.

Mom stiffens.

"What do you mean?" Caution coils around Dad's words.

I sniff. "We were arguing."

"Oh, Darby." Mom eases away from me—the beginning of her withdrawal from me. Good. This fits our normal script better. While it hurts, it also makes more sense.

I hug myself to hold in the bits of me that are crumbling off. "He's dead because of me."

Mom tucks a strand of my icky hair behind my ear. "It was an accident. The roads were icy. You had nothing to do with that."

"I distracted him."

"What were you fighting about?" Dad retreats to the window and rests his butt against the sill. He rolls up his sleeves. Time to get to work on solving the puzzle of Darby.

I suck on my bottom lip, hesitating. It's too embarrassing to tell. My brother's dead because of a couple pictures and a lame revenge plot. Maybe putting it out there will be the final blow. Mom and Dad will have to leave once they find out what I did.

Mom stands. "Did you get in trouble at the game?"

"No, I wasn't *in trouble*."

She returns to the chair, taking her warmth with her. As foreign as it is, I miss it. "Then what happened?"

"It was stupid." Bile rises to my throat.

Dad lowers his chin. His face is all wrinkled forehead, squinted eyes, and thin lips, cancelling out his "we love you" line from a minute ago. Love shouldn't have conditions, but it does for me. "That makes no sense, Darby. Why pick a fight when the weather was so bad? Couldn't it have waited until you got home?"

This is what I'm used to. Anger. Confusion at my stupidity.

"Phillip, go easy on her," Mom says.

"She just said she caused the accident, Annette!" He shoves off the windowsill. His eyes are sharp and piercing. "Why is it that you're always in the mix when bad things happen?"

"*Phillip*." Mom scrunches her face like she's going to be sick.

I stare up at him, shaking. "You wish I died instead, don't you?"

"Jesus, Darby." Dad runs his hand through his thick black hair—care of Just For Men hair dye—and paces the small area between my bed and the window.

"We don't wish you died," Mom says. She slides to the edge of her seat, but doesn't reach out to touch me. Maybe it's finally dawning on her that life will be smoother without Darby to mess it up.

"Yes, you do."

"Listen to me, honey. Accidents happen." Mom's

not letting go.

I can't understand why.

Dad pauses, tipping his head back to stare at the ceiling.

"Daniel's death was not the end for him. His heart went to someone right here, in this hospital. He gave the gift of life to so many others." Mom expression brightens with hope. Soon she'll start talking about how he's looking down on us from Heaven.

Dad covers his mouth with a hand. His face goes red. He sucks in a shaky breath. I doubt he feels the same way.

"I have to hold onto that and you should too," Mom adds.

I toss the blankets aside and stand. My greasy hair covers my face in chunks. I feel crazy. I probably look crazy. "You let the doctors cut him up in pieces and give parts of him away? Is this hospital running a chop shop?"

Mom recoils. Horror snaps through her eyes, widening them with disgust. "How could you say something like that?"

"He wasn't dead. You had to pull the plug." Someone else has Daniel's heart. It beats in his or her chest, strong, alive. *Stolen.* And my brother is lying dead in a coffin.

Mom slumps into the chair. Her whole body shakes.

Dad circles to my side of the bed. "He was brain dead, Darby."

"He was alive!"

"He wasn't, honey. His body was, but his mind was gone. *He* was gone. H-he's in Heaven now." Mom's voice shakes like she's grasping onto what she's saying with her fingernails. Problem is, her hold is slipping. The rock under her hands is sand, and there's nothing to steady her.

A chill shudders down my spine. I don't believe in life after death. Once your heart stops beating, that's it. Game over. And I certainly don't buy the whole silver lining bullshit. I mean, she's happy that Daniel's organs were donated? Doesn't change the fact that he's dead.

He'd dead. He's dead! *He's dead!*

I yank on my c-collar, gasping for breath. I pull until the Velcro tabs loose.

Mom launches from her chair. She clamps her hands over mine. "Phillip, help."

Dad pries my left hand away from the collar while Mom does the same with my right. "Darby, stop."

"Get off me!" My screech pierces my ears, but I don't care. I twist and bend, but Dad manages to pin my wrist behind my back. He wraps his other arm around me while Mom calls for help.

It's too much. I break down into sobs.

About six nurses and aids rush in, ready for action. Nissa, a petite woman with a bubble gum pink stripe in her hair takes the lead. "What happened?"

Mom quickly explains while the group yanks on rubber gloves. It's about to get down and dirty.

"You have to leave the collar on, Darby." Nissa speaks in a calm voice.

It breaks through the noise in my mind. I go rigid in Dad's bear hug. "Get them out of my room."

Nissa's brow furrows with confusion. "Who?"

I wiggle against Dad's solid hold. "My parents."

"Why?"

I stare at Mom. I have to get her out. Dad's already

teetering on the edge and if she leaves, he'll follow. "They killed my brother, that's why."

My words are a fist that crumples Mom's face. Her jaw lowers in shock and she collapses back into the chair, winded, broken.

Dad's hold falters. He steps away from me.

I turn to face him. "He was alive."

He squares his jaw, turns on his heel, and grabs Mom's arm. "Let's go, Annette."

Mom follows him.

I get what I want.

I'm alone.

* * *

The next morning, a tall, thin woman walks into my room while I'm towel drying my hair. Such fun showering with a c-collar on.

Sunlight peeks through the window and the woman steps into the spotlight it creates. Everything about her is rich and stuffy, from her slick bun to her designer clothes. She extends her hand to me. "I'm Doctor Shaw. I work with the heart transplant team and provide psychotherapy for donor families and recipients. You must be Darby."

I eye her while tugging on the end of my towel. The transplant team. Are they fishing for more organs? "You're a shrink?"

"A psychiatrist."

"Who sent you?"

"Your parents called this morning. They told me

what's been going on and they asked if I could help you work through things."

"Did they mention I'm crazy?"

She lowers her brows to a straight line. "No. Not at all. Losing a brother—a twin at that—is such a painful thing to go through, no one should have to do it alone."

"Glad you know everything about it." I roll my eyes.

She tips her head to the side. "I'm not feeding you a line, Darby."

"Whatever." I toss the towel to the end of the bed and pick up a comb. I drag it through my hair. The tines catch on a knot. *Ugh.*

"You said some hurtful things to your parents last night."

I drop the comb. It plops on my lap. "Are you here to yell at me?"

She face softens. "No. I'm here to help you."

"I don't want your help."

Shaw pulls up a chair. "I work with grieving people every day. Take my word, you will get through this."

I go back to detangling my hair.

"I have to say though, you're the first twin I've worked with."

"I'm not a twin anymore."

Shaw drags her chair closer, scraping the metal legs across the tile floor. The wail sounds like fingernails on a chalkboard. "You'll always be a twin, Darby Fox."

I twist my entire upper body to face her. It's the only way I can move with the c-collar holding my neck straight.

Dr. Shaw leans forward, her elbows on her knees, fists tucked under her chin. Her dark eyes radiate warmth and something else I can't quite name. "Nothing can break the bond you and your brother shared."

"Death can."

She doesn't flinch. Mom would have. "Your parents said you're not taking Daniel's organs being donated well."

My throat tightens.

"It must have felt like your own heart was carved out of your chest when you found out."

I twist the comb with both hands. It snaps in two.

"I'm so sorry." Her voice is soft. Soothing. Judgment-free.

"It hurts so much I can't breathe sometimes." The sharp edge of the comb digs into my palm. I press the pad of my thumb against it until I draw blood.

Shaw stands and gently rests her hand over mine. "I know what it's like to lose someone."

I drag my gaze away from our hands to her face. "Who?"

She eases the broken comb pieces from my hands. "My mother. She died when I was thirteen. Her heart was donated to someone too."

Her confession settles over me like an ice bath. I shiver. "How'd you deal with it?"

She puts the broken ends of the comb together so it looks whole. "I didn't at first. I remember feeling a lot of anger over how unfair it was that someone else got to have their mother while I lost mine." The edge of her mouth curls up in an I-can't-believe-I'm-admitting-this half-smile. "I believed the woman who received my mother's heart stole it from her."

I had the same thought! The ice bath of pain I've been wading in swells over my head and pours down my throat. It sloshes in my guts, chilling me from the inside out. I suck on my bottom lip.

"It's okay if you've felt the same way. Thoughts and feelings are normal. It's how we deal with them that makes the difference."

"You got over it?"

The half-smile fades. "No, not entirely. I don't think you ever do. But I've found a way to cope. I've worked through it. I've survived. And so can you."

I can't live like this. Ripped apart. Empty. Alone. I can't bear the thought of leaving Daniel behind, in the ground, while I live on. Then again, he spent half his time watching out for me so I'd have a good life. I'd be a pretty crappy sister if I let his death destroy me. "Will you help me?"

Shaw stands. "Of course, honey. That's why I'm here."

Chapter Eleven

Adam

Shaw shows up a bit early, carrying a tray with two venti coffees. She catches up to me on my final lap around the ward and walks me to my room. I don't bother greeting her. She doesn't bother with small talk.

I kick off my slippers, yank off my facemask, and retreat to my windowsill nest. It's stuffed with a pillow, blanket, a few books, and my schoolwork. I fumble with my copy of *Frankenstein*. Still she says nothing. She just stands there at the end of my bed, staring at me.

It's creepy.

I toss the book aside in favor of the facemask. Bit by bit, I tear the mask to shreds, letting the tattered pieces fall on my lap, the windowsill around me, and to the floor.

My hands shake. Actually, my whole body quivers as if I've drank three espressos. My legs itch to run and

I haven't run in years. I tighten my muscles, close my fists, and grit my teeth.

The next fifty minutes are going to be hell.

"You're giving that mask the what for," she says, breaking the so-called ice that seals the beginning of our sessions.

I shrug.

"So you're really not going to talk to me?"

"Wasn't planning on it."

"At least tell me why you're so angry with me."

I splay my fingers on my thighs. "I'm not angry."

"Repressing it doesn't make it go away."

I make eye contact with her, reluctantly.

"It's better when you're honest, Adam. And not just honest with me, but with yourself." She holds a coffee out to me. "Decaf, light and sweet."

I toggle my lip ring, caught in indecision.

"Go on. Take it. I feel bad about what happened yesterday. Consider this an amends."

"Thanks." I accept the peace offering. It's easier than keeping the fight going.

She takes a sip of what I assume is a latte, failing to hide her satisfied smile. "What should we talk about today?"

Instead of answering, I take a long, long drink from mine. The same grit from yesterday's coffee is in this one. Seems more bitter today. I grimace, chewing on the sandy substance.

"Maybe we should review the coffee shop incident."

I set my coffee aside. "Incident?"

"I didn't expect you to walk out on session. Something must've really triggered you. We should process it."

I rest my skull against the wall. Shaw's right. Something had triggered me. She had asked a good question yesterday and the answer is, no, I didn't expect things to be this way. I didn't expect to be accused of ungratefulness. I didn't expect to cast out my mother. I didn't expect Dad to blab to Shaw.

I didn't expect things to be worse.

"I don't want to talk about it."

She taps her palm against her cup. "I'm not opposed to giving you some space. Why don't I come back tomorrow and we can try again? You can use today's session time to think about what you'd like to say."

"Look, I meant what I said yesterday. I'm done with therapy."

The brightness in her expression fades, fractured by the hard lines of her thin face. Her almost black eyes dig into me. "I'll have to speak to your parents about this."

"Fine." Let her talk to them. They can't make me continue therapy. She can't force me to process anything. I can make my own decisions.

Point made, she retreats out of the room.

I exhale with relief and chug the rest of my drink. In the end, it's a total disappointment. The rich coffee flavor I crave is there, but the chalky bits floating at the bottom are beyond bitter. I have to brush my teeth twice to erase the grit.

Ricky, the physical therapist knocks on the door about an hour later. He doesn't wait for me to answer, but comes striding in with a smile plastered across his face like it's part of his uniform. His sweatpants swoosh as he walks. There's a hole over his right knee. His polo shirt—which has the hospital logo stitched on it—looks like it's been washed ten thousand times. His brand name trainers don't have a speck on them. Priorities, I gather. "Morning, Adam. Finished with Doctor Shaw?"

In more ways than one. I tip my head in his direction to greet him. "Yes."

"Ready for your daily dose of PT? I won't let you beg out of it like you did yesterday, killer headache or not." He rubs his hands together. Reminds me of a tiger licking its chops before leaping at its prey.

"I thought my head was going to explode." I did. Damn thing lasted most of the afternoon and nothing made it go away until the doctor ordered some Percocet.

"Fair enough." He spots the shreds of mask litter. His eyebrow ticks up. "What the … ?"

"It's a mask. I was bored." He doesn't have to know the real reason I tore the thing to shreds.

He chuckles. "Guess you'll need a new one, then."

After grabbing a new mask and fitting it over my face, I follow him to the PT room. It smells like rubber, old sweat, and dried bleach. Other patients are working on various exercises to regain whatever skill they lost. Most of them are wrinkly old men. One of them wears a Vietnam Veteran hat.

Ricky leads me directly to a treadmill in the far corner. A bank of mirrors lines the wall so I get to watch myself work out. Yay.

For good measure, he breaks out a disinfecting wipe and cleans off the handholds and controls of the treadmill. "Have you been doing laps around the unit?"

"Every couple of hours."

"How many circles do you do?"

"Five."

He nods. "Good. Hop on."

I plant my feet on either side of the belt and grip the handholds for balance. Air stutters in my lungs. I'm out of breath and I haven't started exercising yet. This should go well.

Ricky presses a few buttons, selecting a circuit. "Gonna walk uphill today."

The motor's whine joins the other machines. The belt whips to life, winding around the track in a blur. I set my right foot on first, then my left. It starts off slow and increases to the designated speed.

At five minutes, the hydraulics elevate the platform to simulate walking uphill.

I follow along, a good little gerbil. Walking, but getting nowhere. Kind of the story of my life.

It doesn't take long to generate a burn in my calves and hamstrings. I'm huffing pretty hard, too. The mask holds in too much heat. Sweat breaks out all over my body. My palms sweat, slicking the handholds.

I pray for the next phase of the program, the part where the incline reduces so I can walk on a flat surface. My lungs hurt from expanding more than they're used to. I try to take steadier breaths. The wires in my sternum should hold, but it seems like their edges are tugging apart. My oh-so-helpful brain conjures images of them popping open and my heart leaping out to plop lifeless on the belt.

"How you doing?" Ricky watches me from the treadmill's side. He's holding a clipboard and pen, ready to catalogue my stats.

"Fantastic." I pant. A drop of sweat trickles into my eye. It burns and I try, unsuccessfully, to rub it out.

"Let's check your heart rate. Grab the sensors."

I wrap my fingers around the handles on either side of the control panel. The screen flickers and a little heart pulses in the right corner like a cursor. After a few seconds, my heart rate pops up.

"One-twenty-seven. Good." Ricky scratches the number down on his tracking sheet.

I jerk my head up and down a couple times. My heart thumps wildly against my sternum. My pulse rushes through my ears like an out of control tidal wave. Heat encases my body. The room starts to swirl. Before the surgery, this all added up to a warning that my heart was about to trip into an unstable rhythm and if I didn't heed it, I could collapse.

I squeeze the handles, mentally strangling my worry. This heart can handle the challenge.

If that were true, then the encroaching shroud of blackness shouldn't be descending over my eyes.

Something's wrong. I need to stop. Get off this hellish contraption. I must quit … or I'm going to die.

"I need a break." I desperately want to punch the stop button, but if I let go of the handles, I'll lose my balance and fall. My heavy feet slam on the belt, a compliment to my pounding heart. *Ba-boom-ba-boom-ba-boom-ba-boom*. I drag my toe with every step as if I'm walking through wet concrete.

My heart rate spikes up to one-forty-one. The darkness at the corners of my vision spreads.

"Deep breaths. You can do this. No pain, no gain." Ricky watches it, his dark hawk-like eyes trained on the number.

"I can't." My mouth is dry, but the air behind my mask is humid. Salty sweat coats my upper lip. I lick it away as I huff and puff. Air snags in my throat, like brittle leaves scratching along a sidewalk. My knees wobble. "Please."

Ricky presses his mouth into a thin line. "Tough it out, Adam. Thirty seconds."

"I'm going to pass out." I take deep breaths, but can't get enough oxygen in my lungs. My legs shake from fatigue.

I trip over my toe and drop to my knees. The belt keeps looping. I slide down the track onto my stomach, then land prone on the floor. Something crunches in my breastbone. I gurgle out a scream.

Ricky slaps the stop button, but the belt skids along my chin. All my weight is pressed on my upper torso—against the incision Dr. Jervis so expertly carved into my body. My arms are sprawled wide as if I'm about to take flight. I flap them, completely useless.

Ricky is at my side, kneeling. He places a hand on my left shoulder. "You okay?"

I press my cheek against the cold tile floor. "Can't … move."

"Roll on your side."

"C-can't … "

"Yes, you can. Pull your arms in, tighten your abs, and roll." He bends my left elbow so my arm is parallel with my side.

I mirror him with my right arm. "Careful, something popped in my chest."

"It's okay. You're fine." He slides a hand under my shoulder and hip and pries me over.

I groan with the movement. "Something's not right. The wires broke." My voice is shrill from panic.

Ricky lifts my shirt. "Everything looks good. Where'd you feel the popping?"

"There has to be something wrong." My shirt is in the way. I can't tell if my wound is open or if shards of my breastbone are peeking through my skin. I lift my head and point a shaky finger just above my stomach. Intense burning radiates out from the spot—the point of impact.

Ricky hefts me upright so I'm sitting up. He angles me toward the mirror. "Nothing's damaged. See?"

I stare at my reflection. My scrawny, pale, hyperventilating, bug-eyed reflection. Such a coward.

The wrinkled faces of the old guys are turned toward me too. They study me through their milky cataracts, their dentures hanging loose in their gaping mouths. The elderly peanut gallery is getting a front row view of me, the pansy-assed weakling who can't handle five minutes on a treadmill.

"I think we've had enough for today." Ricky pats my back.

He's right. I've had enough. Of everything. I rip the mask off and run my fingers along the incision line. Dozens of stitches pucker my skin. None of them have torn. No wires stick out of my body. The burning that had me in such panic eases. I'm okay.

And I'm chicken shit.

Wait until Shaw hears about this.

* * *

Shaw doesn't visit during our normal session time the next day. At first, I'm relieved. Then as the hours push on, my stomach starts to writhe with anticipation, much like swirling clouds on the edge of a hurricane.

Sure enough, she arrives after dinner, when Mum's there. It's a good plan. Mum will back Shaw up, for sure.

"I heard you had a panic attack in PT yesterday." Of course it's the first thing out of Shaw's mouth.

"He refuses to talk about it," Mum sets her Kindle aside and slides to the edge of her cot.

All evening she's lobbed fiery arrows at me—sometimes in the guise of small talk and sometimes not—in hopes of breeching my outer walls. I've resisted, but it's come with a heavy price. My appetite refuses to return. I can't focus on homework. Nothing interests me on TV. I can't focus on the Maugham book I'm reading. (Perhaps too late, I've abandoned *Frankenstein* in the hopes of leaving visions of the doctor's monster behind.)

"Nothing happened. Let's just forget about it." I rest the back of my head on the wall, clutching my heart pillow to my chest, the silly little thing I have to carry around as a reminder not to use my arms too much lest I actually do and pop open my wounds. It's my shield, my plate of armor. I've been reluctant to set it down since my fall. Wind lashes the window, howling against the sill. A slight shift of air brushes my side. Gooseflesh erupts along my arms. I should've wrapped a blanket around myself, but then again the cold from sitting in the windowsill gives me something to focus on besides my traitorous body.

Mum stands. "I'll leave you two alone. Do you want anything from the cafeteria?"

I try not to gape at her. She's leaving me alone with Shaw. No double confrontation. Shocker. "No."

"I think you should join us for session today." Dr. Shaw gestures for Mum to sit.

"Really?" Mum eases onto the cot, her brow warped into a questioning arch.

Back to two against one. I slump and let my feet dangle over the sill's edge. My knees are sore from crashing to the floor. "I don't want to meet with you anymore, remember?"

Shaw gives a surprised laugh. It has to be part of her act—for Mum. She knows exactly how I feel about therapy so the chuckle isn't for my benefit. "You have to be in treatment. It's part of the program."

Mum folds her hands in her lap, but sits so straight it's like a metal rod is lodged in her spine. "He told you he wanted to stop therapy?"

I curl my fingers around the sill's ledge. Shaw hadn't told Mum already?

Shaw dips her chin. "Yes."

"Why, Adam?" Mum picks at a fingernail.

"You guys think I'm not making any progress anyway, so what's the difference?" I say.

"I'm not giving up simply because you want to." Shaw, so confident, so matter of fact.

One battering ram of a sentence brings down the outer wall of my fortress.

"Doctor Shaw is right. You need treatment more than ever." On cue, Mum backs Shaw up.

"I don't need the two of you ganging up on me." I rub my finger along the stitches of my heart pillow. They're rough, like the sutures in my chest.

"Why do you think we're against you? We're trying to help you, but all you do is shut us out." Mum goes for the center gate.

"Maybe I need to be left alone for a while instead of constantly being—" I pause, catching myself.

Shaw crosses her arms. She hasn't taken off her coat yet. "Constantly being what?"

I suck on my lip ring.

Mum mirrors her by folding her arms across her chest. "Answer the question."

I can't handle a battle on two fronts. "Nothing."

"See? There he goes again." Mum smacks her thigh.

"It must be so frustrating, Lisa."

I glare at Shaw, but she's giving Mum her undivided attention.

Mum's forehead furrows. "Very. It makes me so … *upset* to see him come so far and yet be so … *unhappy*. Why is this happening?"

Shaw sets her purse on the bedside table and sits. She crosses her ankles and tucks her feet to the side, all formal and proper. Except for the side slit in her skirt that gives me an arrhythmia-inducing view of her thigh. "When depression takes hold it can be extremely difficult to pluck it out."

She talks about it like it's a wart or parasite that needs excavating. It's more than that. It's a part of me, indistinguishable from normal Adam. To separate us would mean destroying me. If a whole me can even be teased out of this mess I've become.

Mum abandons her cot to sit on the windowsill. She clamps her hands over mine, looking me straight in the eye. "Please, Adam. Come back to us. Leave the pit of darkness you're drowning in and *live*."

My inner defenses, fatigued from constant erosion, flee. A rush of emotion swells until my entire body shakes with it. Heat rushes to my face. Tears explode from my eyes. "You think I want to feel this way? That I want to carry around this … this … " I stumble in the dark, grasping at the rubble of my fortress, which in reality is my prison, digging my fingernails into the dirt. I've sentenced myself to this hell and locked myself away. In my own head. And there's no key to unlock the door. No chance of escape.

"This what, honey?" Mum's grip tightens.

"I can't get out myself. Help me." My voice is thick with exhaustion and surrender.

Mum turns to Shaw. "Tell us what to do, doctor."

Shaw uncrosses her ankles and slowly stands. A satisfied tic to her mouth spreads into a full smile as Mum delivers me to her without a fight.

Chapter Twelve

Darby

It's day two of Darby being alone in a small room. I'm about ready to bug out.

Mom and Dad stay away like I ask. The nurses and aids check on me a few times, but they're in and out to check my vital signs, comment on the food I'm not eating, and remind me to shower.

Mostly I'm waiting for Dr. Shaw to come back. She said she'd help me and then she'd disappeared. Maybe I dreamed her up.

I slide off my bed and peek out the window. Outside, light and dark fight. Black sky argues with yellow office windows. Red, yellow, and green stoplights yell at blue neon signs hanging over the stores' front doors. Headlights from the steady flow of cars slap the wet road. Rain flecks over the whole scene like static on a TV screen.

I climb back into bed and tug a lock of hair apart

from the rest, dividing it into three sections. It only takes a few seconds to braid it, so I get busy sectioning off and twisting strands until half my head is in loose, half-unraveling twists.

"I like the new look."

I startle.

Shaw leans against the wall with her arms folded across her chest. Her hair is down. Loose curls touch her shoulders. It softens her sharp cheekbones and pointed chin. I could never hope to be as beautiful as her. She's like art. "Didn't mean to scare you."

I tousle my hair to undo the braids. "Just messing around. Not a lot to do here."

My gaze lands on the pile of lonely art supplies dumped in the corner. I wouldn't even know where to start if I picked up a brush again.

She takes off her pea coat. Her cream cable knit sweater compliments her porcelain skin and her skinny jeans highlight how slim and tall she is.

God, it's like she's stepped out of *Vogue*. I, on the other hand, could barely make the cut for some heroin-junky-busted-for-shoplifting-crime-bulletin-photo on the local police Facebook page.

She twists her mouth to the side. "Have you left your room at all?"

"No."

"Well that's terrible."

I snort.

"Would you like to get out of here for a while?"

I stare at the doorway. Do I deserve it? "I don't know."

"You have a jacket?"

"In the closet."

"Get dressed." She twirls her coat like a bull fighter and slides her arms in the sleeves.

"I, uh … "

"Come on. We won't be breaking any rules, if that's what you're worried about." She fastens her buttons. "I'll wait outside for you."

I sit there, stunned, as Shaw shuts the door behind her. A smile plays at my mouth. She's really serious about going outside.

I lower my feet to the floor. The tiles are cold on my bare feet. I pad to the closet next to the mini-bathroom—with the locker-sized shower—and open the door. Mom organized what she brought—a couple shirts and sweatshirts on the left, jeans in the middle, and underwear, bras, and socks in a mesh bag on the right. A pair of boots and sneakers wait neatly on the floor. Not one piece is stain-free, all wearing paint or turpentine.

I grab jeans and a zippered sweatshirt so I don't have to tug anything over my c-collar and dress quickly. The smell of fabric softener and home mixes with the bleach-y hospital scent. For a fraction of a second, I get a flash of my old life, pre-accident. A life where I plot revenge against a know-it-all cheerleader, doodle in my notebook during school, and party hard at the club. In that life, Daniel is always there to swoop in and save me from crashing and burning.

My safety net is gone now.

I open the door and take the first step out of my hospital room turned jail cell.

Shaw's talking to a nurse by the nursing station. Rosa. Her laughter pulls a small smile from me even though I have no idea what's funny.

Rosa catches me walking up to Shaw. The lights rimming the station along the ceiling reflect off her glasses. "Oh my goodness, she's out of her room!"

Shaw turns to me. "Darby, I'm glad you decided to join me."

I tuck a loose chunk of hair behind my ear. "Yeah."

"It's chilly out. You might want to layer. Do you have a hat?"

I'd tip my chin up to glare at her, but my neck brace stops me so I lean back instead. "I don't need you to act like my Mom."

She raises her hands in surrender. "Not my intention."

I tug the hood of my sweatshirt over my head. "Let's get out of here."

Shaw flashes her perfect teeth. "As you wish."

Rosa leans over the counter. "Have her back in an hour?"

"Of course." Shaw waves goodbye to Rosa and we're on our way to the elevator.

My stomach flops on the ride down. I haven't been outside since the accident. Thankfully, the hallways are nearly empty as we walk to the front entrance. Only a couple people rush along the sidewalk, collars turned up and heads ducked against the chilly rain.

An icy breeze blows, shoving cold air into my lungs. Even my skin tingles. It's not painful, though. It's refreshing after so many days of stale hospital air.

"Feels good, doesn't it?" Shaw says in my ear.

"Yeah." There's a lightness to my voice I haven't heard in weeks. Despite myself, I'm enjoying this. I pause. Am I supposed to be liking this?

Shaw and I duck out of the way of a woman with

a giant umbrella. Seriously, she could fit a bus under that thing.

Shaw hooks an arm through mine so I don't step into a pothole. I hadn't noticed it and if I'd fallen ... well, it wouldn't have been pretty, even with the c-collar to protect me.

"Thanks."

She squeezes my arm. "Anytime. Where would you like to go?"

I lift my hood. Not too many options. A cafe across the street. Yuck. Or the sandwich shop between a pharmacy and bank. Generic. "I don't care."

"There's a diner at the corner."

More like a mess of chrome and neon. I can taste the French fries from here. Tempting. As much as I don't want to go inside so soon, I'm shivering from the damp. "Okay."

The diner is pretty quiet when we enter. Bitter coffee, fresh grease, and decades of customers wrap us in a suit of odors that'll stay in our clothes.

A perky waitress with big hair seats us at a table next to a window and hands each of us a menu. Her uniform is the same pastel blue as the vinyl booths ... and her chipping fingernail polish. Her nametag reads Celia.

Shaw orders a tea.

I ask for water.

"Sure thing." Celia bounces off to get our drinks, popping her gum along the way.

Shaw shirks out of her coat, grinning. "We break out of a hospital and you order water? Pick out something fun. My treat."

I dig a twenty out of my pocket and slap it on the

white table. "I have money."

"All right. We'll go Dutch."

"Huh?"

She giggles. "I'll pay for mine and you pay for yours."

Celia returns with our drinks and silverware on a tray. After setting the items in front of us she says, "What can I get you?"

Shaw squints at me, but her smile is all fun and light. "Apple pie with vanilla ice cream, please."

Celia scribbles down the order, though I can't imagine she'd have trouble remembering it. She turns to me. "What'll you have, hun?"

I scan the menu, lost in all the choices. It's been so long since I wanted food that I can't decide from the pictures of juicy burgers, overflowing fries, and sundaes.

"Rosa said you didn't eat dinner," Shaw says.

Celia sucks on the end of her pencil. "Oh, you must be starving. How about mac and cheese? Randy makes it extra cheesy. It's delicious."

Shaw watches me.

"Sure. Sounds good." I hand Celia my menu, not sure if I really want food, but I can't refuse either since this is what we agreed on.

Doctor Shaw adds a packet of sugar to her tea and stirs it slowly with a spoon. "So, what's it like for you?"

I peel the wrapping off a straw. "What do you mean?"

"Being outside." She blows on the tea. Wisps of steam curl into the air and disappear.

"It's … weird." And it is.

"How so?"

I chew on my straw. "I don't know. Everything feels different. I mean, it's the same, but not." I sigh. "That's pretty lame."

Shaw takes a sip of tea. "Not at all. People who suffer trauma often feel the way you do. The world is the same, but you're different and it makes things seem *off* somehow."

I drag my thumb along the side of my glass, tracing the outline of ice cubes. Some are square, some more rounded, and others are simply shards. The memory of the Mustang's broken windshield flashes before me. "Exactly. And I don't think things will ever be right again."

"You're very brave."

I tear my gaze from the water. "What do you mean?"

"It's not easy to jump back into life." She rolls up an empty sugar packet between her thumb and forefinger.

"I haven't."

She drops the tiny ball. "But you have. By stepping foot outside your room. By trusting me enough to talk."

I shrug. "We're at a diner. It's not like we're heading to a rave or something."

"You like raves?"

"I like parties. Or I used to." I jab the straw into my glass. Ice cubes shift out of the way. "And I don't do drugs, so don't label me as one of *those* kids."

"I haven't. You like to be in control too much to use drugs." She takes another tiny sip of her tea. It's not steaming anymore so she doesn't have to blow on it first.

I lean against the vinyl-covered bench. It creaks. "I'm not in control of anything."

"I'm not sure I believe that. You're a fighter, Darby Fox."

"What makes you say that?"

Celia returns with our food. "Here you go, ladies. Can I get you anything else?"

"No, thank you. This looks great." Shaw smiles at her.

"Let me know if you need something." She returns to the counter, busying herself with filling salt and pepper shakers.

Shaw cuts into her pie with a fork and adds some vanilla ice cream before sticking the bite into her mouth.

I eat a spoonful of macaroni, waiting for her to answer while I chew. Maybe she won't. Maybe she forgot I asked.

She licks her lips. "How's the mac and cheese?"

"Good."

She sets her fork down with the tines resting on the plate. "I think you're brave because you are unapologetically you."

I swallow. "You don't know me well enough to say something like that."

"Am I wrong?"

I can't bear keeping eye contact with her, so I turn to my food. Celia's right. Randy does make it cheesy.

"Besides, your mom and dad told me about you. They showed me some of your paintings. They're brilliant."

I ignore her compliment about my art. It's not a part of me anymore. "I'm sure they gave me glowing reviews."

"They mentioned your tendency to get in trouble at school."

"Did they also mention how I'm Daniel's opposite? Did they say how perfect he was? Did they say how much they wish I'd act like him?"

"They're … frustrated with some of the things you do, but they love you very much."

"Right." I drop my spoon. I get it now. Her plan is to show me my mistake so I have to apologize to Mom and Dad. Nope. Not gonna happen.

"It's true."

I slide to the end of the booth. Coming here is the mistake, so is listening to this woman.

"Darby, don't go."

I face her.

She slides her half-eaten pie to the side. The ice cream has melted, creating a pool of sugar and milk. "Your parents wanted me to tell you that and a lot of other things, but I have something more important to say and I hope you give me the chance to speak."

"Go ahead."

A secret waits in the full blackness of her eyes. "I know who received your brother's heart. Would you like to meet him?"

The air goes thin. My head swirls. "I thought they kept that stuff locked up, secret."

"Oh. Well, if you don't want to find out. Never mind." She drapes her napkin over the pie.

I hold the tabletop so I don't explode. "Why would you even offer if you're not allowed to?"

"You don't strike me as the type of person to follow the rules if they don't suit you." She waves to catch Celia's eye. "You sure you won't let me pay for this?"

"I, uh … "

She pushes my twenty to my side of the table. "Put

your money away."

Celia has the check in hand. "All set?"

"Yes." Shaw gives her a credit card.

"Be back in a jiff." Celia whips off to run the card.

"So you'd be doing something wrong by telling me who has Daniel's heart."

She shoves her arms into her coat sleeves. "For the most part, the anonymity of donors and recipients is a policy I support. But there are exceptions to every situation. Like I said, I've never worked with a twin before and this is a unique circumstance."

"What about Mom and Dad?"

Celia drops off the receipt and Shaw's card. "Have a good night and stay dry."

"You too." Shaw signs the bill. "What about your parents?"

"Will they know?"

She lays the pen diagonally over the receipt. "Everything we discuss is confidential. If you won't tell, I won't tell."

Doubt tangles its slippery fingers around my guts. I've never hesitated on doing something I want to do. This seems different. It's not some silly rule we're breaking. It's a real one. Families aren't supposed to know who gets donor's organs. Period. I'd have to trust that Shaw isn't trying to trick me. Then again, she has to trust me not to tattle on her.

Shaw stands and buttons her coat. "Well?"

I slide out of the booth. "I want to know."

Chapter Thirteen

Adam

S haw takes me to the visitor lounge for our next session. It's a semi-private area at the back of the unit where docs and patients and families can talk about treatment, procedures, and prognoses. Anybody can come in at any time, but for now we're alone.

She dives into it as soon as we sit. "What's the first thing you remember after surgery?"

"Beeping." It's the truth. The heart monitor is what guided me out of the haze of anesthesia, each beat a tiny audible crumb leading me to consciousness.

She shifts in her chair. "And then?"

I pluck at the Ficus cowering in the room's corner, its leaves dry and dusty from neglect. The last thing I want to do is relive my hallucinations. I push it aside, allowing something else to surface. A girl's cries tore through the unit shortly after I woke. The nurse said she was in the adjoining ICU. Her shrieks were so agonizing I'd thought she was being skinned alive. It made me believe for a little while longer that I was indeed in Hell, at least until the tranquilizer had pulled me into a deep sleep.

"Adam?"

"A girl was screaming." I want to cover my ears, but I can't unhear a memory.

"How did you feel when you heard it?"

"Scared and … sad."

"Say more."

"It sounded like she was in Hell and I wondered if I was there too. I figured it looked like a hospital because it was familiar. I thought maybe my spirit was cursed to wander an ICU like her because we refused to believe our lives were really over. Then I wondered what had ended her life and why she was so upset about it. Had she left behind someone she loved? Had she expected to meet them in Heaven? Had she left something unsaid that she'll never be able to say?"

The pause between us absorbs what I say, molecule by molecule, syllable by syllable.

"You're extremely poetic. In a few sentences, you've given so much material to work with that we could spend an entire session on this."

I slide my gaze to her. "Glad I'm so interesting to you."

"This isn't for my benefit, it's for yours." She crosses her legs. The hem of her skirt hikes up a couple inches.

"Right."

"The last comment you made, about something unsaid. You struggle with voicing your thoughts to your mom and you're suffering in some self-imposed purgatory because of it. What holds you back from telling her how you really feel?"

"I don't want to be nagged."

She purses her lips. "There's more to it than that."

"Mum wants a fairy tale ending. Reality isn't like that. It's hard and ugly and painful. When she quotes some self-help, feel good saying it's like she's putting on blinders."

"She doesn't see you for who you really are."

I shrug. "I think it's because she's afraid."

"I'd agree with you." She laces her fingers around her knee.

"It's sort of crashing down around her, though. She thought everything would be happily ever after. And it makes me angry that she still won't see things the way they are. She thinks I'm depressed and I'm the one causing all the problems."

"You are depressed."

I pick at a snag on my sweatpants. "What if I'm not and this is just *me*?"

"Say more."

Bollocks, I *hate* it when she says that. "I can't put on a happy face like her. I can't fake it. Why can't she accept that, accept me?"

"You've been sick for so long that you've never had the opportunity to really discover who you are. Maybe the real Adam isn't depressed, and I don't think you should cut yourself short because you are capable of growth." She stands. "It's time for you to learn how to live and today is the first step."

I tilt my head to hold her gaze. "What do you have in mind?"

"I can't tell you how to live your life."

"Then what are we doing this for?"

"Here's what I want you to do. Imagine some things you'd like to try, even if they seem silly or impossible. We can review them tomorrow."

A thousand possibilities should be clamoring at me, but my mind is like a vacant cavern.

"Deal?" She smiles down at me.

"Alright."

"Good."

I follow her out.

She pauses at the door. "You've done good work today, Adam, and I want to reward your efforts." She draws something out of her pocket. A tiny square of pale blue fabric with a length of white ribbon tied in a bow. "This is for you. It's a token for what you've been through. A reminder that you're not alone."

I turn the gift around in my palm. "What is it?"

"Open it."

I untie the knot and unfold the fabric. Nestled inside is a silver butterfly pin. Thin blue veins fan out along its wingtips. They race toward the center toward a pale pink heart. The butterfly's body is made up of a line of sutures to represent an incision. "Um … "

"Everyone in the program gets one after they receive a transplant." She plucks the pin from my palm.

I sit perfectly still as she fastens the pin to my shirt. She's leaning so close I can smell her perfume and make out the fine hairs at the edge of her temple. Such personal details that for a brief moment I see her as human rather than cutthroat clinician. "Why a butterfly?"

She smirks. "Not very manly, eh?"

I cover the pin with my hand. "Well … "

"You don't have to wear it if you don't want to.

Maybe you could put it on your heart pillow."

I slide my fingers over its surface. Smooth, like Shaw's delivery. "Yeah. Thank you. It's nice."

"Did you know butterflies represent metamorphosis and the psyche?"

"No."

"Apropos, then, don't you think, that the program chose to incorporate a butterfly into the design as a symbol of new life?"

"Was it your idea?"

"Yes. As was the incision cleaving the heart." She traces the line with her finger. "Even beautiful things carry scars."

"Where are yours?" The words fly loose from my tongue, slippery and rebellious.

Her face closes into an unreadable mask. Without a word, she turns her back on me, and strides down the hallway.

* * *

Ricky greets me in full armor—the polo shirt and sweatpants uniform and a dazzling smile. "PT time."

I'm tempted to crawl under the bed like a little kid hiding from monsters. Mum demands I strip away my shroud of depression. Shaw expects me draft a list of things the New Adam would do. And Ricky here is ready to drag me to the deathtrap he calls a treadmill.

Ricky props his hands on his waistband. "Hop to it, kiddo." He adds a clap for emphasis.

Excellent motivation, but frankly, PT is the last

thing I want to do, especially after what happened last time. I hug my heart pillow to my chest. "I don't know."

"The only way you'll gain strength is to exercise. You don't want to let a little panic attack stop you, do you?"

"Little? I thought my heart was going to burst out of my chest."

"That's a little dramatic, don't you think?"

"Not particularly."

"You've associated an increased heart rate with something going wrong in your ticker, but you've got a new heart. It can take the stress. You need to build tolerance to it … you know, get used to the sensation and learn that it's not bad." He rubs his hands together.

"Sounds like a Shaw-ism." I slide to the edge of my windowsill and set my pillow aside.

"A what?" He stops working an invisible lather with his hands.

"Something Doctor Shaw would say."

He laughs. "Yeah, I suppose it does. The woman is brilliant, so I'll take that as a compliment." He waves his arm for me to come along.

I don't bother clarifying that I didn't mean for it to be a compliment and follow him down the hall after grabbing a mask from the box by the door.

My heart is already revving by the time we reach the PT room. Ricky's no pain, no gain babble drifts through my mind. Maybe I *am* psyching myself out. My reaction last time was a simple panic attack, nothing more, and certainly nothing dangerous. Like Ricky said, my new heart is strong, show room new.

I stride toward the treadmill with my hands fisted and jaw clenched.

Ricky immediately redirects me to the stationary bike on the other side of the room. "We're trying something different today."

Instead of a standard bicycle seat, the machine has a full-on chair with hand grips on either side. A towel rests on the center console. Ricky whips it off and drapes it over his shoulder.

"Hop on." Ricky slaps the chair's seat. "Grip the hand holds and work the pedals. I'll increase the resistance to the right spot. I want you to feel like you're working, but not so hard as it feels like you're wading through wet concrete."

"Okay." I slip my feet through the footholds and start pedaling. It's so easy that I actually have to concentrate on not going too fast.

Ricky turns up the resistance dial. "Tell me when you feel the burn." He smiles. The guy totally enjoys this. He'd probably be completely comfortable in a medieval torture chamber. I can imagine him saying in a light-hearted voice, "Let me know when your feel your tendons pop. That means your legs and arms will rip off soon. All you have to do is get used to the pain."

The pedals fight back. I lean into the seatback, tightening my grip on the handles. My thighs start to burn. "I think that's good."

Ricky reverses the resistance a notch and drapes the towel around my neck. "Ten minutes. I'll be back."

I stare at the clock, watching the seconds tick by as I wind the pedals around in circles. One minute feels like a hundred.

Ricky's chuckles carry over the noise of the other machines. He's a guy who enjoys life. I'll have to ask him his secret. Maybe he'll give me a couple of items to add to my alarmingly blank list.

Right now, I'm nothing more than a sixteen-year-old in a physical rehabilitation room with ancient relics who could probably beat me at arm wrestling. Hell, they could probably beat me in a competition of mall walking.

A layer of sweat creeps across my upper lip. Damn mask. I tug it under my chin and take a deep breath of real air. Relief floods me, though my heart continues to pump faster and faster. My pulse rushes in my ears.

I close my eyes, but nothing can dull the competing scents of stale body odor, cleaning fluid, and overused equipment.

This place sucks.

I keep pumping my legs. What would it be like to ride a real bicycle in a park on a summer day? How serene it would be to glide past pastures of green grass, to skim under shade trees, and a pause at a pond to catch the sunset. I almost feel the wind dragging through my hair. All of a sudden I feel lighter, freer. I'm normal. Healthy.

Whole.

"I've never seen someone so happy to be exercising." A girl's voice tears through my fantasy.

My eyes fly open. I'm face to face with a petite girl wearing a plastic collar around her neck. Her baggy black t-shirt and gray sweatpants are covered in paint stains. Her crystal blue eyes study me with curiosity, a striking compliment to the cobalt streaks in her black hair.

I stop pedaling, struck by the clarity of those inquisitive eyes. I open my mouth, but have no idea what to say so I close it again. Lamest of the lame.

The right side of her mouth ticks up. "The silent type. I like it."

I blink.

She slides her fingers along the machine's center console then rubs them together, testing for dust. "Okay, Mister Tall, Dark, and Quiet. You got a real name?"

"I, um … " I clear my throat.

"Um is not a name."

We're face to face with me sitting and her standing, yet it's like she's peering down at me from a tower. "A-Adam. My name is Adam."

"Adam. Like Adam and Eve?"

"No, I mean, I guess."

"Is that a yes or no?" She laughs. It's one of those wow-this-bloke-has-no-idea-how-to-talk-to-girls laughs.

Heat builds in my cheeks. A bead of sweat slides from my temple down my cheek. My hold slips on the bike's handles. "What's your name?"

She shifts her weight. "I'm Darby."

"Why are you here?"

"It's a hospital. What do you think?" Her mouth collapses into a frown.

I imagine kissing the smirk right off her face. The heat intensifies in my lower belly. "Um … " I point to her throat, or, more specifically, the collar around it.

She stiffens. "Oh. Well, I broke my neck and … " Her words trail off and so does her gaze. She ducks her head so her hair veils her face.

"I'm sorry. You don't have to tell me." I don't want to talk about my illness either, so I can't blame her for clamming up. I drag the towel from my shoulders and twist it in my hands, hoping she won't leave. Not yet. If only my brain would come up with something interesting to say.

She watches me work the towel over while sucking on her bottom lip. Then she takes a deep breath, snapping back into the fresh girl who first greeted me. "It's okay. I was in an accident."

She shrugs like it's no big deal but the hint of pain in her eyes tells me otherwise. It's only a slight wince, but it's there. I've gotten used to catching it over these past few months, whether it's from Mum fretting over me during one of my episodes, a doctor delivering bad news about my condition, or Dad letting me know how ungrateful he thinks I am.

"You're not in a wheelchair," I say. Utter brilliance.

"You noticed." There's a playful twist to her mouth now.

"Yeah, but don't people who break their necks end up paralyzed?"

The darkness returns to her gaze. "I was lucky."

"Very."

Just as quick, the hint of pain is gone. "How about you?"

"Me?"

"Why are *you* here?"

"Oh. I had heart surgery so I need to recondition my body." Recondition. I have no idea if I'm using the term right. It's Ricky's. He won't mind me borrowing it. However, the "re" would imply I had some "condition" to begin with.

"Heart surgery." She takes a step away as if I'm contagious

The bike beeps. My ten minutes is up.

Ricky saunters over wearing his permanent smile. "Making friends?"

I nod, though I'm not quite sure what we're doing.

"I see you've already started your break, so let's jump into the next ten minutes right away." He resets the timer.

"Sorry to interrupt." Darby retreats some more.

"Who are you working with?" Ricky asks.

"Uh … Sandra."

Ricky ushers her toward the door. "She's in the other room."

She rolls her eyes. "Yeah, I know, but she started working with someone else, so I left."

Ricky shakes his head. "She's probably looking for you."

"Whatever," Darby says.

Well, well, looks I have something to put on my Live Life List.

Talk to Darby again.

Chapter Fourteen

Darby

Shaw's waiting for me after I shower. She's placed two chairs at right angles to each other. I only need one shot to guess the empty chair is for me.

"There you are." Shaw doesn't bother to stand.

I steady the towel wrapped around my head and sit. "I decided to shower after PT."

"How'd it go?"

"The shower or PT?"

Shaw gives a small smile. "PT."

I shrug—or try to 'cause the c-collar blocks me—and scrunch my nose. I have to wear the thing *all the time*, sleeping, showering, sitting, walking, PTing, and I can't *wait* to rip it off. "Okay, I guess. It's boring."

So boring I had to wait twenty minutes for my physical therapist to figure out what she wanted to do with me. Her excuse? She hasn't worked with spine injury patients much. Not comforting. At. All.

Good thing I wandered and found that weird kid, Adam, in the other room. Talking to him gave me something to do. Sure, he was shy, but kind of cute and his lip ring means he's not a complete loser.

"It's important for your recovery."

"I could recover at home, but I … " I pick at a hangnail. Mom and Dad haven't visited or called since I kicked them out.

"Don't want to go home."

"More like I'm not welcome there."

Shaw's face pinches. It reminds me of when Mom purses her lips or Dad picks his teeth when they see my report card. "What makes you say that?"

I twist away from her.

"Your parents love you."

"Can we get out of here?"

Shaw uncrosses her legs. "You're upset."

I shake out my hair. "I'm sick of being cooped up."

"Our little outing last night gave you a taste of freedom, I see." Shaw stands and snatches her coat off the back of her chair.

I find my sneakers. "I don't care where we go, I just can't stay in this room anymore."

Shaw helps me into my rain jacket. "Okay."

We head in the opposite direction from last time. A light drizzle falls. Dampness seeps into my bones. I don't care. It's better than being in the kiddy room with safari walls.

There are more people on the sidewalk than last night. Makes sense. It's day time. Most rush along, heads bowed or tucked under umbrellas and hoods and hands stuffed in coat pockets. Shaw and I take a right, entering a small park at the bottom of a hill. We pass empty flowerbeds and leafless bushes until we find a bench next to a pond. The wood is worn and wet.

"Not the best place to sit," Shaw says.

I tuck the back of my coat under my butt and sit anyway. "My jacket's waterproof."

She sits next to me. "So is mine."

My nose runs from the cold. I wipe it with the back of my hand.

Shaw rubs her hands together. "Chilly out here."

"I can't go inside."

"It was cold like this the day my mother died."

I stare at her out of the corner of my eyes.

"My mom and I were in a car accident, like you and Daniel. Somehow, she lost control of the car and we crashed into a lake. Water started rushing in almost instantly." She closes her eyes and hugs herself.

I want to say something, but what's there to say?

"Mom's head hit the steering wheel. She was knocked out. I shook her and shook her, but she wouldn't wake up. I managed to drag her out of the car and to the shore. It must have been a rush of adrenaline. I was just a little girl." Shaw pierces me with her dark stare.

"Why are you telling me this?"

"I know how painful it is to lose someone you love and I know how painful it is to be separated from your mother. Yours is still alive. You should savor every moment with her."

I pull my cuffs over my hands. "I'm sorry about your mom. What happened was horrible. But you don't know anything about my life or about my mom, so you shouldn't tell me what to do."

Shaw stands. She stares down at me, her face

clouded, even in broad daylight. "You're a sharp girl, Darby Fox. Seems I underestimated you."

"Most people do."

She lifts her chin. "Even your parents."

I stand so we're more on equal ground. Doesn't matter. She's still a foot taller than me. "Right."

"I apologize for overstepping my bounds. I shouldn't have assumed."

"Isn't it your job to know better?"

She runs her tongue over her teeth. My jab stung. "Indeed. Sometimes I take a chance and sometimes it doesn't work out."

I drop my gaze to the pond. She's not the only one who's failed at taking chances. "Yeah, well, I'm pretty good at making mistakes, too."

"Like what?"

"The accident was my fault. If I hadn't been arguing with Daniel, maybe he wouldn't have … " My throat closes, strangling the end of my sentence.

"Hit that patch of ice? The roads were horrendous that night. You can't blame yourself for the weather."

I make eye contact with her. "Like you can't blame yourself for your mom not surviving."

The edge of her mouth ticks up. "Never said I did."

Confusion fuzzes my head. "Oh."

She crosses her arms. "It's easy to assume, isn't it?"

I snort. Boy, she's good. "Thanks for making me look like an ass."

She lowers her chin. "That was not my intention."

I scratch my jaw. "No, I deserved it. Especially after I snarked at you for telling me about your mom."

She extends a hand. "Truce?"

I shake. "For what?"

"We have a lot more in common than you think. I know what it's like to have a loved one's organs be donated. My mother's heart was given to someone else. I never knew who they were and it kills me to this day."

The more she talks, the more gutted I am. "What am I supposed to do with all this stuff you're telling me?"

"I don't want you to feel bad for me. That's not why I'm sharing."

"Then explain it to me."

"We need to work together, not against each other."

"How?"

She laughs. "Not used to collaborating?"

I start walking up the hill. "If we're going to 'work together,' I need you to lay off the loving parents angle, okay?"

She takes easy strides next to me. "Okay."

"And how long are you going to make me wait before you tell me who had Daniel's heart?"

"I'll tell you when you're ready."

I halt. "When will you know that?"

"I'll know."

* * *

I stir the gloppy, overcooked pasta around my plate, pushing watery green beans to the edge. A couple of them splat onto the plastic tray. Since I haven't picked things on the menu, the kitchen sends up whatever they have. I glare at the lime gelatin for desert. Gross.

I push the plate aside. It bonks against a can of Boost. If Mom were here, she'd force me to suck it down.

But she's not here and I doubt she's coming.

I slide out of bed and shove my feet into my slippers. Shaw had paid for my food the other night, so I still had twenty bucks. I tug on my hoodie and make sure the money is in the pocket.

The hallway is empty. Two nurses at the nurse's station have their backs to me. I sneak off the unit without being seen.

Shaw's right about me sweating the taste of freedom.

My stomach growls. Holding my belly, I step out of the elevator on the main level and follow the yellow signs to the cafeteria. A few visitors wander around, talking about fountain soda versus canned and what their favorite pudding flavor is. I do a lap myself to scope the place out. Pizza, burgers, salads, soups, ice cream, sushi. *Sushi?* Yuck.

I settle on a slice of white pizza with broccoli and a half pint of caramel swirl ice cream. A group of staff take up half a dozen tables near the registers. They complain about double shifts on weekends.

After checking out, I pick a table on the empty upper level. I point the chair so it faces the window. The lights are dimmer inside and the streetlights are brighter outside, so I get slight hints of myself—the petite girl with a huge c-collar swallowing her up. The drizzly rain from before has turned to sloppy snow. Flakes cling desperately to the dead grass and bare tree limbs for a second, then melt into nothingness.

I have to wonder if I'm doing the same—clawing

onto a life I don't deserve by going out with Shaw …
and letting myself look forward to seeing a boy with a
double lip ring.

Adam.

The kid is cute. In an odd sort of way.

Bet it's his British accent.

I sink my teeth in the pizza. Much better than the
slop that was on my tray. I nosh until I get to the crust,
then pry open the ice cream container. It's soft from
sitting out, but not soupy. I take a ridiculously large
bite. Rich caramel coats my tongue. I close my eyes
and savor another spoonful.

"I've never seen someone so happy while eating
ice cream." The guy's voice has a clear accent.

I fumble my spoon. It bounces off my thigh before
clanging to the floor. "Dammit."

I twist, half-surprised and half-pissed at the
interruption. My jaw drops. It *is* him. "Adam."

"Hello." He drops a heart-shaped pillow on the
table and sits across from me. He's got a facemask on,
though it's tucked under his chin. "Mind if I join you?"

So proper. "You already have."

He snort-laughs. It's shy. And adorable. "Yes, I
guess I did. I can leave, if you want."

"No," I blurt. Way too fast. Heat burns my cheeks
and I hope, no I pray, the dim lighting hides it.

He uses his tongue to wiggle his lip ring. I can't
stop staring. OMG.

"What're you doing here?" My question comes out
barely more than a squeak.

He frowns and leans forward. "Come again?"

I clear my throat. "Why are you here?"

His gaze wanders around the room. "I'm sick of

being cooped up in my room."

"I know the feeling. How come I haven't seen you on the Pediatric unit?"

"I'm on the cardiac floor. The staff is more trained if my heart decides to go wonky."

"Wonky?"

"Odd term, eh?"

"Does it scare you? Your heart, I mean."

He scratches the back of his head. "Yes. A lot. But my heart is supposed to be … better now."

"Good." I tip the ice cream container in his direction. "Want some?"

One corner of his mouth slides up. "Need another spoon?"

"Since you made me drop mine and I didn't grab two, yeah."

This pulls a full smile out of him. "Sorry. Didn't mean to scare you."

I stand. "It's okay. Wait here. I'll get two spoons."

"Okay." He settles deeper into the plastic chair. Comfortable. Not awkward at all like he was in the exercise room. What a quirky boy.

I force myself to take my time over to the plastic utensil dispenser, but I let myself rush—a little—back to the table.

"Here." I offer him a spoon.

Our fingers brush against each other. My skin tingles from the contact.

"Thank you." He stares up at me. The light above him catches his eyes. They're a color I've never seen before, a mixture of blue, green, and brown. Didn't look that way yesterday. Chameleon eyes. Beautiful.

I sit, trying to settle the somersaults in my stomach.

A simple idea hits me: Paint them.

Guilt stomps it out. How can I think about picking up a paintbrush when my brother is dead? He'll never shoot a basketball again, or drive his precious car, or get the sports scholarship Dad's been rooting for. I don't have a right to enjoy anything if he can't.

"You alright?" Adam asks.

I chew on the spoon. "Y-yeah … Hey, you wear contacts?"

"No. Why?" The lean muscles in his forearms ripple and the tendons in his hands work as he fiddles with the ice cream container.

I sort out the color combinations I'd have to mix to get just the right shades to match his irises. I can almost feel my fingertips sliding across a blank canvas, reading it, urging it to tell me its story. My fingers twitch, aching to hold a brush again. Can I?

"Nevermind. How come you're not with your parents?"

He offers me the carton. "I made them go home. Needed a break, you know? I'm sure they needed one too."

I dig into a ribbon of caramel. "Yeah, I know."

"How about you? Where are your parents?"

"Home."

He sets his spoon down. "I think I've forgotten what home is like."

"Me too." It's not a lie. I've been in the hospital so long, I've gotten used to the smell, the dry air, the noise all night long, and the craptastic color scheme.

"How long do you have to stay here?"

"Probably forever."

He puffs his cheeks. "Sometimes I feel that way too."

I wipe my mouth with a napkin and ball it up. Home is the last thing I want to talk about, or even think about. My stomach curls with anxiety. It won't be too much longer before the doctor will say I'm ready to be discharged. Mom and Dad will have to pick me up. I'll have to get used to living in the house, going to school, and just being … all without Daniel. "You supposed to wear that mask?"

He tugs on the elastic hooked around his left ear. "Yes, but it's kind of hard to when I'm eating."

"You weren't wearing it when you came up to me."

He twists his mouth to the side. "Touché."

The angles of his cheekbones and chin contrast with the softness of his mouth. His black lip ring pops against his skin. I drool, thinking about the brushstrokes it'd take to capture his face. I could do it. He'd fit in my Fire and Ice collection.

I toss the container on my plate next to the pizza crust. "Why do you have to wear it? Are you contagious or something?"

He tugs the mask into place. "No. My immune system is crap because I have to take a bunch of medicine … "

"Why?"

He slides his chair back and crosses his arms, stuffing his long, thin fingers into his armpits. "I don't like to talk about it."

He's not the only one. "It's too bad the mask hides your lip ring, because it's bad ass."

The corners of his eyes wrinkle with a smile. His laugh is muffled from the mask, but its warmth reaches me. "My mum and dad hate it."

I giggle. "My parents hate my blue hair."

"You have to keep it. It's ace." The joy in his eyes is genuine.

"Ace?"

"Um, yes. I think you Americans call it awesome?"

"Oh, yeah. Thanks."

He tips his chin down. "Let's get something out in the open, yeah?"

I stiffen. He's going to make me talk about Mom and Dad or the accident. "O-okay."

He moves the chair to the table and leans his elbows against the tabletop. "Neither of us wants to talk about why we're here."

"Uh-huh."

"So I say we call a moratorium on the subject."

This kid uses some weird words. "A what?"

"A moratorium. It means we both agree not to discuss it."

As long as he doesn't dig into my story, I won't dig into his. I stick out my hand. "Agreed."

He slips his hand into mine. His skin is warm. "Ace."

"Ace." That tingle I felt before when we touched comes back, twice as intense. I pull my hand away even though I don't want to. "You're different, Adam. I like that."

"You're different too, Darby. I wish I could be as straight forward as you."

I raise an eyebrow. "Uh, you just were."

He gives his soft laugh again. It's so simple, like peanut butter and jelly sandwiches or eating buttered popcorn in a movie theater. "I should probably get back before the nurses send a search party."

"Good point. Don't want to be counted as going AWOL."

Adam insists on picking up the garbage. After dumping the leftovers, we head to the elevator.

We hit buttons for different floors.

"Too bad we're not on the same unit," I say.

"Agreed, though I kind of like these clandestine meetings."

"I like your vocabulary."

My floor comes first. The doors open and I hesitate.

"This you?" he asks.

"Yeah."

He presses the door open button. "See you at PT tomorrow?"

I'm not ready to leave. But I have to. I lean into him, rise up to my tippy toes, and kiss him on the cheek. "Yep."

Hyped on adrenaline, I dash out of the elevator before he can respond. I can't breathe normally until I step into my room.

I'm used to kissing boys, but it's different with Adam. I don't know why, but things mean more with him.

I snort. Things mean more with a boy I don't know. But somehow it's like I've known him forever. Maybe I'm just desperate.

I mean, really. I'm getting all romantic and sentimental. What would Shaw say about that?

In the bathroom, I stare at my reflection. I draw my fingers along my upturned lips. It's a smile. Haven't used one of those in a while. I'd forgotten the pull and tug of muscles. The tingling in my belly from the urge to laugh.

I can't wait to see Adam again.

Chapter Fifteen

Adam

Shaw and I visit the hospital's atrium during our next session time, taking full advantage of every spare nook and cranny of the hospital with every passing day. We sit on a bench under a pergola ringed by holly. A fountain sits dry in front of us. Water isn't flowing from it and the flowerbed at its base is empty, already cleaned out for winter. The slate under our feet is a dull gray, but the square of sky above us is a vibrant blue. Sunlight bathes us in warmth so it's not too bad sitting here in a longsleeved t-shirt. Since we're surrounded by the interior hospital walls, we're sheltered from the wind.

Shaw takes a sip of her latte, then opens the session by saying, "How's your Live Life List coming along?"

It isn't, but I can't tell her that. I could mention Darby, not that there's much to say. Well, nothing I'd want to share with Shaw anyway. I rub my cheek where she'd kissed me last night. My skin tingles at the memory of it. I wish I could so easily embody her ability to take any moment and turn it into opportunity.

"Earth to Adam." She nudges me with her shoulder.

I swirl the coffee Shaw brought for me—I wonder if this is some new tradition—and take a tentative sip. Less grit than before, but it's still there. I prop the cup on my heart pillow that's resting on my lap. "This is a bit gritty."

"Must be the sweetener. So, are you actually going to talk about what's on your mind? Because you have to if this is going to work."

I'd prefer sitting here for the entire session in silence, but Shaw will keep prodding until the words pour out of me. I don't have the mental energy for another drawn out battle with her. "I met a girl."

Shaw shifts position to catch my sightline. "Really?"

"She isn't like anyone I've ever met before."

"How so?" Her gaze falls to my coffee. She purses her lips slightly, then adopts her usual clinical flatness.

A smile plays at my mouth as I take another sip—I don't want to give Shaw another reason to think I'm resisting her by refusing to drink it. "She's interested in talking to me," I joke. Only it doesn't come out as a joke. It sounds pathetic. Internally, I groan, knowing Shaw will delve deeper into my lack of self-esteem.

Shaw relaxes a bit. "I'm sure a lot of people want to talk to you, but you don't let them in. What about your friends? Have you reached out to them since you were admitted to the hospital?"

"You know I haven't."

"Right, which means you push people away."

"Uh-huh."

"Just like you're doing now. You're afraid of

letting people in." Shaw picks a piece of fuzz off her wool jacket. Imperfections aren't allowed in her world. Maintaining an immaculate persona must be her way of dealing with the messy lives of the people she treats. I wonder what she'd think of my pop psychology interpretation of her.

I give a non-committal shrug, even though she's wrong. I'm not afraid of letting people in. I'm afraid of letting her in. Doesn't matter. She'll burrow through anyway. She always does.

"So what's different about this girl that you've decided to bring her up?" She takes another sip of her latte, then bonks her cup against mine. "Cheers, by the way, for stepping out of your comfort zone."

I chew on my lip ring. Every word I say has significance. I can say I hate hangnails and Shaw will interpret it to mean I hate a part of myself and fantasize about ripping it off. Ordinary conversations don't go like this. They're spontaneous, words are just that—words, and there's no pressure or wondering if what you say will be torn apart and analyzed bit by bit. Finally, I say, "Meeting people is living life."

"True. But you didn't have to talk to her."

"She came up to me first. I couldn't ignore her."

"That's not what I'm getting at. What was it about *her* that drew you in?"

That couldn't possibly be important for Shaw to know. I consider asking her, but my last question got shot down so I'd be wasting my time by following up with another. "She's direct. Says what she means. She doesn't twist my words around or analyze them. And I don't have to talk about the surgery or my heart or anything."

Her lips thin into a line of displeasure. "You think I'm forcing you to share your most secret thoughts and emotions and you think I twist them around, and you like her because she's the exact opposite of me."

How'd she turn this into being about her? I examine my last words like a scientist reviewing test results. ... "*twist my words ... or analyze them.*" Oh. Crap. I've done a brilliant—and by brilliant, I mean awful—job of screening what I say. I need to hit the brakes and shift into reverse if I want to prevent this session from spiraling out of control. "No, I didn't mean you..." I pinch the bridge of my nose. "It's your job to analyze what I say."

And I hate every single minute of it.

"I don't need you to be considerate of my feelings and I know what my job is." She runs her fingers along the rim of her cup.

So much for smoothing things over. I slump into the bench, resting my coffee on my pillow again. "How am I supposed to be open with you when you attack everything I say?"

"I'm not attacking you."

"Feels like it."

"Sometimes therapy is painful."

I debate if she's offered a white flag, then say, "Sometimes it's nice to hang out with someone who doesn't know a lot about my heart condition."

"How much have you told her?"

"Not much, but the subject had to come up." I lift the pillow, feeling a bit like a toddler with a security blanket.

Shaw pins me with her needle-like gaze. "Tell me exactly what you told her. I need to know everything."

I shift to the left until the armrest stops me. It digs into my side. Still less painful than talking to Shaw. "Why is it so important?"

"This is a new potential relationship and I need to know how it may impact you and our work."

I never should have said anything. My stomach curdles. I don't need Shaw meddling in whatever I might have with Darby. If I have anything.

I hug the pillow tighter. Maybe it *is* a security blanket, or in the very least a shield against her ... a rather ineffective one. "She knows I had heart surgery, but I didn't say anything about the transplant."

"What else?"

Maybe she'll drop her inquisition if she knows about Darby's and my moratorium on the subject of our illnesses. "We decided not to talk about why we're in the hospital."

"So she's a patient. What's her condition?"

Again, I have no idea why Shaw would need to know that, but I have no hope of dodging her question either. "She broke her neck in an accident."

Shaw's on her feet in a flash. "I'm glad you didn't tell her about the transplant. You have to be careful who you share that information with."

I peer up at her, startled. "Why?"

"Some people don't understand it. They think it's unnatural."

I frown. Up until now, she's been trying to get me to accept a new heart as a gift, not as cheating death, and now she's telling me I have to keep it a secret so I won't be ridiculed.

"Everyone at school knows." Sure, the other students have given me odd stares or pity glances, but they've never called me out for being "unnatural." I was the one who did that to myself.

"Just be careful with this girl." She turns and walks away from me, her heels clicking on the slate tiles.

I stare at her back as she yanks open the door and slips through.

What the hell?

I run my fingers over my lip ring, replaying the conversation in my mind. Things were okay—well, for our sessions—until she found out I discussed my condition with Darby. Like it pissed her off I talked with someone else about it besides her.

Weird.

* * *

Mum and Dad are waiting for me when I return to my room. They're hovering by the window. Mum holds onto her purse like I hold onto my pillow.

I pause inside the doorway. Seems like it's been forever since we last spoke. Finally, I drop my coffee in the waste bin and say, "Hi."

Brilliant, I know.

Mum strides toward me, then halts, uncertain. It reminds me of a deer scoping out a new situation. I'm not a threat, per se, but I can be unpredictable. "How are you?"

"Fine." The word reflexively flies out of my mouth. I've said it so often it's my tic.

Dad crosses his arms. The downturn of his mouth tells me he's not pleased.

Mum slumps onto the cot. "We haven't spoken in days and all you can say is 'fine?'"

"But I am. I'm doing everything I need to do. I'm exercising, taking my meds, talking to Shaw. She's making me write a Live Life List. Is that what you want to hear?" I lean against the wall, pining for my coveted windowsill seat, and fumble with the pin Shaw gave me. I attached to the pillow like she'd suggested. It's surprising she didn't mention it.

"Live Life List?" Dad asks.

I don't miss the sarcasm hanging on every "L" with dirty claws.

"It's part of therapy. I'm supposed to make a list of things I'd like to do with my life. You know, hobbies, goals, that kind of stuff." It's an easy thing to explain, yet an impossible thing to complete.

Mum leans forward. "Can I see it?"

And here's where my argument faceplants. "Well, I haven't actually written anything on it."

Dad puffs his cheeks out and exhales.

"But I'm getting out of my room and … I don't look depressed, do I?" I toss my pillow on the bed and spread my arms wide to match the toothy grin I bare to them.

Mum's scans me up and down. "No. You don't look as depressed as you did."

I lower my arms. "See? I'm alright."

"I wouldn't go that far." She mimes Dad's posture.

"I wish you guys would give me a break."

"We'd ask the same of you."

"Right."

"Don't talk back to your mother," Dad says.

"I'm not."

"It's okay, David." Mum stands again. "Honey, this isn't how I wanted our visit to go. I'm glad you're doing what you need to do. We worry about you, is all."

"You don't have to."

"I'm not sure we know how to stop." Mum gives a little chuckle.

"Maybe Shaw could give you some tips."

"Maybe."

Mentioning Darby might perk them up, but it didn't go so well when I told Shaw about her and I'm not sure I'm ready to take the risk with Mum and Dad. On the other hand, telling them about her might give them a reason to lay off me a bit. "If it helps, I've been hanging out with someone."

Mum perks up. "Is that where you've been? Who is it? I hope you didn't have caffeine in that drink."

I hesitate at her flurry of words. I could confess Shaw's new habit of bringing me coffee, but don't want Mum to question me about that. Every time we talk about Shaw, it turns into an argument. Darby it is then. "She's my age. Her name is Darby. She's a patient here, too. Well, on the Pediatric wing. She got hurt in an accident."

Relief softens her face, makes her look five years younger, easy. "That's so wonderful, honey. Not that she's hurt, of course, but that you enjoy spending time with her."

"She's so different from anyone I've ever met." It's the truth. Talking seems easy for her, like swimming is for fish, or flying is for birds. I'm more like an ostrich flapping my useless wings.

"Are you going to see her again?"

"I hope so." We'd planned on seeing each other during PT. I glance at the clock. Ricky should be showing up any minute now.

"That's great." Mum's face shines brighter than the sunlight streaming through the window.

Dad breaks his crossed arm stance and hooks his thumbs through his belt loops. "You should get her number so you can keep talking after you come home."

Both of their defensive strategies are softening. Good.

"Yeah." I try to suppress the smile tugging at my mouth. I've never asked a girl for her number before. I'm checking items off my Live Life List before I have a chance to write them down.

Mum pulls me in for a hug. After patting my back a thousand and one times, she says, "Is that a smile I see trying to break through?"

A rush of heat blossoms in my cheeks. "Um ... yes."

She laughs. It's the genuinely happy.

I dip my head to hide my fiery cheeks and hope we're heading for more steady ground.

Chapter Sixteen

Darby

I stand in front of the stack of art supplies tucked into the corner. They're as lonely as I am. A foldable easel sits on the bottom. On top of that are a dozen canvases—some works in progress, some blank, and all different sizes. My wooden briefcase of paints, brushes, and palettes leans against to the pile.

For years, painting has been natural to me. I need it to breathe, to survive. But that part of me died with Daniel and left a wide, rotten hole behind. In two short meetings, Shaw cleaned it out. Then Adam started healing it.

Maybe that's why the burning desire to break out my paints came back.

Carefully—I can't lift too much weight—I pick up the case and set it on the bed. Then I peel back the layer of canvases one by one, picking a blank one. After setting up the easel close to the window, I lay the canvas on it and open my case. Familiar scents of oil paints and turpentine greet me like a long lost friend. I draw my fingers over the row of paint tubes, a smile playing at my mouth.

My heart pumps faster, ready for an adventure of color and brushstrokes. With a shaky breath, I grab a handful of paints, dab them on my palette, and choose a brush.

Facing the canvas, I close my eyes to remember the tones of Adam's unique eyes. Pale brown with flecks of gold form an inner ring. A sea of green-blue makes the outer. The circles bleed into each other, uneven and messy. Ordinarily, I'd sketch out a drawing first and plan where I want each color to go, but I'm afraid I'll lose the freedom of dabbing my brush in a pigment and sliding it across the canvas if I wait.

I'm afraid I'll lose my nerve.

I confront my fear and dip the bristles in gold.

* * *

I ditch my Physical Therapist the second she turns her back to work with another client. The way I see it, painting counts as arm exercises.

I knead my shoulder as I walk across the hall to the other gym. Too bad PT doesn't include massages or soaks in a hot tub. At least, it hasn't for me and I don't see any massage tables or tubs around.

Like before, I find Adam pumping his legs at a stationary bike. He's staring at the monitor, though his eyes have that far away look of someone who's left their body to free-float somewhere else. His mask hangs on a knob and his pillow is propped in a pocket hanging off the monitor.

I approach slowly, uncertain of if I want to bring him back to reality or let him stay in whatever world he's flown off to.

The timer on his bike buzzes. He blinks and shakes his head. It reminds me of someone coming up from a dive underwater. He wipes his face with a towel.

I saunter over to him. "I wish I liked PT as much as you."

He fumbles with the towel, then dips his chin with embarrassment. It's adorable. "Oh, hello."

"You finished?"

He glances around. "Not really, but my therapist isn't here." His brow furrows. "Wonder where he went. He's usually on top of me like Marmite on toast."

"Mar-what?"

"Um," He twists his mouth like he's trying to figure out how to explain what he just said. Finally, he gives up with shrug. "Nevermind."

I catch him by the wrist and yank him toward me. "Let's go."

His eyes widen as he flails to keep up with me. "Where?"

I shake my head. "Anywhere but here."

We halt at the door. I check to see if the coast is clear. The hallway is empty. I lead us to the elevator. Adam doesn't make any moves to free his wrist from my grip. A tingle of excitement works through my belly and threatens to burst out in a giggle.

While we wait, Adam holds his palm to his chest like he's lost something. Then he covers his mouth with his free hand.

"What?"

"I'm supposed to wear a mask and carry my pillow." He chews on his lip ring.

"Why?"

"It's so I don't get an infection or pull out my stitches and wires."

The elevator dings and the door slides open.

"I don't have cooties, you know." I drag him onto the elevator. "And you have to carry a pillow to walk? You're a bit delicate, aren't you?"

He winces. "I … um … you think I'm delicate?"

I let go of his hand and press "G" for ground floor. "I didn't mean it as in weak or bad or anything."

"Yes you did," he says quietly. He stares at his feet, hiding his multicolored eyes behind his long lashes.

God, it doesn't take me long to ruin things. Especially if it's good. "Sorry. I'm a jerk."

"No. It's okay. You're right. I'm weak." His Adam's apple bobs as he swallows. "I should go back to the gym. Or my room."

"Don't be silly. And you're not weak."

"I probably wouldn't be any fun to spend time with anyway." He taps his right heel to his left toe. It reminds me of a little boy who's apologizing for stealing a cookie out of the cookie jar. He hasn't even done anything wrong. And not wearing a mask for a few minutes isn't that big a deal, is it?

"Come on. Forget what I said, okay? And forget the rules. Have fun." I want to say, "Please don't ditch me. Not now. I need this." I curl my hands into fists. He's not weak. I am.

The elevator slips from the fourth floor to the third. I count the seconds between levels. Soon, we'll be at the first floor and I'll step off and Adam will probably return to his eighth floor tower.

The number "2" lights up.

Then "G."

Like everything else, I'll have to let him go. Move on. Stay alone.

I step out as soon as the doors open without saying a word or looking back. I keep walking, straight through the sadness filling my lungs and stinging my eyes. It slows me down, but I don't stop. I'll be able to breathe once I get outside in the cold, numbing air.

Easy-strided footsteps keep pace.

I face whoever it is, ready to lob a fireball of snark at them.

Adam halts. We're shoulder to shoulder. Well, more like my shoulder to his elbow.

The corridor is crowded, full of employees, visitors, and patients. We're boulders in the stream of bodies. They break against us, twisting sideways and side-stepping like swirling currents.

"What are you doing?" I ask.

He laces his fingers with mine. "Living life."

The emptiness inside shrinks a bit. "I don't understand."

"I said I'm *supposed* to wear a mask and carry my pillow. I didn't say I wanted to. I'd rather be with you."

His proper accent tickles me. I try to steady my breathing and fail. "It could be dangerous."

"That's exactly why I'm doing it."

My heart jitters, high on his touch, his warmth, and his bright gaze. I hurt him, but he didn't lecture me on how I should think before I speak. He didn't yell. He didn't break.

He stayed.

I squeeze his hand. "Sometimes I say dumb things."

"Me too."

"Sometimes I ruin things."

"I find that hard to believe."

"That makes you pretty dense."

"Would this be an example of saying something dumb?" His tongue finds his lip ring again.

"Funny." I give him a half-smile.

He takes the lead, holding fast to my hand. We make our way outside. Though it's chilly, the sun's brightness makes me happy.

Oh hell, who am I kidding? Adam is holding my hand. He's breaking whatever rules he's *supposed* to be following to be with me. It could be a blizzard and I'd still be ecstatic.

"Where should we go?" he asks.

"There's a park around the block."

"Ace."

My heart does another somersault. One word and the kid's got me crushing on him harder than ever.

More people visit the park today. The lack of rain must have something to do with it. A couple sits on the bench Shaw and I had huddled on. Fine with me. I'd rather find someplace new to share with Adam.

Past the pond behind a group of trees, we find it. A swing set.

"When was the last time you swung?" I ask, sitting on the plastic seat. I hold onto the chains.

Adam settles into the swing next to me, but sits still. "I don't know, maybe when I was five."

I kick off my feet and pump my legs. "I always loved this feeling. Sort of like flying."

"Careful."

I slow down a bit. "Do you see everything as a risk?"

He scuttles in the track like a crab crawling on the ocean floor. "I've been sick a long time, Darby. It's not so easy for me to jump into things as it is for you."

I let the swing come to a stop. "You sound so much older than most kids our age."

"Sometimes I feel it."

"Well, I can make you feel young again." I swing, ignoring the tension building in my shoulders.

He works his lip ring with his tongue.

I imagine what it'd be like to kiss him. On the mouth, not his cheek. I could hop off this swing, throw my arms around him, and suck on that piercing until he melted. On the other hand, I'd probably shock him so much his freshly operated on heart might trip all over itself.

Down Darbs, down. One step at a time. Start with something light and work your way up. "This is a judgment free zone, right?"

He angles his face toward me. The sunlight catches him just right. "Absolutely."

"Then we can say anything we want to each other, no pressure."

"I'd like that."

"Okay, then. Try this one on for size. You have the most unique eye color I've ever seen."

His eyes widen, but his mouth curves up at the corners. "Yeah?"

I stand and move in front of him. "Definitely."

He tips his head back, not that I'm much taller even with him sitting. "Most people think they're light brown. Boring."

I hook my index finger under his chin and lean closer, making sure not to block the light. "They're so much more than that. I see brown, gold, green, and blue. They're beautiful."

He blinks, but doesn't shy away. "You see a lot."

"I … paint. I'm an artist."

A spark of curiosity flickers in his gaze. "What do you paint?"

I trace my fingers along his jaw and cup his cheek with my palm. "I like contrast and the way things blend when there's conflict. I smoosh opposites together and let the paint sort out the details."

He covers my hand with his. "Juxtapose."

"Huh?"

"Putting things close together."

"My, my, your vocabulary is showing."

He blushes. It's so sweet that my stomach grows warm and tingly.

I have to take a step back to stop myself from locking lips with him right here and now. But I don't want to ruin this moment with rushing things.

Huh. Me, hesitating.

That's new.

* * *

Instead of going directly to my room after Adam and I return from our walk, I wander the hospital, searching for a quiet corner. I finally find a chair next to the outpatient pharmacy. It's closed now, so no one is waiting for a prescription.

I'd rather hang out with Adam, but he's expecting his parents around dinnertime, so we decided to part ways. It's okay. For now. In the meantime, I can plan my next series of paintings.

I immerse myself in the contrast of Adam's eyes. The way the sunlight highlighted them. How a cloud shadowed them. I hope I can capture his raw emotion. Sincere, sensitive, and shy, but also quiet and steady. More contrast.

Footsteps approach. An employee—I can tell from the scrubs and name tag—stands over me. She peers over her wire-rimmed glasses to look down at me. "You can't sit here."

"Why not?"

Her gaze lands on my wristband. "You're a patient? You should go back to your room."

I roll my eyes. "Fine."

Mom is staring at my painting when I return to my room. Her profile is backlit by the window and she's covering her mouth with a hand, so I can't read her expression.

I don't think she heard me arrive. It'd be so easy to turn around and walk away. On the other hand, I've got to talk to her sometime.

"Why are you here?" I ask. It's as good an opening line as any.

She startles. "I didn't hear you." She points to the painting. "Did you do this?"

"Who else would do it?"

"*Darby*."

I tuck my hands into my sweatshirt sleeves. "I worked on it this morning."

"It's beautiful. All the colors. Did you make this up,

or is it someone's eye?" Mom—the detail person. She probably thinks she's showing interest by asking me about my art, but I think explaining a painting anchors it, chains it to reality, and prevents it from just being.

"Actually, it's a boy's eye."

"From school?"

"No. From here."

She circles the bed. "The hospital?"

I move to avoid her. "Yeah. His name's Adam and he's a patient. We met at physical therapy."

"Really?" Shock clips her question.

"Surprised that someone would want to talk to me?"

She slaps her thighs with her hands. "No, Darby, but I *am* surprised that you went to PT. Doctor Wong tells me you haven't been compliant with your treatment here."

Oh, gee, I'm in trouble again. I fluff my pillow. "The therapist totally ignores me. What am I supposed to do, sit there and do nothing?"

"She has more than one patient." Mom logic. No point in arguing.

"Whatever."

"Right, whatever. If something doesn't go your way, your response is to push it aside and ignore it." She fiddles with her bead necklace—her own creation. Creativity is something I inherited from her. She works with jewelry and I work with paint. My mouthiness, on the other hand, is from my dad. The dyslexia ... well, that's pure Darby.

"Fine, I promise to do my exercises then."

Mom crosses her arms. "Doctor Wong has decided to discharge you. She says you can do outpatient physical therapy and follow up with her at the clinic."

I gape at her. "That's news to me. When was the

doctor going to tell me, the patient? Guess it doesn't matter."

"Don't tell me you want to stay here." Mom gestures to the room.

I don't, but … "It's better than home."

Her face falls. The weight of dealing with me, the snarky, non-compliant, bad twin, must be unbearable. "You can't mean that."

"It's obvious you don't want me there. How many days has it been since you've visited? Have you buried Daniel without me? I bet the whole town showed up." My heart shivers at the thought of missing Daniel's funeral. Then again, I don't think I could've handled it anyway. "Is he in the ground?"

Mom nods. "Yes. We thought it'd be easier for you to focus on healing."

"Thanks for giving me the choice."

"You kicked us out. Honestly, I don't understand you at all."

"I'll try to make better sense from now on." I pick at a pastel giraffe applique (surprise, the mural isn't painted at all, but is a bunch of stickers glued on the wall).

Mom huffs. She yanks open the closet door, drags the duffle bag from the top shelf, and starts stuffing my clothes inside.

"What're you doing?"

"Packing. You're coming home tonight."

I scramble to her, tweaking my neck in the process. Jolts of electric fire scream down my arms. My head swirls. I retreat to the bed. "Whoa."

Mom drops the bag and rushes over. "What happened?"

I'd shoo her away, but the idea of moving right

now brings a fresh layer of sweat to my skin. "Nothing. I twisted my neck wrong."

She sits next to me. "You have to be careful."

"I know."

"Sometimes I think your emotions erupt from you like lava and then you act without thinking." She rests her hand on my knee.

I study her hand, the fine wrinkles in her skin, her flawless French manicure, and the amber ring on her middle finger. I've always admired her hands. They're so graceful, clean, and delicate. The opposite of me. "I'm a volcano."

"Sometimes."

I bite my lip.

"You could use your fire for so much more productive things than fighting."

I try not to groan. "*Mom*."

She pats my thigh. "Your father's coming soon. He'll bring your art supplies to the car. Want to help me pack?"

If I leave tonight, I'll never see Adam again. I don't have his number, address, email, nothing. This can't be happening. I can't let someone else leave my life. I refuse to let it.

Mom goes back to packing.

When I can feel my toes again, I stand up gingerly and take a few steps toward the door. No zaps, thank goodness. At the doorway, I say, "I have to say bye to Adam."

I'm down the hall before Mom can say anything. She can chase me if she wants, but nothing's going to stop me.

This volcano is erupting.

Chapter Seventeen

Adam

Doctor Jervis stops by after dinner. His scrubs are wrinkled and his face bears the lines of wearing a surgical mask for hours on end. Today, his surgical cap has racing flames on the sides instead of skulls. At least he has a theme.

Mum and Dad greet him like the god he is with double-fisted handshakes and bursting smiles.

"How's our young patient?" Dr. Jervis unwinds his stethoscope from his neck and motions for me to lift my shirt. "Let's have a listen."

I pull my t-shirt off, exposing my scar. A puffy, red line marks the center of my chest, puckered by black sutures. Underneath lays my treasure, my new heart.

Dr. Jervis presses the stethoscope to my skin. Mum and Dad huddle at the end of my bed, gazes locked onto the doctor's every move.

After listening to my heart, Dr. Jervis slaps on a

pair of gloves and gingerly prods the wound. "Any pain, trouble breathing, shortness of breath, dizziness, black outs?"

"No." Not since the day I snuck out for coffee and fell off the treadmill.

"You use the pillow?"

"Yes." It lies next to me on the bed, so I pat it like it's a dog. My companion.

"Taking your meds, wearing a mask in public?"

Quick questions means I can give simple answers. It's the one thing I like about surgeons. Other than the life-saving operations they do, of course. "All the time."

Mum and Dad nod in agreement, eager to please him.

"Ricky says you're progressing quite nicely in PT. Feels good to have a functioning heart, doesn't it?" Jervis pats my shoulder, all atta-boys and look-what-I've-done-for-you.

"Can I put my shirt back on?" I ask.

"Sure," Dr. Jervis says.

Mum grips the foot of the bed with both hands. "What happens next, doctor?"

"Since Adam's doing so well, I think we can plan for discharge. We'll do one more biopsy tomorrow to check for rejection—I doubt there is any—and once he wakes up, you can take him home." He rubs his hands together. It's a done deal.

"That's wonderful, doctor. Thank you. For everything." Dad extends his hand for another shake.

Jervis gladly accepts it. "No problem. It's what I do."

After Jervis leaves, Mum skirts around the bed and

hugs me. "Isn't that fantastic news? You're coming home tomorrow."

I immediately think of Darby and the excitement that charges through me when I'm with her. My new heart skips right along with me. But if I'm discharged, we can't share ice cream in the cafeteria or sneak away to the park or commiserate about being stuck in the hospital.

Or kiss.

I bite my lip ring to suppress the smile that wants to burst across my face. Next time, I'm going to kiss her first.

If there is a next time.

My stomach folds into knots.

I *must* get her number or email before I leave.

Mum keeps squeezing me. "I'll make your favorite dinner. Then we'll pop popcorn, veg on the couch, and watch movies. How does that sound?"

"Yeah, great," I mumble. All I can think about is shrugging out of her grip and dashing to the Pediatric floor.

Dad frowns. "You don't look excited."

Mum peers down at me. "What's wrong?"

I try to animate my face. Make it look like I'm happy. "Nothing's wrong. I'm just surprised ... shocked. Didn't think I'd be leaving so soon."

"You didn't think you'd be here forever, did you?" Dad chuckles. "I thought you'd be chomping to get out of here."

"Yeah, I am, but this seems so sudden."

Mum fusses with my hair. "It'll be good to have you home. Things can go back to normal."

Normal. Mum's fantasy turns into reality.

The only thing I can say for certain is Darby has made me feel more alive than anything—or anyone—else. Forget Shaw's stupid therapy, Ricky's grueling PT sessions, or drafting a Live Life List. None of it is real, like really real.

Except for Darby.

Without her, I'm not sure which way to go. It figures that I'd finally have a glimpse of what my life could become and it gets mowed down before it can grow. The seedling of optimism I dared to cultivate starts to shrivel.

I slide to the bed's edge, leaving Mum's embrace.

Nope. I shake my head. I will *not* give up so quickly. If I'm going to take full advantage of this second chance, I need to take a cue from Darby and *act*.

"Adam?" Mum tentatively puts a hand on my arm. Her wide eyes search Dad's face for support.

"Son, what's going on?" Dad comes closer.

Flanked by them, I fidget even more, like a thoroughbred at a starting gate. I need to find Darby now. Launching myself off the bed, I rush out of the room before Mum and Dad can stop me.

Mum follows. "Adam! Where are you going? Your mask and pillow!"

I pick up my pace. "I'll be back in a minute. I need to talk to Darby."

Mum's heels *click-click-click-click*. "You have to talk to her now?"

At the lift, I press the down button several times. "Yes."

Mum catches up to me, huffing a bit. She leans against the wall. "I'm not used to you running."

"You didn't have to chase me."

Dad rounds the corner. He's carrying my pillow and mask. "Thought you might need these."

I put the mask on and clutch the pillow to my chest. "Thanks."

He turns to Mum. "Where's he rushing off to?"

Mum shifts from leaning on the wall to leaning on him. "He's going to visit Darby."

His brows crawl up his forehead. "Now?"

Mum stares up at me, her eyes filled with confusion and maybe a hint of excitement. "I'm not sure what's going on with you right now, but … I'm going to trust you."

My chest swells with hope. "Really?"

She nods.

"Can someone explain what's going on?" Dad asks.

Mum pats his belly. "I told you, Adam's going to see Darby."

He raises his eyebrows like he's caught on, but he hasn't. I can tell by the frown tugging at his mouth. True to form, he doesn't argue or keep questioning. That's Mum's job and for once she's letting me do what I need to do.

The lift's doors open.

Filled with a lightness I haven't felt in months, I rush inside and press the button for the Pediatric floor. "Thank you."

Mum smiles up at me. And she's proud.

Dad's expression remains confused. He circles an arm around Mum's shoulders and plants a kiss on her head.

The doors close, leaving my past behind me.

When I step off the lift, I'm on my way to Darby and a new life.

* * *

I round the corner and almost smack directly into Darby.

Her eyes widen. "Adam."

"Darby." I breathe out her name, tugging the facemask off.

"What're you doing here?" She grabs my wrist and drags me to a dimly lit alcove.

"I love it when you do that." I blurt out the words, then hold my breath.

"Do what?"

"Take charge."

She giggles. "Seriously?"

I laugh. "The truth is, I came to see you."

Her smile widens. "You did?"

I toss my pillow to the floor and lace my fingers with hers, suddenly sobered. "I'm being discharged tomorrow."

Her smile fades. She shifts deeper into a shadow. "I'm being discharged tonight. Now."

"*Now*?"

She presses her lips together. "Mom is packing my things, but I left her to find you. I couldn't go without seeing you again."

"So you came to see me too?" More lightness infuses my body. I'd levitate if I could. Instead, I plant my feet firmly on the ground, swallowing down the hope building from my feet, up my legs … No. I shouldn't get carried away. She might simply want to say goodbye and good luck and all that.

"Of course." She peers up at me through her eyelashes and rests her palms against my chest. Heat radiates from her, igniting a fire deep in my belly. "This is happening too fast. I thought I—I thought we'd be here a lot longer."

"Me too." I want to hook my finger under her chin like she did mine when we were in the park, but I'm not sure how with the neck brace and all, so I tuck a blue lock of hair behind her ear and let my fingers linger on her skin. She doesn't shy away. "We agree to be honest, right?"

"Yes." She answers without hesitating.

"Good because I want to say something." My heart pounds. Practicing a New Life can take its toll. This heart should be able to handle it where my old one couldn't.

"Say it."

I creep my toes to the proverbial ledge, stare out at the horizon, and leap off, spreading my arms wide to fly. "I'm not ready to leave you."

She shivers. I pull her closer to me. She clasps her arms around my waist and presses her face against my chest. "Me neither."

I ignore the pressure it puts on my sternum. She wants to be with me. *Me*. The sick, delicate, awkward guy who doesn't know how to live. I catch an air current and float. "We can exchange numbers and emails and ... "

She hugs me tighter. "Uh-hmmm."

"I was thinking ... " I pause, hoping an upwind will catch me so I don't crash.

She giggles. "You think too much."

I hold my breath. Can't falter now. I unwrap Darby's arms from my waist and bend my knees so we're almost eye level, holding onto her hands. "You're probably right."

A troubling darkness deepens her crystal eyes. I can't tell if it's sadness, regret, or both. "Sometimes thinking is good. I don't do enough of it."

"Too much thinking is just as bad."

She blinks away the shadow in her gaze. "So stop it."

I toggle my lip ring. My gaze falls to her mouth. "Okay."

I lean in, hovering close to her lips. Her breath warms my face. My heart goes crazy.

It's now or never.

I press my mouth against hers. She's soft and smooth and perfect. I settle on her bottom lip until the kiss turns urgent and bold, and oh god, she slips her tongue in my mouth and kisses me back.

We're here, together, two opposites, a thinker and a doer, a rule-follower and a rule-breaker, meeting in the middle, living in the contrast.

Chapter Eighteen

Darby

I think about Adam's kiss for the entire ride home. He whispered, "Ace" when we finally broke apart. I didn't think he had it in him, Mr. Thinks-A-Lot.

He's so different from anyone I've ever met. He's smart and innocent all at once. Bet he reads a lot, with all those big words he uses. Bet he likes Shakespeare and Hemmingway and boring things like that.

His kiss wasn't boring. At all.

I suck in my bottom lip to keep from smiling. I'm usually the one who starts the lipfest.

Okay, so it was obvious it was his first kiss. He wasn't sure which way to angle his face so our noses didn't bump, but whoa, he picked it up quick. He wasn't a dead fish and he wasn't a slobbery dog either. And hands didn't wander too much.

Plus his lip ring? *Awesome.*

Mom parks in front of the garage. She cuts the

engine and cups the keys in her palm, but doesn't make any move to leave the car. She must be cooking up something good to ream on me about. I'm surprised she isn't waiting until we get inside.

The engine pings and pops. I can't even think about the empty spot where Daniel's Mustang should be.

Mom sniffs. The car gets cooler with every passing second. Like a damp grave.

Well, I'm not going to sit in here all night. I unfasten my safety belt, letting it slide across my body. It's gonna be weird inside the house, without Daniel there.

I curl my fingers around the door handle. Why'd I have to go and think that? Now I don't want to leave *and* I don't want to stay.

Mom jiggles her keys. "I thought it'd be important for you to continue counseling, so I scheduled an appointment for you with Doctor Shaw tomorrow afternoon."

How thoughtful of her to make that decision on her own.

"Gee, thanks for the head's up." I open the door with a yank of the handle. The quick movement sends jolts down my arm. Yep, I was ready to leave the hospital. Sure.

She pulls the lever that opens the trunk. "This *is* a head's up, Darby. You should take this opportunity to work through whatever it is you're going through."

I stiffen. "*Whatever it is I'm going though?* Because it's such a puzzle."

"You can't keep blaming yourself for Daniel's death."

Heat flares in my cheeks as tears prick my eyes. "And you can't tell me how to feel."

"I'm not. That's why I'm sending you to doctor Shaw."

"Stop trying to fix me." I slide out of the passenger's seat and head for the porch.

"Darby!" Mom calls.

Dad opens the door before I get to it. He leans to the side to let me in. "Welcome home." His tone is light. Fake.

I start climbing the stairs, ignoring him.

"Where are you going?" he asks.

"My room." I bark.

Daniel's bedroom is the first one on the left and mine is the second. His door is shut. It's for the best. I can't face its emptiness.

I slam my door and twist the lock in place. Here I am. Home. My head whirls. I shouldn't be here. I don't belong. Not when half of me is gone.

With a shaky hand, I flick on the light. Bed tucked into the corner—the comforter is still pulled back from when I got up the morning of the accident. A pile of flannel shirts, silkscreened t-shirts, and paint-stained jeans on my desk instead of textbooks. Finished paintings cram every spare inch of wall. An easel stands in front of my bare window. A blank canvas sits on it, waiting.

The room is the same, but I'm not.

Shaw understood. Maybe I should talk to her about it tomorrow.

A knock comes at the door. "Darbs?"

It's Mom.

I stand in the middle of my room, feet rooted into the carpet.

"I brought your things. Dad has your art supplies."

The hallway floor creaks.

"Open the door," Dad says.

"Leave it there."

"Don't shut us out." Mom's voice is shaky.

"Leave. It. There." I fist my hands.

Something thuds to the floor. It's followed by a cascade of objects thumping against the door—probably my easel and canvases.

"We have to leave by one o'clock tomorrow if you want to keep your therapy appointment," Mom says.

"Fine."

The stairs creak and moan from Mom and Dad heading downstairs. I wait a few minutes before dragging my things inside.

Mom and Dad's voices echo my way, but it's too soft for me to make out what they're saying.

Slowly, I creep toward Daniel's room. My heart plays a game of dodge ball with my ribs. The door falls open with a slight push. I hold my breath and turn on the light.

Daniel's room is clean and organized. His bed is made, desk clean, and clothes organized in the closet. A bookshelf in the far corner holds trophies, books, and pictures of him and his buddies. His flat screen TV and game station sit neatly on his dresser.

Holding a hand over my mouth, I stuff down a sob and shuffle to the beanbag chair. I pick up a plush basketball and cradle it to my chest like Adam hugs his heart-shaped pillow. Walking backward, I retreat from the room, shut off the light, and close the door.

I don't bother undressing or straightening out my bed.

Lying on my back, I stare at the ceiling, dig my fingers into the toy, and cry myself to sleep.

* * *

Shaw's office is much like her—sparse, elegant, and upscale. A wall of windows behind a glass and metal desk. A sleek laptop on a bamboo blotter. A silver cell phone next to it. The only natural thing is a little bonsai tree with a carved wooden box in front of it.

Shaw gestures to two leather chairs. The modern bookshelves behind them hold a bunch of psych books written by people I've never heard of and a couple of abstract sculptures. At least they're interesting.

I dip into the chair closest to the door and fold my hands in my lap. With paint stains on my jeans and wrinkles in my t-shirt, I'm a zit on her perfect room.

Shaw sits and crosses her leg. She belongs here. This is her world, and the hint of Chanel No. 5 hovering around her confirms it. "You seem quiet."

"Do I?"

"How was it being home?"

"Okay."

The tan swirls weaving their way across her white area rug spin like my thoughts. I press my fingernails into my palms. Shaw's here to help me, right? So I should tell her about my *un*happy homecoming.

"The way you're sulking makes me think differently."

I shake out my hands. "You calling me a liar?"

The corner of Shaw's mouth turns up. "Ah, there's the Darby I know."

I squint at her. "You tricked me."

"Had to get you talking somehow."

I cross my arms, pissed, though I have to give her credit for getting one over on me. "Hope you're proud of yourself."

"I was surprised when I heard you were being discharged."

I huff. "I wasn't being *compliant* so the doctor kicked me out."

"That's what your Mom said when I spoke to her."

"I'm sure she told you everything, so why do you need to hear it from me?"

"Everyone has their own version of events and I'm working directly with you. That means whatever you say is of utmost importance. I'm all ears."

Sitting in Shaw's office reminds me of Principal Shepherd's. What's different is Shaw seems to be on my side. At least, so far. "Then why bother mentioning what Mom tells you?"

"We have to build our relationship on trust. I want to be an open book with you."

I draw my hands through my hair. No sense in holding back if she already knows what happened. I'm sure Mom has put her own spin on it though. Let's see what Shaw thinks of my version. "Well here's my open book. I got home, locked myself in my room, refused to talk to Mom and Dad, and cried myself to sleep. The end."

Her brow furrows a bit, like she's actually concerned. "Sounds rough."

"You don't know the half of it."

"Tell me."

"It's pathetic." I grind a toe into the carpet.

"Darby, you're not pathetic." She clamps her fingers around the arm of my chair. "You're strong, independent, and resilient."

I haven't done anything to give her the impression I'm any of those things and they're definitely not words Mom would use to describe me. I suck in a breath. "I went into Daniel's room and took his toy basketball. I hung onto it like a five-year-old. That's not very resilient."

She's quiet for a long time. But it's not an embarrassing quiet, or a judging quiet. It's a hug of silence. A chance for me to decide if I want to say more.

After a while, I add, "You want to know what else? His room was immaculate. There wasn't even any dust anywhere. But my room? It's like no one's been in there since I left. Like I've been forgotten while Daniel's been memorialized."

"I can't imagine how painful that must have been."

"I thought Mom would make the bed or vacuum or something. She had to go in there to bring clothes to the hospital."

"Is that what you were hoping for? That your mom would make things nice for you."

"I don't know." I shove off my heels and pace the room. "I don't know anything."

"You know plenty."

How can this woman really keep seeing good things in me? I spin on my toes to face her. "Yeah, like what?"

"Your Mom said you picked up painting again." She slides to the end of the chair, moving closer.

I retreat to the window. "So what?"

"It's a gift to be creative."

"It doesn't matter to my parents. They want good grades and popularity and medals and *perfection*."

"Have they said that specifically?"

"No. They don't have to." I slide my fingers along the window ledge.

Shaw appears at my side. She doesn't give up, that's for sure. Mom would've stormed out of the room by now. "You know what you need?"

"No, but I'm sure you'll tell me. Mom does. She tells me all the time. Darby, you need to study. Darby, you need to clean up your room. Darby, you need to stop getting suspended. Darby, you need to get over your dyslexia."

"I won't say any of those things to you, but I will say this: You need to feel secure, accepted, and loved."

I point to her books. "You get that from your library?"

"What prompted you to pick up the paintbrush again?" She taps my hand with a finger.

If she were Mom, she'd flinch at my brushoff and launch into some lecture on how I should be acting. But she's not Mom. She keeps proving it more and more by the second. Maybe I can trust her.

"If you must know, his name is Adam," I say.

She squares her jaw and sits at her desk.

The vibe in the room flips to pure ice.

"Who is he?" Her tone is much more clipped.

I stuff my hands in my pockets. "What's with the sudden change of temperature?"

"Answer my question." She reaches across her desk for the small box. Her fingers hover over the latch.

"I met him in the hospital. He had some heart surgery or something, I don't know. But he has the most beautiful eyes I've ever seen. I had to paint them."

She opens the lid. "He's your muse."

"Muse? I don't know about that. Sounds too fancy."

"He inspired you." Her voice is softer.

I take a step toward her desk. "I guess so."

She picks up something from the box and holds it out to me. "Maybe this will inspire you to."

I examine it. A butterfly pin with a heart in the middle, held together by stitches. Adam has the same pin on his heart pillow. "Oh my god."

"The butterfly represents change. You've certainly experienced a lot of change in the past couple of weeks." She closes the box and sets it back in its place.

"What's this for?"

"I told you my other work is with the heart transplant team at the hospital. I treat transplant recipients and each of them gets a pin when they undergo the procedure. It helps them feel like they're part of something and reminds them they are not alone. I want you to have one so that you can remember the same thing."

The pin weighs down my palm like lead. Adam has a pin. He's had heart surgery. No, he's had a *heart transplant*. And he's been in the hospital for about the same amount of time as me. "Doctor Shaw ... "

"You wanted to know who received Daniel's heart."

I suck on my bottom lip, squeezing the pin until the edges of the butterfly's wings dig into my skin. "Yes."

"His name is Adam."

My knees wobble. I shatter. The next second, I'm on the floor in a puddle of hands and knees and tears and sobs.

Shaw is at my side in an instant. "What's the matter, honey?"

A wail oozes out of me. All I can do is rock back and forth while hugging myself.

"Darby?" She makes little circles on my back with her palm.

"Why him? *Why?*" I cough and sniff, wipe the snot and tears from my face, and writhe some more. Sweet and shy and hopelessly quirky Adam. I'd dared to open myself up to him, to let myself like him. Only to find out he has Daniel's heart.

Shaw doesn't let go. She stays at my side, quiet, letting me get it out without telling me to stop, pull it together, or get over it. When I finally catch my breath, she says, "Maybe I shouldn't have told you."

"I wanted to know." My voice trembles, like my heart.

"You're fond of Adam."

I shut my eyes. "Y-yes."

"He's a sensitive boy."

"Y-you work with him?"

"He's as conflicted as you. He often wonders if he's stealing life and for the longest time was uncertain if he deserved a donor heart."

I open my eyes and press my palms onto the floor. "What does he think now?"

"I think he's happy to be alive."

"With my brother's heart beating inside him." I dig my fingers into the carpet.

Shaw had asked me what drew me to Adam. I'd said his eyes, but I hadn't noticed them until after I started talking to him. At first he was just some random kid in PT I'd decided to bother because I was bored. Or so I'd thought. What if I was somehow *connected* to his—Daniel's—heart?

"Are you going to keep seeing Adam?"

I sit back on my butt. "I don't know if I can. He has

Daniel's heart. He's alive and my brother isn't."

Shaw stands and extends a hand. "It's not fair."

I let her help me up. "You know what's not fair? He wouldn't have had a second chance if Daniel hadn't died and I would've never met him if the accident hadn't happened."

She opens her mouth, pauses, then says, "It messes with your mind."

I affix the pin to my shirt. My hands shake so bad it takes a couple tries for me to do it. "I'm glad you told me. Adam didn't want to. Guess I know why now. He's a liar."

"He betrayed your trust."

The clock chimes. It's the end of the hour.

I walk out of the room, calm on the outside, and a raging sea of lava on the inside.

PART THREE

REQUIEM

Chapter Nineteen

Adam

The first day back at school races by. Kids who've never talked to me before give me grand handshakes and several hearty, "Welcome back!" greetings, complete with brotherly slaps on my shoulder. The teachers are full of smiles and outlines to help me catch up. Best of all, the guidance counselor has decided to pair me with a peer tutor during study periods so I can get caught up ASAP.

It's all bloody brilliant.

On the drive home, Mum makes me give a detailed account of my day. At the end of it, she insists on hiring a professional tutor instead of one the school provided.

I carry on the conversation inside, after pulling off my mask as soon as I cross the threshold. "I don't need a tutor."

"Did you use your pillow today?"

I sigh. Nice of her to ignore me.

She halts me in the hallway and stares up at me, waiting for an answer.

"Yes, all day." I didn't, but she doesn't need to know that. It would've been weird explaining it to everybody. It was bad enough wearing a mask.

I drag my rolling suitcase around her toward the living room. The doctor suggested I use it instead of a backpack until my sternum fully heals. I wanted to use the stairs at school, as sort of a triumphant comeback, but couldn't because of the rolling suitcase. At least the lift worked.

"Where is it?" She settles into an armchair.

I sit on the couch and pull the pillow out of my suitcase-bookbag, snagging the pin on the wire of a spiral notebook. "Here."

"Good. Do you keep an extra mask in there too?"

"Yes." I grab my copy of *The Razor's Edge* by Somerset Maugham and kick the suitcase aside. Like me, the main character is a bit disillusioned with life and, unlike me, he travels the world to find himself.

"Are we really sliding into one word answers again?" She pats the arm a few times in frustration.

I crack open the book. "I told you everything in the car. Not sure what else to say."

"How about writing your friends at home? I'm sure they'd love to hear how you're doing."

"Uh-huh." I agree, even though I have no intention of doing so. Writing to them would be weird, especially since I've ignored them for so long. What could I say? Something like, "Hey, I've ignored you for a few months but I finally got a new heart, yay!" just doesn't cut it.

I rub the book's spine, itching to pull out my mobile

and dial up Darby. She's the only person I can turn to. I chew on my lip ring, caught in a sudden attack of nerves.

"What about Darby? Are you going to call her?"

My mother must be psychic.

"Maybe."

Mum stands. "I think you should."

I pretend to read.

She waits for a moment, perhaps giving me extra time to answer, then walks out of the room.

I skim the page, but I'm not concentrating enough to follow the words. Instead, I keep picturing Darby and all the things that make her, well, *her*. Blue and black hair, pouty mouth, and bright personality. Most of all, the paint stains that cover her clothes. She wears her love every day. I could never hope to embody such passion. It's not like I can staple pages of my favorite books to my shirt.

I toss the book onto the coffee table. My most interesting hobbies are reading and, well, reading. Lame with a capital L. Darby would be crazy to want to hang out with me outside of the hospital. I have nothing to offer.

Swallowing a lump of self-doubt, I press my fingers to my lips, remembering our kiss.

"Stop thinking, Adam, and *act*," I whisper.

I grab my phone and retreat upstairs for some privacy.

It's so simple to pull up her name and press *call*. Yet it's also terrifying. My throat goes dry.

I smile, hearing Darby's words, *you think too much*.

She's right. Thinking gets me more confused and anxious.

I dial.

While my heart thrums, the phone rings.

And rings.

And rings.

Finally, voice mail picks up.

Darby's throaty voice yaps at me to leave a message. "It's Darbs. You know what to do."

At the beep, I say, "Hey, Darby, it's me, Adam. Um, from the hospital. Yeah, so I wanted to talk to you. How's everything?" I suck in a breath, cringing at myself. "So, ring me when you get this message."

I hang up and groan. I can't have sounded worse if I tried.

Jagged energy courses through me with a conversation left unsaid and uncertain possibilities. She could've seen my number and decided not to answer. It wouldn't surprise me if she didn't want to speak with me. Bet she'll get a good laugh from my stupid message.

I peer into the mirror hanging over my dresser. "Um, dur, it's Adam from the hospital." I add a lisp and cross my eyes for good measure.

"You're such an idiot." I push off the dresser and wander to my dormer window. Branches from an ancient oak tree stretch toward the glass, desperately grasping at the air. They're reaching for nothing. Sort of like me.

Larry Darrell, the main character in *The Razor's Edge*, wouldn't mope on and on like this. He'd go off on some adventure, travel foreign lands, visit Paris, ride elephants in India, blend with the local cultures. He'd seek out wise men and search for the deeper meaning of life. I can't even figure out what to do with a free afternoon.

My gaze falls on a gap in the fencing marking the side yard's perimeter where a thin dirt path sits nestled between a pair of evergreens. It takes a sharp curve to the right then disappears into shadow. I wandered the woods there a little bit when we'd first relocated and it reminded me a bit of home. As a kid, we'd summer in the country and I'd play under the trees, pretending I was a knight in search of a dragon or a space pilot stranded on a distant planet. During dinner, I'd tell Mum and Dad about my voyages. They'd laugh. Mum would kiss my forehead and say I had a wild imagination while Dad mussed my hair and mentioned something about Only Child Syndrome.

I had a life before I got sick. It was full of fantasy and idealistic white picket fences and quality family time moments, but it was mine. All that stopped when my heart decided to go on strike. The thing is, I can't relive those years. I can't pick up where I left off. I'd never be able to bridge the gap of lost time. Sickness changed me much like World War I changed Larry. The promise of imminent death would do that.

Larry was able to redirect himself, figure out what to do after he faced his mortality. I haven't yet. How did Larry do it? He simply went and did it. Well, so can I, since I can walk now without getting short of breath. I stare down at my shoes. "Alright, feet, let's get journeying."

Decision made, I creep downstairs, grab my jacket from the coat rack in the foyer, and slip outside, rushing to the path. I don't slow down until I'm well out of sight. I hate sneaking, but I don't need Mum offering to come along with me. I can see her now, walking in her heels and bundled in layers of clothes, a thick coat, scarf, and a hat and gloves, taking two steps to my one.

It's late afternoon. The sun falls steadily toward the horizon. Deep shadows claim most of the woods. It's only a few acres of land between suburban cul-de-sacs and housing developments, but already it seems a world away from where I've been.

Fallen leaves and loose stones crunch under my feet. My pulse whooshes in my ears, no hitches or unnatural pauses. It matches the rhythmic brush of my breath in and out of my lungs. The farther I go, the more surrounded I am by an earthy mixture of sharp pine, bitter dirt, and rotting leaf matter.

This is what I'm looking for, isn't it? Being in nature, witnessing the elements directly instead of through a TV or computer screen or reading it in a book.

I shiver off the descending chill as I wind my way down the sloping trail. A small pond is at the bottom. Pale tan reeds line the far side. Some are bent over, as if tired from fighting the cold. Although it isn't officially winter, some snow has fallen (and mostly melted off again) and the nights are frosty enough to freeze the pond's surface.

The last time I went skating my head barely reached Dad's hip. At first, he skated behind me, holding me up by my armpits. When I got my footing, he'd let me go a few feet on my own. I fell a lot, but it didn't matter. I craved the wind against my face and the feel of floating as I skimmed across the ice.

I close my eyes, trying hard to remember the sensation. Like the oak branches straining for the sky, I grasp at the memory, but can't reach it. It's from my past life. Too faint. Almost dream-like. Intangible.

Toggling my lip ring, I open my eyes.

Living means action. Living means taking chances. Living means doing stupid things and getting high on the rush.

I ease one foot onto the ice and slowly put some weight on it. It holds firm, so I add my other foot, inching forward a bit. No cracks, no pops. A smile pulls at my mouth.

Like an old man without a walker, I slide ahead and make my way across the surface. Soon, I'm standing in the middle, free and trapped all at once. Free because I'm actually doing something, by myself, without Mum's watchful gaze, without the chance of my heart flipping into a lethal rhythm. Trapped because the only way off is to complete the trek or return the way I came.

I tip my head back to the darkening sky. What's the hurry? I'm making my own life. I can stay here as long as I want.

Snap!

I startle, scanning the surrounding ice for a crack.

Pop!

Sure enough, there's a fracture line extending from my right foot, forward and back.

More rattles and rumbles shudder across the pond. The vibrations tickle my feet.

My whole body tenses. I'm in trouble.

I squint into the reeds ahead. Dusk is upon me and I can't clearly make out where the shore is among the brittle spears. I glance over my shoulder. The shore is flatter and more open there.

Okay, I've got two options. Make a run for it and risk stomping into a crack or inch my way in reverse and hope the ice holds out long enough for me to make it. Sudden movement seems like a bad idea.

I slide one foot toward the shore to start my retreat. That's when the ice gives way and I plunge in. The little harmless pond instantly becomes a death trap. I gasp at the cold and suck in slimy water. Submerged in a few feet of dark water, I lose my orientation. My clothes weigh me down. I force my eyes open and flail my arms and legs.

I break the surface and spit out a mouthful of frigid algae-laden pond water. Grunting and choking, tongue and face covered in slime, I latch onto the jagged edge of ice to slide onto it, but it gives way too. Like a cutter ship breaking a path along a frozen river, I chop my way to the shore. All with a lot of splashing, gasping, groaning, and crying.

Exhausted, I roll onto the shore wheezing.

My first attempt at living life, really living life, brought me closer to death than my crappy old heart did.

The irony.

I laugh and laugh and laugh. It's coarse at first, gravelly from the grime and dirt I choked on, then clearer and more high-pitched with every new breath.

"*Adam!*" Mum's screech cuts through my maniacal barking.

I cough some more and roll onto my side. "Mum."

"David, he's over here." Mum crashes through the woods. Her flashlight beam bounces around until it lands on me.

I squint, lifting a hand to block its piercing brightness.

Mum drops to her knees at my side. "What are you doing?" She drops the flashlight and cups my face with both hands.

"I fell in," is all I can manage to say.

Dad jogs up to us. He kneels next to Mum. "What the hell are you doing out here?"

Mum grips my jacket. "He's soaked. Let's get him inside, then we can find out what happened."

I need their help to hold my weight on the walk back to the house. Mum wants to supervise me in the shower, but I don't let her. Even with the water on the hottest setting, it takes a long time for me to thaw. When I finally make it downstairs, Dad has built a roaring fire in the fireplace. Mum forces me to drink a steaming mug of chicken noodle soup and two cups of tea. She checks my temperature every fifteen minutes, asking me a thousand and one times if I swallowed pond water.

While I roast by the crackling blaze covered in three blankets, she paces the room, wringing her hands. "I should ring Doctor Jervis. You may need to be checked out. Maybe we should go to the ER."

"I don't want to go to the ER. I'm fine." I peek up at her, then to Dad.

He scratches his chin. "We can call the doctor tomorrow."

"What if he has hypothermia?"

"His temperature is normal, Lisa."

Mum stops wearing a rut into the carpet. Dad's level-headed tone seems to calm her. She sits next to me on the ottoman. "What on earth possessed you to go out there and walk on the ice? Any fool would know it wasn't solid enough." She all but screeches.

Maybe I spoke too soon about the calm part. "It was pretty stupid," I admit.

Tears well in her eyes. She brushes my hair away

from my forehead. "Were you trying to kill yourself?"

My breath catches. "Wh-what?"

"It's just … from everything Doctor Shaw was saying, to you being depressed and distant, and not talking to your friends … what am I supposed to think?"

Whatever pond scum I ingested bubbles in my stomach, spiced with Mum's words. "I'm not suicidal." I launch to my feet, casting off the blankets.

Dad stumbles back. Mum leans away, wide-eyed.

"I'm trying to live."

And totally sucking at it.

Chapter Twenty

Darby

I give Mom the silent treatment on the way home after session. I skip dinner too. Mom knocks on my bedroom door and announces she's left a plate for me on the floor. I wait for her footsteps to fade away before opening the door to drag the tray in my room.

Two slices of greasy cheese pizza—definitely delivery—crowd the plate. A container of chocolate milk sits next to a bowl of homemade butterscotch pudding. Silverware is wrapped in a linen napkin tucked neatly between the plate and bowl. I balance the tray on an uneven stack of books on the floor.

While chewing on a bite of burnt cheese and gummy dough, I listen to Adam's message. Then play it again. He trips up so many times it's like he can't get out of his own way. I must've been out of my mind to think he was cute.

I toss the pizza aside and do the same with my phone.

The painting, the first I've done since Daniel's death, the one that brought me back to life, leans against my dresser. Adam's beautiful eye—as I see it with a bold mixture of colors and brushstrokes—watches me, bright and open, but also mocking and taunting. Adam has my brother's heart. He's alive because Daniel is dead. The boy "muse."

Adam's eye calls to me. Squeezes my head. I fight the tug of anger snaking across my shoulders, down my arms, and to my hands.

My c-collar seems to close tighter around my throat. Sweat slicks my skin underneath it. So itchy. I tug at the Velcro straps, tearing them open. I drop the collar on the floor, gaze superglued to the painting.

I'm torn between swooning in the depths of the multicolored iris and shoving my fist through the pupil. Shit, why'd I have to recreate his eye so perfectly? It's like Adam himself is staring at me through the layers of paint.

I replay his stuttering message. The softness of his accent melts me. He soothes my pain.

And, somehow, he's also causes it.

I can't face him again knowing a part of Daniel is inside him. I can't. Not after he lied to me about it.

Enough! I flip the painting over so if faces my dresser. It cuts the connection and I breathe with relief, free from my own creation.

The break won't last. I'm in the canvas too. And some of Daniel, because he's now a part of Adam.

We're all anchored to one another.

I drop to the floor, empty.

I don't know if I'll find the strength to stand again.

* * *

A bunch of bangs at the door wakes me.

"Darby!" Mom knocks some more.

I curl onto my side and groan. Pain shoots from my hip to shoulder. Sleeping on the floor. Bad idea. "Mom."

"Open the door or so help me, I'll rip off the lock."

I clear my throat. God, my neck feels like a loose rubber band. "Give me a minute."

"*Now*, Darby."

Mini shocks bite at my fingertips as I push off the floor to sit up. I use the bed to climb to my feet. The c-collar lies next to me. I stumble to it and put it on before opening the door. Mom already has enough reasons to be pissed at me. I don't want her to freak out about not wearing the damn thing. "What?"

Mom's lowered brows and thinned lips switch into a wide-eyed, wrinkled-forehead mask of concern. "You look awful."

"Thanks." I tug on the hem of my shirt.

She exhales through her nose. "You're going to be late for school."

"I'm not going." I swing the door to close it.

Mom blocks me with her toe. "Yes, you are. Get washed up, or at least change out of those clothes. Weren't you wearing them yesterday?"

"So?"

"You have ten minutes. I'll meet you in the car."

"Whatever." I slam the door.

Doesn't take long for muffled shouts start downstairs. Mom's high-pitched whine mixes with Dad's deeper barks. Soon after, heavy footsteps pound up the stairs.

I sit on my bed, waiting for the tornado to hit.

Dad bursts into my room, chest-puffed out and face red. "What's this about you not going to school?"

"It's simple. I'm staying home."

"You need to catch up."

"I missed over two weeks, so what's the difference?" I cross my leg and swing my foot back and forth.

"The difference is you were in the hospital and now you're not. Skipping will only get you further behind." He straightens the knot of his tie, even though it's already centered.

"I don't care." I crawl to the head of the bed and hug Daniel's plush basketball.

Dad strokes his shaved chin. "Is there anything you *do* care about?"

I squeeze my eyes shut. "Go away."

A shadow creeps over me. I open my eyes to Dad looming over me.

He grabs my arm and hauls me off the bed. "You're going to school, even if I have to drag you kicking and screaming."

I squirm, but he's at least twice my size and three times as strong. My arms throb from his iron grip. Tears scald my eyes. "Let go. You're hurting me. Dad!"

He releases me. "I'm sorry."

I stumble backward, rubbing my upper arms. "No you're not,"

"Can't make it easy, can you?"

"*Easy*. You think losing my brother is easy, or

wearing this fucking neck brace is easy, or that being in this house, knowing you and Mom would rather have Daniel here, is easy? No, it's not."

He huffs and puffs like the wolf in *Red Riding Hood*. "You don't know the half of it, little girl. You're not the only one who's lost someone. My son is dead, my wife is so riddled with grief I don't know how to make her feel better, and my daughter is circling around the drain. So it'd be wise of you to realize you're not the only one suffering here."

"It's hard to tell."

He squares his jaw. His fisted hands shake. "When will you realize we love you?" He spins on his heel and walks out of my room.

The blaze from Dad's anger remains after he leaves. It burns the walls. Creates smoke. The air is heavy and hot. Suffocating.

I stuff my feet in a pair of ballet flats and flee.

In the foyer, Mom is twisting her hair into a bun. Her wool coat hangs open and her crocheted bag drapes limply over her shoulder.

"Will you drop me off at school?" I ask.

Mom freezes. "Uh … s-sure."

I follow her outside.

We're both quiet for the entire ride. I don't mind.

After pulling up to the school's main entrance, she unlocks the doors, then grips the steering wheel like she's choking it. Instead of saying goodbye or wishing me good luck, she stares straight ahead at the bus parked in front of us.

I leave everything I want to say unsaid in the car seat and I don't look back. Mom can eat the conversation we didn't have all the way to work. It can get stuck in her teeth, scrape down her throat, and upset her stomach, just like it's doing to me.

With a hand pressed to my belly, I head toward the art room. The idea of sitting in homeroom, going to classes, fake listening, and acting like everything is normal sounds like Hell.

Since art class is only offered in the afternoon (the teacher works part-time here and at another school), I have the place to myself. The room is dark. I flip on the lights and stride to my stack of canvases. A cloth with my name painted across the surface covers them. I drag it off the pile and fold it. The ritual calms me. So does organizing my drawer of brushes and pigments.

I flip through the series I was working on before the accident. They all suck. A different Darby painted these. She used too bright colors, overly blended, too happy.

I pile the canvases on a bare table, then search for the biggest pair of scissors I can find. Holding the handle in my fist, I swing my arm up and bring it down against the first painting, puncturing its center with a satisfying *thwump*. I yank the scissors out and open them to drag the blade through the woven fibers. The painted cotton resists my carving, but I don't stop until it tears and frays. It screams and I cry in reply. I'm killing a part of myself. The old self. The part that was whole and then was fractured like the Mustang's windshield when Daniel's skull collided with it.

I don't stop until all of them are in tatters. Their wounds are too deep to heal.

Like me.

I toss the scissors on the pile of carcasses and leave the building. Outside, I brush loose pieces of paint and fibers off my clothes.

"Darby Fox."

I freeze.

Principal Shepherd. She's wearing a navy blue suit, sensible heels, and a scowl that would make Mom proud. "Where do you think you're going?"

I kick a pebble onto the grass. "For a walk."

"Why didn't you attend homeroom?"

"I've been here for less than an hour and you're already tracking my every move?"

"I saw you on the video camera. Why'd you destroy your paintings?" Her scowl loosens into pity.

"They're crap."

"The art teacher says you have more talent in your pinky than all her other students combined."

I roll my eyes. "Spare me the cliché."

She tugs on the hem of her jacket to straighten it out. "Do I have to suspend you for skipping class on your first day back?"

"Do what you want."

"I'll have to talk to your parents."

I sigh and stare at my nails. I still haven't added new polish.

"Perhaps they should consider home schooling for you."

"You want me to wait in your office while you figure it out?"

"Are you okay?"

Is she serious? I stuff my hands in my pockets. "Oh, I don't know, my brother died, I broke my neck, and everybody's pissed at me. Sorry I'm not all sunshine and giggles and skipping around with joy."

She closes her eyes and hangs her head. "I'm sorry, Darby. I didn't mean … "

"Forget it. Nobody does."

"Come inside while I decide what to do with you."

Surrendering this round, I brush past her and head for the entrance. I'd rather be where it's warm. It makes listening to yet another person tell me how messed up I am a teeny tiny bit easier.

Shepherd escorts me to her office. We take our usual seats, her at her desk and me in the chair across from her. Some things don't change, like me spending time in the principal's office. I suppose going AWOL is as a Bad Girl thing, but wrecking my own paintings shouldn't count against me. They're mine. I could argue it's a new part of my creative process.

I sit quietly while Shepherd calls Mom at work, right there in front of me. She must want to be an open book like Shaw.

Shepherd gives Mom the run down super quick. The call lasts less than five minutes. "Your mom is on her way."

"Is she pissed?"

She folds her hands on top of her desk. "I think she's more at a loss as to what to do with you."

"I'm hopeless."

"I wish you wouldn't make such disparaging comments about yourself."

"It is what it is."

"Through a tainted lens."

"So I'm not seeing clearly."

"That's not what I said."

"Sounded that way to me."

Shepherd exhales, then attacks her keyboard with her fingers. Probably writing a nice summary for my file. The corner of her mouth pulls into a smirk as she types. Yep, whatever she's working on is definitely about me.

Darby Fox, human sandpaper. I slide deeper into the seat. The only person I don't piss off is Adam.

He's immune to me, like Daniel was. I wonder if it's because he has Daniel's heart, if something like that is even possible.

The question is: Can I be immune to myself?

Chapter Twenty-One

Adam

I'm perfectly fine, but Mum makes me stay home the next day. I veg on the couch while she conferences with Dr. Jervis. By the end of all her fretting, Jervis has deemed me stable, although promises to call in a script of antibiotics just in case I swallowed some demon bacteria along with the pond scum. It'll pair nicely with my cocktail of anti-virals and immunosuppressants. A trifecta of rejection and infection killing pills that blasts my stomach to bits each time I send a volley down my throat.

Mum rounds out her agenda by calling Dr. Shaw. I end up with an emergency session.

Anyone with half a brain wouldn't have walked out on that ice and now I get to explain my stupidity to Shaw.

Although the sun shines bright and the late autumn air is uncharacteristically warm, I'm freezing in my layers of a long-sleeved t-shirt, hoodie, and vest.

Seems the frigid pond water has infused every cell in my body.

Mum drives us to my appointment early. We sit in the car park for twenty minutes before starting the slow march to Shaw's office. She hooks her arm through mine. To others, it must seem like we're close, but I know the truth—she doesn't want me running off. Perhaps she's afraid I'll find another pond and dive in face first.

Shaw is standing by her receptionist's desk. She greets Mum openly. While Mum pays the fee, Shaw turns her steely gaze on me. Always assessing. Always keeping me on my toes.

I bet she won't have a cup of coffee for me today.

"Lisa, why don't you join us for a few minutes?" Shaw escorts us into her office. She drags her rolling desk chair to the pair of armchairs in front of her bookshelves and sits.

Mum crowds me toward the farther chair and takes a seat. "Thank you so much for squeezing Adam in. He scared the bejesus out of me yesterday."

"It was an accident," I say.

Shaw raises a hand to shush me. "Tell me what happened, Lisa."

I can't help but interject. "Didn't you discuss it over the phone?"

"I think you need to hear your mother's side here, in a therapeutic environment, so we can process it together," Shaw says.

Surprise, surprise, she shot me down. Mentally, I fold in on myself like Origami paper. Larry from *The Razor's Edge* faced opposition and he overcame it. I have to hold onto the fact that I can too.

I think.

Mum gives her version of what happened, which includes her panic about me not being in the house and then finding me soaking wet and gasping for air near the pond's edge. She fills the middle of her tale with her all-night vigil and frantic call to Dr. Jervis this morning. She wraps up with my utter lack of concern about my own wellbeing. At every turn of her story, her voice goes up a notch and peaks to a stringy pitch by the end. Poor Mum. I've put her through the wringer.

"Your turn, Adam." Shaw laces her fingers in her lap. She lifts her chin, scrutinizing me.

Bollocks. "It's been so long since I've been able to do anything, I just wanted to *move*. Feel my legs swing, feel my feet pounding the earth—"

"Walk across thin ice?" Mum's voice reaches a breaking point. She shifts in her seat.

"I didn't think it'd break." I answer in a soft voice.

"No, you didn't think."

Dr. Shaw hands Mum a box of tissues. "Lisa, tell Adam how you felt when you saw him on the ground."

"I was terrified. I thought he tried to kill himself. After everything we've been through, *he's* been through, he's really giving up." She snags a tissue from the box and dabs at her eyes. "Things were supposed to be better, not worse."

Shaw slides her gaze to me. "Your mother doesn't want you to die."

I shoot to my feet. "I don't want to die either!"

Shaw lifts her chin. "Your actions don't support what you're saying."

I stalk to the window. "Then why'd I crawl back to shore?"

"The instinct to survive is powerful. People often panic during an attempt, but sometimes the will to live happens too late. You were lucky."

"How many times do I have to say I'm not actively plotting my death?"

"There are other concerning behaviors."

"Such as?"

"I see you haven't brought your pillow and you're not wearing a mask."

"Bloody hell," I murmur. My pillow is neatly packed in my rolling suitcase and I haven't worn a mask since school yesterday. "I forgot."

"I was going to tell him to wear it, but I thought you should see what he's doing." Mum oh so conveniently throws me under the bus. Fan-freaking-tastic.

"You've made up your minds, then, so what do you want me to do?" I ask.

Mum blows her nose. "He needs another medication. The anti-depressant isn't working enough."

"Perhaps you're right, Lisa." Shaw fetches a pill bottle from her mahogany cabinet. She hands it to Mum. "Methylphenidate Hydrochloride. It's usually prescribed for ADHD, but it can also be used to augment anti-depressants, and it can work quickly. Considering yesterday's scare, I'd say time is of utmost importance and it's a good thing I have these samples. Lisa, give him three tablets every morning."

"Yes, doctor." Mum holds the bottle like it's her salvation.

"What will it do to me?" I eye the thing, my new adversary.

"If you're so worried about the pill's effects, why don't you take a dose here and I can observe you for an hour or two? You and your Mum can sit in the waiting room."

I'd rather not.

"Good idea," Mum says.

Shaw walks to the door. "Hang on a minute. I'll get some water."

She reappears a few minutes later. "Here you go." She offers me a paper cup of water and a smile.

With both of them watching, I swallow a pill and chase it down with the entire cup of water and a prayer.

Mum tucks the bottle into her purse. "What happens if this doesn't work?"

"We may have to consider psychiatric hospitalization."

As the new medication dissolves into my system, so does my newfound freedom and new life, evaporated by Mum's worries and Shaw's dictates.

* * *

My heart pounds in my chest, thumping away as if it's running for its life. No matter how much deep breathing exercises or how still I try to lie in bed, it keeps racing. These unsteady arrhythmias were supposed to be a thing of the past, something buried with my old heart.

It has to be the medicine. I'd Google it, but the last time I did that Shaw argued her way out of it and Mum didn't believe me. Besides, refusing to take it will earn me a one-way ticket to the psych ward.

I launch out of bed, hyped on whatever the bloody hell is in this pill. I pace the floor, cringing at every creek and moan of the hardwoods. It's half past two in the morning, so Mum and Dad are asleep, but I'm sure Mum's got her ear trained on me. I could sneeze and she'd be at my door.

I spin around the four walls of my room. My new prison.

"It's alright, Adam. Just calm down," I say.

My heart pounds harder, laughing at me. *It's not okay*, it says. Poor thing wants to escape too.

I dash to my dormer window and unlock it. The seal groans a bit when I lift it. Cool air streaks in. I take in giant lungfuls of it.

I dig around my closet for a torch—flashlight as Americans call them—and train the beam on the oak tree. The trunk bifurcates half way up. One long, thick arm leans toward my window. On windy nights, its smaller branches strike the pane. Little talons scratching for entry.

None are thick enough to hold my weight.

I track the torch beam along the roof edge. The pitch isn't too steep. I can walk on it, no problem.

Charged on adrenaline, I yank on trainers and a pullover, and make like a tightrope walker. The torch is my spotlight and the night my audience. I make it to the top, then straddle the peak. Larry would be proud.

Ambient light from the nearby city washes the eastern sky in a peachy glow. It's a false sunrise. I'd love to watch the real one. With Darby.

I click off the torch and scratch the back of my head with it. What would she think of me treading on the ice? She'd probably laugh or call me an idiot. It wouldn't be a judgmental laugh though and I doubt she'd accuse me of attempting suicide.

The chimney is a short butt slide away, so I scoot over to it. I shiver against the cold brick, tucking my hands in my sleeves.

While my heart freaks out in its nest made of lungs and vessels, I tip my head back and search the cosmos for answers. How many sleepless nights did Larry spend huddled on frozen mountain peaks, desperately trying to discover the meaning of life? The stars inspired him. They led him on a journey around the planet. Would my parents and Shaw be placated if I told them I wanted to travel, wander ancient ruins, seek guidance from the wise, and photograph the natural wonders of the world?

A slight twinkle peeks through the inky black above. It's a star, inviting me to chat.

I extend my hand up toward it. "What am I supposed to do?"

It twinkles again. A steady whisper. A hiccup of light.

A figment of my imagination.

I close my eyes and lower my chin. Stars are volatile, fusion-fueled fireballs of energy—equally involved in bestowing life as they are at destroying it. Stars don't have consciences or motivation. They just are.

Darby is like a star in her own way. She is who she is and however someone reacts to her is of no concern to her. Maybe I can take a cue from her and the trillions of suns making up our universe and forget about writing a Live Life List. I can just be. I don't have to do anything grandiose to prove myself to Mum, Dad, or Shaw.

I can be me.

Whoever that happens to be.

Chapter Twenty-Two

Darby

Day two of home schooling. I'm already daydreaming of playing hooky, but skipping out when I'm the only student is a bit problematic. Mom set up the dining room as a home office for Dad and a classroom for me so Dad can make sure I didn't blow off studying. Every so often, he glances at me over the edge of his laptop.

He points at my tablet. "How's it coming along?"

Small talk with Dad. Ugh. Gag. I twirl a strand of hair around my finger. The mess of letters and words on the screen makes no sense. Even though I've been Skyping with a live tutor, it's obvious I'll never figure it out. I replay the tutorial he recorded for me *again*, taking slow, deep breaths, internally screaming every curse word I know.

Dad clears his throat. "I asked a question, Darby."

I imagine punching my fist through the screen or

bashing the tablet on the table until it breaks in half. "Fine."

He closes his laptop. "I haven't seen you do anything for the past fifteen minutes."

"I was watching a tutorial."

"Show me."

"*Dad.*"

He circles the table to peer over my shoulder.

I tip the screen up. "See?"

The doorbell rings.

I'm half out of my seat before Dad stops me.

"Sit tight. I'll get it," he says.

I tiptoe behind him, hanging back a few feet while he answers the door.

"Is Darby here?" Stephanie Veene slides past Dad without waiting for him to invite her in. She carries a large, flat package wrapped in hot pink polka dot paper.

"What're you doing here?" I'm tempted to shove her outside so I can slam the door in her face.

Stephanie's heels click on the floor. "I'm sorry about Daniel. He was a good guy."

I pick some paint off my jeans. All colors I used on Adam's painting. "What do you want?"

"*Darby.*" Dad scolds. He shuts the door and props his elbow on the newel post.

"It's okay, Mr. Fox. Darby and I aren't very close in school." The perfect little angel gives Dad a sweet smile.

I want to gag.

"Well, it's very nice of you to stop by and offer your condolences." Dad shoots a "be nice" look at me.

I sigh. "Come in, Stephanie. Would you like something to drink?"

"No, thanks. I can't stay long."

Thank. God.

We head to the dining room to sit. Dad quietly slips into the kitchen—blessedly out of sight.

Stephanie sets the gift on the table. "I thought flowers would be weird, so I brought you a canvas because I know you like to paint. I asked the art teacher what kind you use. Hopefully the size works."

If it's what I think it is, then Stephanie paid a lot for it. I reach out to touch the wrapping paper. "You didn't have to do that. A card would've been fine."

"I got a bunch of generic cards from my best friends when my grandmother died, like it was an obligation or something. It kind of pissed me off, so I didn't want to do that for you." Stephanie avoids eye contact with me by taking in the room and Mom's kitschy décor. Mom dresses like an artsy hippy, but her decorating tends toward farmhouse country. She says it reminds her of growing up down south. Whatever.

I do my best to suppress a blush. I doubt Miss Rich Girl Stephanie's home looks like this. "Sorry about your grandma. I didn't know."

"It was a couple years ago during summer."

"Look, we're not friends and there's no sense in pretending otherwise. Tell me why you're really here."

She rolls her eyes. "God, Darby, don't be paranoid. I feel bad for you, okay? You lost your brother and he was a twin. That's like harder and stuff."

I wince. She's right. I just didn't expect to get sympathy from her. "It sucks. A lot."

"It's so terrible. The whole school is shaken up."

"Everyone loved Daniel." And they hate me.

"Have your friends called or stopped by?"

I almost say "what friends," then stop myself short. "No."

"That's lame. What's wrong with them?"

I shrug. The only kid I actually want to hang out with is Adam. Or, I used to, before Shaw told me he has my brother's heart.

"Are you ever going to come back to school?"

"Dunno."

"It's so weird without you guys." She drags her fingers along the table edge and scrunches her nose.

Checking for dust? "Yeah, it's a tragedy to lose an MVP and an outsider on the same day."

She makes eye contact. "You're only an outsider because you put yourself there."

"Thanks for the tip. So ... how's your new boyfriend?"

She frowns with confusion.

"Eric."

Her mouth forms an "O," then widens into a smile. "Eric was a project."

"Huh?"

She pushes the wrapped canvas aside. "Yeah, his buddy—the guy you danced with at that party—and him tried to double team Mads. They got her drunk and I think they tried to rufie her. It didn't go anywhere because I showed up before they unzipped their pants, but Mads was pretty upset and nobody, I mean *nobody*, messes with my friends."

"They tried to rape her?"

Stephanie's face darkens. "Yeah. I stopped them."

Jeez. My stomach curdles. Madeline was ... well, she didn't have much of a personality, but that didn't mean she deserved to be taken advantage of. To think Stephanie rescued her. "I ... I didn't know."

She spins the bracelet around her wrist. "He goes to a different school. And they weren't dating."

"So why'd you rag on me? We just danced."

She bites her lip. "Look, I know now that you had nothing to do with it or with that guy and I'm sorry for calling you out for no reason. You have your brother to thank for setting me straight."

I lower my gaze. I have Daniel to thank for a lot of things. How am I going to manage without him? Tears spring to my eyes. I clench my jaw. I can't break down now. Not with Stephanie Veene watching. "How?"

"He explained everything to me before the game. That you didn't know the kid and stuff."

He'd tried to help me when I'd accused him of doing nothing. I clear my throat, choking on my grief. I dig my fingernails into my thighs to stop the memories and tears from flowing. "So where does throwing yourself at Eric fit into all this?"

"You got ringside seats for that outside the second floor bathroom." She barks a laugh. "For a minute, I thought you'd totally screw it up."

I think of the mess of pictures clogging my camera phone app.

She leans on her elbows and tucks her chin conspiratorially. "What's the best way to get a guy back? Make him fall in love with you, and then crush him. Mads is too sweet and innocent, so I had to do it. Eric was totally wrecked when I dumped him. He sobbed. *Sobbed.*" A mischievous twist takes over her mouth.

"Wow. But what about Guyliner?"

"Who?"

"The guy I danced with."

She narrows her eyes. "Oh, he's next."

She stuck up for the underdog and took some asshole down a few pegs. Sounds like something I'd do. Stephanie and I can't possibly something in common. I must be in some sort of nightmare.

She laughs, clapping her hands with satisfaction. "I. Can't. Wait."

"You know, in a different world, we might be friends."

"Why not this one?"

I don't have an answer for that, other than because she hates me, but I don't really feel like heading down that road, so I stay quiet.

She stands. "Look, when you're ready, give me a call. We'll hang out. But it's totally up to you."

I stare up at her, shocked.

"You look like you don't believe me and that's okay. I know we're not close. But I'm not tricking you. The mask I wear at school is just that—a mask. I'm a normal person underneath and I suspect you're a normal person under your mask. I just hope you let someone in, even if it's not me." She flips her hair cheerleader style and heads down the hallway.

I peek around the doorway.

Dad meets her in the foyer. "Thanks for stopping by."

"Have a nice day, Mr. Fox. I'm sorry for your loss."

I scramble to my seat before Dad locks the door. He joins me a moment later and returns to work like nothing happened.

Not long after, Mom comes home. She greets Dad with a kiss. "Darby, we have to get going or we'll be late for your therapy session."

"I'll order take out so it's here when you get home," Dad says.

"Good idea."

Mom rushes me to the car like she's afraid I'm going to skip out.

In Shaw's office, I immediately gush about Stephanie. Shaw sits with her ankles crossed and eyebrows bent the whole time. At the end of it, I let out a long breath, finally empty.

"Sometimes people treat you differently after a tragedy or loss. Do you think you'll take her up on your offer and call her?" Shaw asks.

"No, it'd be totally weird. I mean, she was Daniel's friend, not mine. Besides, we hate each other."

"If she hated you, she wouldn't stop by your house or bring such a thoughtful gift."

"Unless she's trying to trick me." I chew on a hangnail.

"What motivation would she have for that?"

I tell her my revenge plot of sharing photos of Perfect Stephanie in a tongue war with Baddy Eric. "I thought it would destroy her popularity and make her understand what it's like to be a nobody."

I expect Shaw to give me a look of disapproval—a raised eyebrow, an unsettled twist of her mouth, or even a distinct lifting of her chin. She doesn't do any of those things. Instead, she says, "Justice is different for everyone. How would taking her down make you feel?"

"At the time, I thought it'd make things right. I wanted to see her suffer."

"And now?"

"She was nice."

"You don't trust nice."

"Not after she told me about manipulating Eric."

"What about Adam? He's nice."

My breath catches. He is nice. But so what? He's hiding a secret inside his chest, like Stephanie kept a secret from Eric. She ended up wrecking him in the end. Adam's secret nearly destroyed me too. So much for *nice*.

"Does he know he has my brother's heart?" I ask.

Shaw hesitates, then says, "No, but that doesn't change the reality of it. Someone else has your brother's heart."

"Yeah, but if he wasn't told … " … then I can't hold his secret against him. I scrunch my nose.

"Ignorance isn't innocence," Shaw reasons.

I stand and pace the room. "You were willing to bend the rules for me. Why not tell Adam whose heart he has?"

Shaw sighs. "I've been second guessing myself the moment I shared it with you. I thought it'd be helpful, but now I'm not so sure. It seems to have complicated things."

"I'd rather know. Maybe he would too."

"That's admirable, Darby, and that's what makes you unique. Adam can't handle the truth." She presses her fingers to her temple. "I never thought you'd actually meet Adam. What are the odds you'd befriend the very person who has Daniel's heart?"

"I'm not sure we're friends."

"You're not?"

I sit, out of breath. "I liked Adam. I still do. I think. But I'm totally pissed too. I just don't know how to fit this whole transplant thing into it. I miss my brother. He shouldn't have died."

"It's not fair that Adam has his heart."

"I guess."

Shaw slides to the end of her chair so our knees almost touch. "You said you felt like he stole Daniel's heart. How can you be friends with someone who did that? How can you still like him?"

"He's sweet, he doesn't judge me, and he's *himself.* He probably doesn't even know the meaning to the word fake."

"So it doesn't bother you that he has Daniel's heart."

"It does bother me. A lot."

"Then how can you say such good things about him?"

I stand again. "Why not? Unless you have something against me liking him. Don't you want me to have friends?"

"There is more to it than that."

"Like what?"

"You're sense of justice means someone has to pay for Daniel's death. Wouldn't that person be Adam?"

I take a couple steps back. "If anyone is to blame for Daniel's death, it's me."

"We determined that it isn't."

I drag my fingers through my hair. Shaw is so fast I can't keep up with her. I close my eyes to stop the swirling thoughts scrambling my brain. "I can't blame Adam."

Shaw's heels click on the floor. She drapes her hands on my shoulders. "You already have. I can tell by the way you reacted when you found out the truth, by how you refuse to talk to him, and by how much you're fighting me now. The truth is painful. It's normal to reject it at first. But I know you're smart and reasonable. I know you'll realize your first instinct—the little voice in the back of your mind telling you Adam *stole* Daniel's heart—is true."

I face her. "No."

Shaw chews on her cheek. A light flares in her eyes. "Maybe Adam *does* know and he *is* hiding it from you."

"*What?*"

"Think about it. Adam is smart. He knows you were in an accident. He knew his donor was in an accident. Perhaps he put two and two together and figured out that you're related somehow."

My head starts to hurt. Could he?

She leans closer. "He heard you screaming in the ICU, you know."

"Me? How?"

"He remembers a girl's sobs when he woke up after the surgery. I can only assume it was you after you learned of Daniel's passing. Your mother told me how hard you cried."

"No."

She squeezes my shoulders. "Yes, it has to be. You were in the ICU together, separated by only a few rooms. He heard you suffering and in that moment, he knew. You'll never convince me otherwise."

I'm shaking all over, so badly that Shaw has to guide me to the chair.

She holds her arm tight around my waist. "He's not even certain he's glad he survived. Can you imagine, a transplant recipient who's upset he got a second chance at life. It's absurd."

"W-what?" My legs buckle. Landing in the seat

jars my neck, sending sparks of pain down my arms. "He has my brother's heart and he doesn't even care?"

"The boy is obsessed with death. I don't think that's healthy for you to be around."

I did scream when I found out about Daniel. I cry out again, here, in Shaw's arms, surrounded by her warmth, the kind that Mom hates to give me. To think Adam heard my sobs. I wonder if he can hear me now. If I'm feeling this in my soul, he has to in his. He knows the truth. He has to.

I know the truth, too. The truth I avoided since meeting the weird boy wearing a mask and carrying around a heart-shaped pillow. The boy with the most honest, beautiful eyes I've ever seen.

It doesn't matter.

I can't like—or love—a thief.

Chapter Twenty-Three

Adam

Delightful sunlight pours through the kitchen window. It's agitating.

I stand at the center island with my hand draped over the bar chair's back, eyeing the line of pill bottles meant for me. This is my new life. Swallowing pills, fending off rejection, and searching for a cocktail of psych meds that makes everyone but me happy.

Mum watches me take the next dose of methylphenidate. It catches in my throat so I chug some orange juice, forcing the tablets down.

"Thank you, dear. I'm glad you're following doctor's orders. It'll help." Mum busies herself with making breakfast—eggs and hash.

Dad has left for work already, so it's just us. I watched him back his car out of the garage and drive down the street from the roof. It was my cue to sneak inside before Mum came in to check on me.

Mum loads my plate with food. "Eat up."

"I've got a whole meal of pills swirling around in my stomach," I say, dipping my fork into the hash.

"It's what the doctors prescribe."

"I'm not sure they're doing anything. The psych meds, anyway."

"It takes time."

"I'd do better without them."

Mum slams the bottle on the counter. The tablets rattle inside. "You call throwing yourself into a frigid pond better?"

"It was an accident. Why don't you believe me?" I shake some ketchup on the hash. I don't have much of an appetite, but pushing the plate away will give Mum more ammunition.

"I would, honey, but you're smarter than to go out on thin ice." She attacks her eggs with her fork.

Each stab jabs me in the heart. Poor Mum. She thought she had to worry about me dropping dead before the transplant, now she thinks she has to worry about me killing myself. While I may have given death a lot of brain time, I always feared it too much to act on any fantasies of suicide.

Finally, she sets her fork down. "Why would you want to leave your Dad and me? We've given up everything for you and all you've done is fight against us."

"I never asked you to sacrifice anything."

She lowers her chin. "You're our son. We'd give our lives for you."

"Then you should believe me. Not Shaw. Did you see the pharmacy filling her drawer? She's a pill-pusher. She doesn't know who we are, nor does she care."

Mum presses the back of her wrist to her forehead. "Oh, Adam, you need to drop your paranoia about her."

"I'm not paranoid."

She sets the dishes in the sink. "I trust Doctor Shaw. She wants to help."

I lick my lips. They're dry, cracking. "Guess we're at an impasse."

"It's your stubbornness that worries me. You never used to be that way."

"Mum."

She waves a hand. "Go get ready for school."

I shuffle upstairs. In my room, I dial Darby's number. Like before, it rings until voicemail picks up. "Darby, it's Adam. I, um … well I'm floundering here. It's okay if you don't want to talk to me. I mean, I'd be gutted, but I'd understand. Either way, I'd appreciate it if you told me. And if you *do* want to talk, give me a ring okay? I just … I need someone to talk to. Someone who'd understand."

I toss my mobile on the bed and take a shower.

On the drive to school, I check my messages a hundred times. Nothing.

She's shut me out. I'm in this alone.

* * *

Two days pass, and no word from Darby. I trudge through my days, crestfallen and amped at the same time. My heart races constantly now. So does my head. All day it pounds, as if a jackhammer is chipping into my skull. I'm not sure if it's from my thrumming heart or my inability to sleep.

Mum thinks I'm slipping further into depression, of course, but I'm too apathetic to care. On the downside, she's convinced Shaw to double the dose of methylphenidate.

By the end of the week, I throw the pills into the kitchen sink in protest. "I'm done taking these. They make me feel like shit." Spit launches from my mouth with my words. Rage courses through me, hot and pulsing. I clench my fists.

Mum's eyes widen. She stumbles away, frightened. I've turned into a frothing beast in front of her. "Y-you must t-take them."

"Even if I can't breathe or sleep or eat or think?" I rake my fingers through my hair.

"It's not the medicine. It's your depression."

"Is that what Shaw says?" I'm panting against the pressure of Shaw's demands, meted out by Mum dose by dose. The room is so hot and dry. My eyes are grainy from being awake for so long without the reprieve of sleep.

Mum retreats around the island to put distance between us. "Adam, please."

My whole body jitters, charged on an unnatural beat created by an unnatural chemical. "I'm *not* taking any more."

She pours out a fresh dose of the methylphenidate. "You have to. Or Doctor Shaw will hospitalize you."

Hot tears sting my eyes. "Defend me and tell her no. I'm begging you. If you could feel half of what's happening inside me right now, you'd flush all those pills down the toilet and curse them to Hell."

"Take the medicine. We'll talk to Doctor Shaw

about changing the dose at your next appointment." Fear has planted itself behind her eyes, but her stance is firm. She believes I'm turning into a lunatic because of depression. She believes in Shaw's dominance. She believes she's doing this for my good.

"Take them." She bites her lip.

My freaking out only makes her dig her heels in deeper. And she says I'm the stubborn one.

I could lob them across the room and we can play this game of tablet table tennis until the entire bottle is exhausted and I find myself on a one way trip to the loony bin. "No."

She pounds her fist on the counter. "*Take them, Adam.*"

My fear of Shaw and the psych ward overrides my fear of the methylphenidate. With a shaky hand, I sprinkle the pills on my tongue. It takes a whole glass of water to make sure they go down.

I plunk the glass in the sink and splay my fingers on the counter. "Satisfied?"

Mum's lips thin. "Seeing you suffer does not make me happy."

"Then you shouldn't force me to do this."

"It's the depression talking. Doctor Shaw said it'd make you contrary and resistant to things that can help." She wipes tears from her cheeks. "I never thought it would warp your mind so thoroughly."

I grab the drying towel haphazardly thrown on the counter and toss it across the room. "My mind isn't warped."

Mum retreats, a painful wince contorting her face. "I barely recognize you."

She leaves. Her clipped footsteps echo down the hallway.

The bathroom door slams shut.

I lean against the counter. I've done it now.

My stomach gurgles with dread as I creep down the hallway. I press my palms against the doorframe. Mum's soft cries filter through the door.

I've ruined everything. Sick Adam or Healthy Adam, it makes no difference—either version is just as destructive.

Maybe Darby is right to avoid me.

Problem is, without her, I'm lost, set adrift to aimlessly wander the choppy seas of life. A life I don't know how to live. A life my parents and Shaw think I want to throw away. A life I don't deserve.

I head outside, leaving Mum to her cry. Wind slices through the fabric of my flannel shirt, but I don't care. It's oddly comforting, actually. The elements are real and no one can dispute them. Thoughts, on the other hand, are individual, locked inside each person's brain, hidden in the dark, secret until uttered. Once spoken, a pervasive magic takes over, lulling the listener into their siren's call. Something evil happens then, when they reach another's brain: Interpretation—an illusion of its own. The speaker is either believed, or disbelieved, and the speaker has no control over which outcome occurs.

The breeze picks up, rustling the last of the fallen leaves. They skitter along the sidewalk, protesting their loneliness and banishment from their former home. The trees lining the street ignore their former tenants. Rejected castoffs. Forgotten. Crumbling.

I feel the same way, discarded by Darby. Each day that passes finds me withering more and more. I could find nourishment elsewhere, but where should I start looking? Larry from *The Razor's Edge* thought he'd find satisfaction in a life after the war, but quickly discovered his career and fiancé left him wanting.

He decided to give up the ordinary life in search of a meaningful one. Everyone thought he was nutters whenever he tried explaining. Another victim of misinterpreted words.

Or maybe the original one.

I step off the sidewalk into an unkempt field and trace my way to a hedgerow. I'm in no mood to search for frozen ponds, but I'd rather meander through some woods than the well-worn sidewalk. The idea of it—following the cultivated concrete, the man-made path—is too cliché and my thoughts are diving straight into philosophy.

No, existentialism. Shaw has a book called Existential Therapy. I'd asked her about it one day and she gave me a cursory description that I later filled in with the help of Google and Wikipedia.

Life, death, the pursuit of happiness. It all fell under the same umbrella of humans trying to figure out their existence. Not such an easy task.

So why is everyone expecting me to have a plan so quickly?

It's unfair, really.

A whisper slithers through the tree branches and tickles my ears. *"Why do you cling to life?"*

I halt. Then spin, searching for the voice's owner.

No one is here but me.

"You should stop wasting everyone's time."

I spin in a circle, gaze volleying between shadows and light. "Who's there?"

"Give up. End it all."

I crash through some underbrush. "Show yourself!"

"*Your life is worthless.*"

I'm alone. There's no devilish taunter hiding in the bushes to torment me.

I answer anyway. "No, it's not."

"*End it.*"

Frantic, I start jogging. Branches slap me in the face and I swat at them as if they're gnats. I slip on some rotting leaves and crash to the ground, landing directly on my chest. Instant fire blossoms in my breastbone, like the day I fell off the treadmill. I roll onto my back, hissing and clutching my arms to my chest.

"*See? You're pathetic. A waste of space.*"

"No," I cry. My mind is turning on me. My own words—my thoughts—are an illusion and it's only now, after being rejecting by Darby, confronted by Mum, and hyped up on Shaw's medicine that I can see it.

I stare at the patches of blue sky through the naked branches, but all I see is the truth I've avoided all along. The truth I didn't want to see, but that everyone else thought was obvious.

I cover my face with my hands and sob into my palms. I've been blind to my own behavior.

"*That's right. You know what to do.*" The voice hovers near my ear.

"Please, no."

"*Kill yourself.*"

"I don't want to die."

"*You don't deserve to live. Death will be easier. You won't suffer anymore.*"

I nod. Maybe the voice is right. I can't handle this *mess* my life has become. "Okay. Okay."

I *do* want to die.

Chapter Twenty-Four

Darby

Mom is quiet on the drive home. Fine with me. Our talks don't go anywhere but to a dead end.

She didn't even bother checking in with Shaw after our session. Then again, I left the room so fast that she had to jog after me. I tried the car door handle a dozen times before she unlocked it.

In my room, I tear off the c-collar and toss it in the garbage. I'm done with it and with everything else.

I rip the pretty paper Stephanie wrapped my gift in. Like she said, it's my favorite type of canvas. Stephanie had to be genuine. No one in their right mind would spend so much on someone they wanted to punk.

I set the canvas on my easel. Stephanie's a puzzle I'll have to sort out later. Right now, I have something else to solve.

Adam.

He's not smooth enough to keep a secret from me.

The kid practically trips over himself whenever he stammers out a message.

The last one—where he said he needed to talk to me …

I shivered at the sound of his haunted voice. Maybe he finally wanted to come clean.

I sigh. No. He'd sounded scared, not guilty of hiding something.

Shaw said he wasn't sure if he wanted to live or not. Can you be scared if you were suicidal?

I have to paint this out. Creating lets my mind slip into another state and when I re-emerge the world looks different. Things I couldn't see before become obvious, simple.

The painting of Adam's eye sits where I placed it, facing my dresser. I fetch Daniel's stuffed basketball, tuck it in the crook my arm, and turn the painting over. The swirls and strokes of greens, golds, browns, and blues invite me in and soon I'm drowning in Adam's stormy iris. Somehow, I'd captured his intense stare along with his wistful, far away, dreamy look.

I set the painting on the dresser, half covering the mirror hanging above it. I study it for a bit longer, then turn to my own eyes, leaning so close to the mirror that I lose track of myself and see only the streaks of blue and silver fleeing my pupil. His eyes are so warm compared to my frozen irises.

We're opposites. Where he's safe and cautious, I'm bold and impulsive. While he's busy thinking over the pros and cons of things, I'm diving in head first.

So why is it I have such trouble deciding whether to love or hate him?

I'll find the answer to my riddle in here, in the

contrast between us.

I swap out two paintings on my wall for Adam's eye and the mirror. With this set up, I can view my subject—my eye—and my inspiration—Adam's eye—while using the remaining daylight. I don't have much time; it's late afternoon.

In the zone, I mix a palette of colors and dip my brush into the pigment and attack my blank canvas. I'm not concerned about mistakes. I want the strokes to be bold and careless, organic and free flowing. *Alive*.

The only sounds are my breathing—which comes out in calculated stutters—and the confident scrape of bristles flying across the cotton canvas. I paint harsh, straight lines streaming from an onyx circle—light erupting from darkness.

When I finish, I clutch the brush as if it's my sword and I'm a skilled warrior. Instead of destroying her, though, I've created her. Darby. On canvas.

I'm shaking and panting, exhausted from the effort. My shoulders and neck are tight, sweat covers me, and chunks of hair cling to my neck and face, but I don't care. I smile.

Daniel found new life in Adam—or at least his heart did—and I found new life through Adam too.

He's saved us both.

Shaw is wrong. He didn't steal Daniel's heart.

And yet, she'd also said Adam didn't appreciate the sacrifice my brother made.

I grip the paintbrush tighter.

Love, hate. Life, death. Warmth, cold.

Opposites.

Each harsh and unforgiving.

But you can't have one without the other.

Contrast needs both sides to exist.
Maybe that's why I need Adam.
For balance.
To find love, life, and warmth in the cold hate of death.

* * *

At the end of the week, I wake up clutching Daniel's basketball to my chest. My alarm is set to go off in two hours and nineteen minutes, but whatever. I carry the basketball as well as a change of clothes into the bathroom and soak in a metric ton of hot water. I let the heat loosen my sore neck and shoulders.

While the stream of water jets over me, I practice the stretches I learned in physical therapy. My headache eases. The tingle in my fingers quiet to a dull buzz. I wonder if it'll ever go away.

The water turns lukewarm. I turn off the faucet and towel dry. My "Loki'd" sweatshirt—Daniel gave it to me on our last birthday—and jeans are well-worn and fuzzy soft. Like always, paint stains decorate both.

Instead of hanging around, I grab my phone and head outside after leaving a note saying I'm walking to school.

The pre-dawn sky is full of bright pinks and oranges. Frost makes the brown grass and evergreen shrubs silvery. I shiver.

By the time I reach the school, I've worked up enough body heat to be warm. I sit on the front steps and pull out my phone. First, I look at my pictures.

Well, the ones of Stephanie kissing Eric. Most of them are grainy and the dim lighting makes it almost impossible to see who's in the photo.

To think, Stephanie was playing Eric for his being a douche. A fair bit of justice.

I tap on the little trashcan in the corner and two options pop up: Delete Photo or Cancel.

The old Darby thought her actions were justified. She thought she was getting Stephanie back for a little name-calling.

The old Darby was so caught up in her stupid plan that she argued with her brother, distracting him from the icy road.

The old Darby was a fool.

The old Darby was just as guilty of killing her brother as Adam was for stealing his heart.

No, not stealing, *wasting*.

In a flurry of taps and swipes, I delete all the photos of Stephanie. I hadn't captured revenge.

If only erasing guilt was so easy.

I sniff, wipe the tears that have traveled down my face, and open my Facebook app. Stephanie hadn't given me her number (maybe she thought I already had it or that Daniel had shared it with me) but I'd bet my best paintbrushes she's posted it on her page. Sure enough, her digits are there. I click it and hold the phone to my ear, breathing in time with the ring tone. I'm not sure if I want her to pick up or not.

"Who's calling me at this ungodly hour?" Stephanie's voice is grainy with sleep.

"Uh … it's Darby. Sorry to wake you, but I need to talk."

"Where are you?"

"School."

"I'm on my way."

Twenty minutes later, Stephanie pulls into the parking lot. Her wheels squeal as she takes the corner too sharply. She stops short in a parking spot and pops out of her car.

I stand and give a wave.

She rushes to me, her ponytail bouncing with each step. Her jeans cling to her in all the right places and her shirt flows around her like a dream. Fashionista-worthy sunglasses sit her head like a headband and her ballet flats have sparkles on the toes. Gawd, the girl had about five seconds to get ready and she looks *this* awesome.

Why'd I ever want to talk to her?

She pulls me into a hug before I have a chance to react. "Are you okay?"

I nod, then shake my head, then shrug. "I don't know."

She leans back. The furrow in her brow seems genuine. "You've been crying."

"Yeah. I've been thinking about what you said about, you know, talking to someone and … "

"I'm so glad you called." She leads me to the bench. "Here, sit. Tell me what's bothering you."

I bite my lip. I *should* be talking to Shaw, but she was so pushy last time. "There's a boy—"

"He didn't take advantage of you, did he?"

"No, no … *no*."

"Are you sure?"

While Adam kept the transplant a secret, he didn't necessarily take advantage of me. I was a stranger to him, so I had nothing to be taken advantage of as far as he knew. "He didn't take advantage, but the whole thing is really confusing."

"What whole thing?"

I vomit the story in a rush of words and hand gestures and end with, "He keeps calling and wants to talk, but I'm not sure what to do. I mean, I like him, but he has my brother's heart and I don't know how to handle knowing it."

She puffs out her cheeks, then exhales. "Wow."

I slouch, hoping for more from her.

She fiddles with the strap of her designer purse. "Do you *like him* like him?"

"God, are we in junior high?"

"You know what I mean."

I sigh. "He's cute, adorable really, and quirky."

Her mouth ticks up. "You'd go for quirky."

I level my "oh, really" stare at her.

She laughs. "It's okay to like a boy. Although, him having Daniel's heart is … freaky."

"My shrink says he's not even sure he wants to be alive, that he's obsessed with death."

She scrunches her nose. "That's way more than quirky."

I tug on a strand of hair. "He doesn't seem suicidal."

"How does he seem? I mean, do you really know him?"

She has a point. I've known Adam for a grand total of a couple weeks. He doesn't give off any weirdo or psycho vibes, though. If anything, he seems like he doesn't know how to live—that isn't the same as being obsessed with death. His eyes certainly aren't dead. Someone who wants to die would have a vacant, hollow stare, wouldn't they? And the way he kissed me. The boy has a lot of life in him, if he just knew how.

"Earth to Darbs. Hello?" Stephanie waves a hand in my face.

"He's a good kisser."

"So was Eric, but he's still a total douche."

"Adam's not douche-like. At all."

"Maybe you should confront him."

I suck in a breath. It's a tempting idea, but we promised not to talk about it. He'd probably flip out if he knew I knew. Still, I couldn't just hang out with him and pretend I didn't know either. So, if we talk, we have to get everything out in the open.

Or I could delete his number, ignore his calls, and forget the whole thing. Never speak to the boy who inspired me to paint again. My entire body stiffens.

I clutch my head with both hands and groan.

Stephanie gasps. "Whoa, you okay? You're not going to freak out, are you?"

"I don't know what to do!"

She wraps an arm around me. "It's obvious that you like him. *Talk to him.*"

Stephanie Veene—the mouthy plague of my existence, the splinter in my thumb, the perfect cheerleader blonde with a sneaky side—is giving me relationship advice.

I lower my hands. The old Darby wouldn't find herself sitting here, looking for advice from enemy. She wouldn't think out options before acting, or open her heart to risk real feelings. Absolutely not!

Yet the new Darby seems to be doing just that.

One thing remains the same—both Darby's fly in the face of reason.

With a trembling heart and wobbly knees, I stand, ready for action.

Chapter Twenty-Five

Adam

I'm lying on the ground curled into a ball, shivering. Over and over again, the same message is repeated to me.

"*Kill yourself,*" it says.

I press my hands over my ears to keep the command out. Doesn't matter. The voice oozes through my fingers, down my ear canals, and into my brain. Its barbs stick into my thoughts.

"Stop, please," I beg, staring at the careless trees above. Birds chirp amongst their branches, staking their territory with their sweet melody. Beauty in conflict.

Glimpses of the lightening sky break through the canopy. There, peeking between crisscrossing twigs, twinkles a lone star stubbornly clinging to the dying night. It shines, despite the losing battle, refusing to surrender.

It shines just for me. Telling me not to give up.

So I don't.

I snake my phone out of my pocket and dial. "Please answer," I moan. "*Please.*"

My heart pounds between rings.

The ringing stops, but my pulse trudges on.

"Hello?"

Relief washes over me. "Darby, thank god."

"Adam, you sound terrible."

"Something's happening. I need your help."

There's a long pause, enough for doubt to creep closer. I squeeze my eyes shut, praying for her to answer.

"You have to be honest with me," she says.

"I swear, I'll tell you everything you want to know. My darkest thoughts, my dreams, everything my crazy mind imagines, I'll tell you, I promise."

She sighs. "You're a poet even when you're freaking out, aren't you?"

"I'll sing you sonnets, anything. I need you."

She gives a tiny moan as if I'm a mewling kitten abandoned by its careless mother. "Where are you?"

"I don't know." The woods somewhere. "Close to home."

"Then go home."

"I can't."

"Why not?"

"I … just can't."

Another long pause. "You've gotten yourself into a mess, haven't you?"

"You have no idea." Sharp pains ricochet through my chest. Whatever poison runs along my veins, saturating my vessels, is stripping my new heart's strength. "Darby, I don't know what I've done to hurt you or make you angry or not want to talk to me, but I'm sorry for whatever it is. Just … do this one thing for me and I'll never bother you again if you want, I swear."

"Hang on."

Something muffles the phone. Her hand, I guess. I hold my breath. Finally, she says, "Can you meet me somewhere?"

"Thank you. Thank you so much." I exhale. "Do you know Mickey's Diner?"

"On Main? That's across the river."

I squeeze my phone tighter. The plastic case cracks in protest.

"Okay. Give me half an hour." She ends the call.

The clock starts ticking.

Shaking all over, I stumble my way to the road. A bus stop shelter is at the end of the cul de sac. I check my pocket. A few coins rub together. I hope it's enough to cover the fare.

The bus arrives. I'm fifty cents shy, but the driver takes pity on me and lets me board. I must look desperate with pine needles in my hair and dirt on my clothes.

Suburbia quickly gives way to deteriorating blocks of Mom and Pop businesses barely holding on since the latest Mega Chain Super Store moved in.

I disembark at Mickey's Diner. It, and it's sizeable car park, dominate the east side of an intersection. I wander past cars, searching for Darby. Perhaps she's gone inside.

To my right, a car door swings open. A girl with paint-stained clothes gets out.

I halt. "Darby."

She's not wearing her c-collar. "Adam. You look awful. What's going on?"

I lean against the car's trunk. "Something's not right."

The driver gets out and joins us, her face obscured by large sunglasses. The morning breeze tousles her blonde curls. "This the guy?"

Darby frowns at her. "Yeah."

"We've been waiting," she says to me.

"Stephanie, you're not helping." Darby palms my cheek and turns my face to her. "Ignore her. Talk to me."

"I *am* helping," Stephanie mutters.

I focus as best I can on Darby's pale ice eyes. A storm brews in them and I swirl along the ribbons of light and silver. "I missed your eyes."

She lowers her brows. "Oh, Adam."

My hand finds its place over my heart, which is pounding harder and faster than ever. At this rate, I'll use up my lifetime quota of heartbeats in minutes. "Shaw prescribed me this bloody awful medicine and I think it's killing me."

"You're not the only one who sees Doctor Shaw." Her gaze turns steely. So much like Shaw's. "So do I." She reaches into her pocket and draws out a pin of butterfly wings in the shape of a heart. A row of stitches runs down its center.

I swallow a cry.

"*They're working together to trick you,*" the voice says.

I jerk my head toward the sound, but there's nothing there. "You're wrong. Darby's here to help," I whisper. I have to believe that.

"No she's not."

I shake my head. "She is," I mumble.

Darby lowers her hand. "What?"

"Don't trust her. She'll bring you to Shaw."

"She won't," I whisper.

"She won't what?" Darby shoots a nervous glance at Stephanie.

"She knows everything about you. You're an evil thief and need to die."

I turn my face to the sky. "I don't want to die!"

Darby gasps.

Stephanie takes a step back. "He's bat shit, Darbs. I think we should go."

I grab onto Darby's sleeve. "No. Please. Don't go. Shaw thinks I want to kill myself but I don't. My parents believe her. I don't have anyone else I can turn to and I can't do this anymore. This medicine. I should've never taken it."

Darby shirks out of my grasp. "Shaw wants to help you."

"See? Don't trust her," the voice hisses.

"Shaw doesn't." I thought Darby would listen to me, but I was wrong. Shaw's gotten to her just like she's gotten to everyone else. I've lost. I slide down the bumper and land on my butt. Coldness from the ground seeps through my jeans. Everything is hard—the pavement, the car, the sun, Darby's stare.

Darby kneels. "Who are you talking to?"

"The voice." I clench my jaw.

"Oh, my god." Stephanie huffs. "This was a bad idea. Get him away from my car. We're leaving."

Darby shakes her head. "Give me a minute. Adam, what voice?"

"It's telling me to kill myself. I don't want to, but it won't stop," I say.

Darby gestures to Stephanie. "We have to get him out of here."

"He's not getting in *my* car." Stephanie juts her hip to the side.

"I thought you were helping."

"I drove you here."

Darby gives a frustrated groan. "Adam, you have to go to the hospital."

I shake my head. "No, I can't. They'll lock me up. Shaw will win."

"Win what?"

"She's trying to destroy me. She's turned everyone against me."

"That's insane. She's a psychiatrist."

"No, she twists everything around. Confuses me. This medicine she gave me … " I tug at the roots of my hair. Why won't she *listen*? "It's making me crazy."

She squares her jaw. "She told me you have my brother's heart, you know."

"W-what? No, that can't be."

"That girl you heard screaming in the ICU? That was me when I heard Daniel had died. We were in the same accident. He died. I didn't."

I drop my hands. Her brother's heart. I have *her brother's heart* beating inside me. Racing inside me. Struggling inside me. My stomach turns to ice. That girl I heard in the ICU … Her pain was so raw it could strip skin and crush bones. The agony of it fractured my soul. That girl was Darby. And I benefitted from her loss. I'm alive because her brother died. "Oh god, I'm so sorry. I would give it back, if I could."

It's not a lie. Things would be so different if I never got a heart. Maybe I'd already be dead and far from Shaw's tormenting mind games.

"B-but if I hadn't lived, I'd have never met you," I say.

Her face softens. "You didn't know, did you?"

I shake my head. My throat is too thick to speak.

"Shaw said you did. She said you weren't sure if you were glad you got a new heart or not." She glances at the pin, her eyes glossy with tears.

"She's told so many lies." I wish I knew why. I bite my lip ring.

"So you're glad you're alive."

"Of course! And I'm glad I've met you."

"*Kill yourself and you won't suffer anymore,*" the voice pushes.

I squeeze my eyes shut. Why is this voice arguing with me? I clamp my hands to my ears and groan. "Stop. *Stop.*"

Darby sniffs. "I'm calling 911."

My eyes fly open. I reach out to grab her wrist. "Don't. Please. I can't go to the hospital. I can't."

She stiffens. "You're not thinking clearly."

Stephanie points her key fob in my face. No, it's a little hot pink can attached to her key ring. "MACE. Let her go, creep, or I'll spray you."

I scramble to my feet. "I thought you were going to help me."

"I am. I'll prove it." Darby tosses the pin into the bushes. Her eyes are wide. "Forget about Shaw. And the hospital. It's just you and me. I'll help you. Tell me what you need." Her mouth trembles.

"I need someone to believe me." I splay my fingers

across my chest. "I need to sit down. My heart won't stop pounding."

"Daniel's heart." She stares at the sky, lost in thought, then pierces me with her gaze. "Your heart now."

My knees wobble. "I'm sorry."

She licks her lips, thinking. "It's not your fault."

"That's not true. I wanted the transplant. I wanted—*want*—life. The way I got it, though, to have someone die in my stead seems wrong." I step toward her. "What if … what if I didn't deserve Daniel's heart? What if I'm being punished for taking it?"

Tears stream from Darby's eyes. "Daniel was braindead. He wasn't coming back." She wipes her face. "You didn't steal anything."

"*Don't listen to her. She's lying.*" The voice turns angry.

Stephanie eases between us while aiming her pepper spray can at my face. "Why are you talking to this freak?"

Darby pulls Stephanie's hand down. "He's not a freak."

"He's crazy. Maybe he's on something. You don't want to get involved with a druggie." Stephanie hooks her arm around Darby's.

Darby breaks free. "It's okay, Stephanie. He's not an addict."

"Are you sure?"

"Just give us a minute."

"I'm not leaving you alone with him."

Darby pats Stephanie's arm. "It's okay. Really."

Stephanie frowns, but nods. "Alright. But I'll be watching you." She retreats to the driver's seat, then twists around to stare at us.

Darby talks to me slowly, like a negotiator trying to convince a jumper to come off the ledge. "The roads were so icy that night. I was arguing with Daniel while he drove us home and distracted him. The accident was my fault."

"Did you yank the wheel or something? Did you make it snow? Did you cause the roads to freeze?"

"No."

"Then it's not your fault."

She snorts. "You're the one who asked me for help and you're trying to comfort me?"

"I'm … sorry?"

Darby sighs. A flash of pain creases her brow. "Guess neither of us is guilty, huh?" she whispers.

"What?"

"I've been punishing myself as much as you've been punishing yourself. Look where it's gotten us."

I open my mouth to speak, but she stops me by planting a finger against my lips.

"I wanted to be mad at you for having Daniel's heart so bad, but I'm not." She lowers her hand. Her dark hair falls over her face. "God help me, I'm not."

"*She's tricking you,*" the voice taunts.

I shake my head. No. The voice is wrong. Darby's not a liar. She's a poor, broken girl who lost her brother. We shouldn't have met—the suffering artist and the uncertain, life-stealing bookworm—but we have. And that's the tragedy of it.

A tragedy that Shaw is feeding off of. She's the one who told Darby about my heart. "Why did Shaw tell you what happened?"

"*Don't be fooled. Darby's working with Shaw.*"

The voice is right there, ready to chime in with its vile poison.

"How do you know what I'm thinking?" I say to it through gritted teeth.

Darby lifts her head, setting her striking azure eyes on me. "I can't read your mind," she says.

"Not you."

"The voice is talking again?"

I nod. "Can you help me?"

She steps into my shadow. "Don't listen to it."

"It's strong."

"It's not real."

"*Don't trust her*," it whispers.

I stare down at her, tempted to touch her face, kiss her lips, hold her. "It sounds real."

"Hearing voices isn't normal. A doctor will know what to do."

"I can't go to Shaw."

"Someone else then." She reaches for my arm.

"*See, she's tricking you.*"

I duck out of the way.

"Come here, Adam," she says.

"You'll bring me to Shaw."

"Just get in the car." Her tone is like warm caramel drizzled over vanilla ice cream.

Soothing.

Dangerous.

If I fall into Shaw's clutches again, there's no telling what will become of me.

Chapter Twenty-Six

Darby

I don't know what's happened. Maybe Stephanie is right—Adam's lost his mind. If I were smart, I'd make like her, get in the car, and take off, never looking back. Forget about Adam. Forget he has my brother's heart. Forget about my brother.

I look at Stephanie. She's given up watching us and is staring in the rearview mirror, reapplying some lip gloss. Guess her "caring" only goes so far. I can't blame her. She doesn't know Adam and she and I have just started, you know, being nice to one another.

Anywho ... more important is Adam. God, I can't leave him here, alone, freaked out. He'd probably end up dead or something.

I have at least get him to help. He deserves that much. He did it for me. Losing Daniel nearly destroyed me. Adam brought me back to life, just like Daniel's heart did for him.

Adam and I are linked together, for good or bad. Who was I to question Adam hearing me wail over Daniel's death and who was I to question finding Adam in the PT room? It was meant to be.

I can't change what happened to Daniel. On the flip side, I can't walk away from the person who has his heart.

"Did you hear me? Get in the car." I gesture to Stephanie's backseat.

Adam shifts his weight from one for to the other. "You'll take me to Shaw."

I rub my temple. He really needs to get over this. Okay, so Shaw bends the rules, but that doesn't mean she's jonesing to make him nuts. Even if the medicine she gave him is causing the voice, that doesn't mean she did it on purpose. She's a doctor, for god's sake. She's supposed to help people. "Alright, I won't take you to her, but have you told her what's going on?"

A mess of emotion rushes across his face—confusion, anger, and sadness. "Are you working with her?"

"I told you she's my therapist."

"That's not what I mean. Are you working with her to trick me?" His eyes dart like he's listening to that damn voice again.

"Of course not. Don't be stupid."

He flinches. Sweat slicks his forehead. He's paler than ever. He's definitely sick and not just in the head.

I have to stop messing this up. I raise my hands, palms facing him. "I'm sorry. Don't go. Okay, how about this? What if we go together to explain it to her? I bet she can fix this."

He clenches his fists. "You said you wouldn't take me to her!"

I stomp my foot. "Do you want to get rid of this voice or not?"

He toggles his lip ring. He tips his head.

"You know what? That voice is totally stupid. You shouldn't listen to it." I step to him, grab his hand, and lay it over my heart. "Look at me. Listen to me. I'm real."

His wounded hazel eyes search mine. "I want to trust you, I do."

"I'm here to help you. Come with me." I tuck a loose bit of hair behind his ear.

"I can't." He yanks his hand away and runs for it.

"Adam!" I tear after him.

Stephanie yells, "Darby!" behind me.

I wave an arm at her. "Stay here."

"Should I call 911?"

"No! Just wait until I get back."

"Be careful!"

Adam's legs are way longer than mine. He's so far ahead, I can't catch him.

He darts into the street in front of a semi.

"Adam, watch out!" I scream and cover my face with my hands. The truck's horn blares. Squealing of tires scrape along blacktop. I'm thrown back in time to the night of the accident. I drop to my knees, caught in memories—blinding headlights, Daniel cursing, me yelling, bending metal, and the shattering of glass.

The angry screech of rubber against pavement stops. The idling truck engine takes over.

Sweet Jesus, I'm afraid to look.

Shivering, I peel my hands from my face to confront my worst fear—an Adam pancake.

He's running down the street, darting between cars.

Horns blare. Someone yells at him out the driver's side window.

"Oh, my god," I cry.

I launch to my feet and run after him. "Adam!"

He ducks down an alley of a cigar shop.

This is impossible.

I stop running and yank out my cell phone. My finger hovers over Stephanie's number. Maybe she left after I chased Adam. I wouldn't wait around, if I were in her place. She certainly wouldn't want to follow Adam in her car. I scroll to Shaw's number. Adam doesn't want me to pull her into this, but she's the one who started it all in the first place. She needs to fix it. I press *call*. I feel like a traitor, but I don't know what else to do and Adam's hell bent on getting himself run over.

She picks up immediately. "This is Doctor Shaw."

"It's Darby. Adam, he's completely insane."

"Adam. You're with him?"

"Sort of."

She sighs, almost like she's been expecting something awful to happen. "What's he doing?"

I give her a quick rundown.

"Where are you?"

I tell her. "But he keeps moving."

"Try to keep him in your sight, but don't chase him. He'll keep running. If he stops and talking to him pushes him away, don't say anything, just listen. If talking calms him, then keep talking. I'm on my way."

"What about nine-one—" The line goes dead.

"That's helpful." I could call 911 myself, but Shaw didn't mention it. She would've told me to do that if she thought that was the best idea, so I grip my phone in my hand and run after him. Again.

It doesn't take long for a giant Charlie horse to knot in my side. I huff, breathless.

Adam slows, then trips, collapsing to the ground.

My heart jumps into my throat. I dive after him. "Adam, are you alright?"

He rolls onto his back. "My heart … I can't breathe … Darby, help."

His cheeks are red. Sweat covers his skin, slicks his hair. It's soaked his shirt. He's panting and shaking.

"Darby, I don't want to die." His eyes go dark.

I bring his hand to my lips and kiss it. "You won't."

"I'm glad you're with me." His eyes slip closed, stealing the unique palette of blues, greens, and golds I love so much.

"Stay with me." I lean over him, pressing my lips to his mouth. He doesn't push me away. Instead, he slowly loosens my hand from his to tangle his fingers in my hair. His mouth opens and I taste him with my tongue.

The kiss is sweet, gentle, urgent … and perfect.

When I pull back, his eyes are focused on me. A flicker of something shimmers in them. Maybe it's hope.

"You're going to be okay," I say.

"As long as I'm with you." He gives a quick smile.

My phone rings. I answer.

"Where are you?" Shaw asks.

I tell her.

"Be there in five." She ends the call again.

Damn, she doesn't waste time.

Adam lifts his head. "Who was that?"

"Shaw."

He exhales. "I wish you hadn't done that."

"I didn't know what else to do."

"It's okay. I know I've gone mad and I've scared you. You don't deserve this."

"As long as you don't run away from me again."

"I couldn't if I wanted to." He laces his fingers with mine. "Darby, I want you to know something." His brow furrows as his gaze searches mine.

"What?"

He swallows. "I don't trust Shaw. I never have. But I do trust you."

I sniff, blinking back tears. "It's going to be okay."

He sighs and closes his eyes.

Five minutes later, Shaw pulls up as promised. Her white Mercedes is spotless, like the rest of her.

The driver's side door pops open. Shaw gets out, her dark hair pulled into a low ponytail. Her light green pea coat flaps around her knee-high boots.

"What happened?" she asks.

Adam squints at her. "The medicine," he says.

"Shhh." She places two fingers on the inside of his wrist and watches her watch. After a few seconds, she says, "You're tachycardic."

"Why do you want to kill me?" Adam swats her hand away.

Shaw gasps. "I don't, Adam. I'm trying to help you." She looks at me like she expects *me* to help *her.*

"You were running like a maniac. Of course your heart is fast," I say.

He groans. "It hurts."

"Oh god. We don't have much time." Shaw draws something out of her pocket. A needle.

I stiffen. "What's that?"

She levels me with her dark stare. "Help me get him on his side." She hooks one hand under Adam's shoulder and another beneath his knee. "Stay still, Adam."

I have to release Adam's hand to roll him.

"What're you doing?" Adam asks. His voice is shaky and high-pitched. He's totally freaked out.

Shaw tugs his waistband down and jabs the needle into his butt. "It's a sedative. It'll calm you down so your heart won't keep being overstressed. It'll buy us some time."

"Time for what?" I ask.

"For me to figure out what to do," she replies.

"I'll call 911."

Adam bucks and flails. "No! No hospital. Mum and Dad'll go bonkers."

Shaw throws her body over his. "Hold him down!"

I do as she says. It's like riding a bucking bronco, he's fighting so hard. Electric shocks travel down my arms. I won't be able to do this for long.

"Relax, Adam." Shaw talks to him with a calm voice. "We won't call an ambulance, okay? No hospitals, I promise."

He stops thrashing. "Please, please, please," he repeats.

"It's okay, Adam. Let the medicine work. You'll feel better, I promise." Shaw coos to him. "Darby, he's acting under the delusions. It's true, I have been challenging his suicidal thoughts. As a result, I think he's internalized it as me trying to kill him, but I'm not. Do you believe me?"

I want to, but his pain is so real. Then again, Shaw's a professional. She knows what she's doing. I can trust her. We're helping Adam. "I believe you."

"Good."

"No, Darby. Don't fall for her lies," Adam cries.

"Nothing bad is going to happen. I won't let it," I tell him. "What do you want me to do?" I ask Dr. Shaw.

Shaw stands. "Help me get him to my car."

Adam needs both of us to get him up. He limply drops into the Mercedes' backseat. His eyes are dulled by the sedative and his lids keep slipping shut. At least he's not panting anymore. He's stopped sweating.

Shaw buckles Adam in. "Hop in the front seat. We have some things to discuss on the way."

I'd rather sit in the back with Adam, but Shaw's right. And she has some explaining to do.

After we're both buckled in, I ask, "Where are we going?"

She grips the steering wheel for a moment. "My house."

"Shouldn't we go to the ER, even if he doesn't want to?"

"It will stress him more. Sometimes depression gets so severe it leads to psychosis. I've been trying to work with him, change his meds, but he's so resistant." She turns the engine on, keeping her focus on the road. "But he trusts you, so with your help, in a quiet, neutral place, I think we can break through to him."

The sun is so bright, we both squint.

"Like an intervention," I say.

A smile. "Yes."

I glance back at Adam as she pulls onto the road. "I didn't know medicine could make you crazy like this."

"I don't think it's the medicine. Adam's become so obsessive, he needed to blame me—and subsequently the meds—for why he's not well. Unfortunately, I've made mistakes with Adam. I thought we could work through them, but then he got too paranoid on me. I took risks, for sure, and none of them paid off. I feel terrible about it."

I rub my temple. Like him, she uses words I barely understand. "So the medicine won't work because he doesn't want it to?"

She speeds through a yellow light and turns onto the freeway. "The mind is a powerful thing. While the medicine works on receptors in the brain, it's more complicated than simple biochemistry. The patient has to believe the medicine will work too."

"Is the medicine hurting him? Because if it is, we have to go to the hospital."

"I'll admit he may be having side effects, but they're not life threatening." She glances at her rearview mirror, then to me before merging into traffic. The bridge looms ahead.

"How do you know?"

She glances at me. "I am a doctor, Darby."

"Yeah, but you said you made mistakes."

She bites her bottom lip. "Touché. But I swear it's not my intention to harm Adam. I'm trying to heal him."

"How did things get so twisted in his mind?"

"Depression is powerful. So are delusions. The sufferer believes them and ignores evidence to the contrary."

"So he can't see reality?"

"Exactly."

"How do we get him to?"

Another glance in the rearview. "Hopefully the

injection I gave him will decrease the intensity of his thoughts, then we'll talk things out when he wakes up."

"That'll really work?"

She nods. "It should."

"And if it doesn't?"

"Then we'll have to go to the hospital." She checks her blind spot and shifts lanes. "Sound fair to you?"

Poor Adam. He thinks Shaw's trying to hurt him but all she's done is try to help. "Yeah, it does actually."

"Good."

Five minutes later, she pulls up to a super modern house with tons of windows and tasteful landscaping. It's beyond nice.

She presses a button to open the garage door. "Ready?"

I unbuckle my seatbelt, taking slow breaths.

Adam will make it through this. He has to.

Otherwise, Daniel will die all over again.

I hesitate with my leg half out of the car. Is that the only reason I want Adam to get better, so I don't have to lose Daniel a second time?

Shaw's already at the backseat. "*Darby*. We'll have to carry him."

I crawl into the seat next to him. "I dunno if I can lift him."

She frowns. "Of course, your injury. Okay. I'll do it. Just get the door and help as much as you can."

I take the keys from her. "Alright."

"He'll get through this. We'll make it work." She rests a hand on my shoulder. She keeps repeating things will get better like saying it over and over will make it true.

"I know," I say, more confident than I feel.

Chapter Twenty-Seven

Adam

I shiver. Wherever I am is cold. My body is leaden and hollow all at once. At least I'm laying on a soft surface. The last thing I remember is Shaw jabbing me in the bottom with a needle and Shaw and Darby restraining me.

Darby, my only hope, the one person who could help me, has turned against me. Guess it was a fool's hope, thinking Darby could resist Shaw's power.

I open my heavy eyelids. The room is vacuous, pristine, and white. Floor lamps anchor the four corners, their soft glow smiling on the pale hardwoods. Windows surround the room's outside walls. Twilight hovers around the house. I must have been out for a while. Mum and Dad must be beside themselves. Oh, what have I gotten myself into?

The steady, confident click of heels makes my blood run cold. Shaw emerges from a dim hallway, carrying a tray with three glasses of water.

Darby follows in her wake, holding a bowl in her hands. Popcorn domes over the top. *Popcorn?*

Across the room, a TV sits above a fireplace. A movie plays on it, muted. Is this what they've been doing while I slept? Not exactly criminal behavior, but odd nonetheless.

Darby catches me watching her. Her eyes widen. A tentative smile plays at her lips. Hope. But hope for what? "Adam, you're awake."

She sets the bowl on the coffee table and kneels next to me where I lay on a couch. "How are you feeling?"

My throat is dry, thick. "Where are we?" I rasp.

"Shaw's house."

I try to sit up, then flop back down, taken over by swirls and dizziness. "No, we can't … "

"Easy, rest. It's safe here." Darby clamps a hand on my shoulder. "You said no hospital, right? Well, this is the only place we could think of."

"This is worse," I say, pinching the bridge of my nose. My head throbs in time with my pulse. "What the bloody hell did you do to me?"

Shaw sets her tray next to the popcorn. "You were in a full blown panic attack. The injection I gave you terminated it and hopefully it will ease the intensity of the delusions you're having. *And* your auditory hallucinations should resolve. Darby told me about them."

I stare at her, mute.

"I'm glad she called me. I never thought this would go so far. Darby saved your life." She sits in a chair next to me.

I find my voice. "N-never meant … *what?* This is all *because of you.*"

Darby bites her lip. "She didn't mean it."

I gape. "Are you serious? Of *course* she meant it. Why else would she prescribe medications that interfere with my *heart*, for god's sake?" My voice raises a couple octaves, stretching to the tops of Shaw's vaulted ceilings.

Shaw furrows her brow. "I should apologize to you. I broke your trust. I thought challenging you would break your obsessions and cure your depression. But it only made things worse. Then with the ziprasidone debacle … I should've seen the mess methylphenidate would make. Your mom begged me for something. I guess I had my own delusion—that it would jumpstart your recovery. I never thought it would make your symptoms worse, that's how much I believed it would work. Seems foolish now, that I've done all this to you. And I'm so sorry for every single worry, every single sleepless night, every single doubt you've had about me, about your parents' fears for you, about your treatment, and about your own mind."

Goosebumps erupt all over my skin. I shudder. She can't be admitting to what she's done. This must be for Darby's benefit. "Then why give me something that could upset my heart? And what about the grit in my coffee? And why'd you convince Mum and Dad I wanted to commit suicide?"

Shaw sucks in a deep breath. "The dose of ziprasidone was low enough to minimize any risk of that. I'd also cleared it with Doctor Jenkins. He had no concerns, so I had no concerns. As far as your parents being convinced you wanted to commit suicide, you did that on your own."

"I never wanted to commit suicide."

She blinks. Nope, she's not buying it. Surprisingly, she doesn't confront me about it.

"And the grit?"

Her forehead wrinkles. "In the coffee."

"Yeah, the coffees you brought me. They were all full of grit."

She squeezes her eyes shut briefly. "Oh, god. The coffee grounds. I had grit in my latte too. I asked the barista about it and he said their machine was on the fritz. And you thought … " She sighs. "You thought I was putting something in your drink."

"You were. What was it?"

"I swear, I wasn't doctoring your coffee." She crisscrosses her heart with a finger, all scout's honor style.

"You're lying," I say.

Darby huffs, frustrated with me. She's falling for Shaw's line of bull.

Shaw shakes her head. "I'm not lying."

I squint at her.

She raises her hands in surrender. "I know, I know. Sometimes I break the rules. Heart transplant work is so unique that it calls for it. There's such a fine line between life and death and people in your situation live in that line. Most transplant candidates would do anything for a second chance at life. You wouldn't believe some of the things people say—that they'd willingly kill someone for their heart, that they'll pay tens of thousands of dollars for a heart. They'll beg, lie, and steal. They'll sell their very souls. But you were different. You were the first to voice your reluctance to accept something that wasn't yours to take. I didn't know what to do with you at first. So I thought outside of the therapeutic box. Clearly, I went too far and it all folded into your irrational belief system. It's not your fault. Everything that happened was proof to you. Misguided, but I can see you'd get it confused. I am such a blockhead for missing the signs. I guess we—*I*—was so scared for you the focus turned to keeping you alive rather than confronting your delusions. A dangerous mistake. I'm just glad you're safe."

Her words are starting to sink in. She's looking me directly in the eye, speaking so earnestly. She's coming clean.

Is it really real?

Shaw goes on. "When I learned you and Darby met, I admit I panicked. It wasn't fair of me to try and keep you apart. I worried it would interfere with both of your treatments and healing. I was so totally wrong. Darby gave me the what for about it."

Darby nods.

I try to sit up again, but I'm little more than a ragdoll. Darby helps me prop myself against the couch's low back. Instead of staying on the floor, she smooshes herself next to me. I'm glad for it. I'm also glad she keeps her hand on my knee. It's warm, strong, and so very necessary at the moment.

"Listen to her, Adam. Give her a chance before you decide what to believe," she says.

"Why do you believe her?" I ask.

"I just do." Darby gestures to Shaw. "Maybe you should tell him what you told me, you know, about what happened when you were a kid."

Tears form in Shaw's eyes. She takes a drink of

water. Her hand shakes so badly that she spills some water on the tray when she sets the glass down. "This isn't easy. Guess I know what it's like to be on the patient's side now." She clears her throat. "I suppose it's best to simply say it. My mother died when I was young and her heart was donated. That's why I went into this work, hoping it would help me process the loss and give me some closure. And I thought it had. But I think your case has affected me so deeply that I've been compromised. I haven't thought clearly. And I've made too many mistakes because I've over identified with you. I just hope you can forgive me."

Darby bites her lip, but she stays silent.

Another shiver works its way down my spine. "I thought you were trying to make me mad."

A single tear rolls down her cheek. "That was never my intention. *Never*. I'm so very sorry to have put you through so much pain."

God, she's leaving me gutted. I press the heels of my palms to my eyes. Nothing's inside my mind except for Shaw's explanation. No voice hovers near my ear. It's gone. My pulse rings steady. The pounding that had me convinced Shaw's meds were killing me is no more. Shaw's not lying. But still …

I lower my hands. "I don't want any more of your meds."

She wipes her cheeks. "You don't have to take anything you don't want to. In fact, I think you should start working with a different psychiatrist."

"You need to tell my parents the truth. What you've done. That I'm not trying to kill myself."

She scoots to the edge of the chair. Her fingers grip her knees so tightly that her knuckles are white. "Of course. I'll tell them everything, with you present."

Darby leans forward. "But she wasn't trying to hurt you, Adam. She shouldn't have to say that."

I lace my fingers with hers. "You're right. I know." I look at Shaw. "I believe you. I'm angry with you, but I don't think you're trying to kill me anymore."

She sighs with relief. "Good. I've been so worried."

Shaw worried. Never thought I'd see the day. "I want to call Mum and Dad. They must be flipping out. I left home without telling them this morning."

Shaw picks at a fingernail. "I kind of already told them."

I raise an eyebrow.

"I figured they'd file a missing person's report the second they realized you'd left the house. They know you're here. They know we're working things out. Yes, they were … " she pauses, searching for the right term, "well, they were more than upset about you running away, but I've done a fair bit of work to smooth things over with them. They're not mad at you, Adam. I made sure of that."

Darby pats my hand. "It's true. I listened to the conversation on speaker phone." She snorts. "I thought they'd show up here anyway, even though they promised not to. They sounded that scared."

My stomach knots up. "I feel like an idiot."

Shaw tut-tuts. "It's not your fault. Delusions are strong." She stands. "And you're not out of the woods quite yet. The medicine I gave you helped decrease the symptoms for a little while, but they may wax and wane. You still need treatment."

I stare up at her. "When will this be over?"

"This is life, Adam. It isn't over until it's over."

"So what do I do?"

"You live it one day at a time like the rest of us." She extends a hand. "Can I bring you to the hospital now? We can call your mom and dad on the way. I'm sure they'd love to see you."

I frown. "I don't need to be admitted, do I?"

"No, but Doctor Jervis will want to see you and he can help recommend another clinician, if you don't want me to refer you to someone."

Darby stands. She's not much taller than me sitting, even at her full height. "What do you say?"

"Other than I feel like an idgit?" I accept Shaw's outstretched hand and get to my feet. "I say, let's go to the hospital. I have a lot to talk to Mum and Dad about. They've been waiting a long time for me to open up to them."

After Shaw calls Mum and Dr. Jervis, we head to the hospital. We're quiet in the car. Darby sits next to me in the backseat, her hand eclipsed in mine. It feels so good holding onto her I don't ever want to let go.

* * *

Unlike what Larry discovered in *The Razor's Edge*, life isn't about searching the ends of the earth for enlightenment. It isn't about checking things off a Live Life List to make your parents (or your psychiatrist) happy. It isn't about pondering, thinking, talking to the stars, or hesitating.

(It isn't about worrying if you're going to become a fictional monster in a horror gothic novel. Really, my imagination does have a tendency to run away from me. Looks like my new therapist and I will have a lot to work on.)

It's about facing the truth. It's about taking a chance on love, even if you're not sure that's what love is. I'm glad I'll be finding it out with Darby.

Mum's face is the first I see when we enter the hospital lobby. Her eyes apologize before she even says anything.

I stop her before she launches into a whole I'm-so-sorry-I-should've-listened-to-my-son speech. It's unnecessary. I don't stop her from fussing over me for the next couple of hours. She's earned it. Even Dad pulls me in for a hug so powerful I thought he'd crush my ribs.

I do, however, launch into my own series of apologies to Mum and Dad, all spoken with Dr. Shaw, Dr. Jervis, and Darby present. In the end, we've aired everything out. Shaw described her role. I cringed at the idea of lapsing into insanity. Mum shed tears. Dad shook his head a lot. But the truth came out. No more secrets divide us.

And no one—including myself—thinks I'm suicidal. Because I'm not.

Dad has to break things up when Shaw and Jervis leave. "Come on, Lisa. Let's give the kids some privacy for a few minutes. I'll buy you some tea." He hooks an arm around Mum's waist.

Mum stares at me until the last possible moment as if breaking eye contact will make me disappear. She says, "I love you."

Darby smiles sweetly at them, then rolls her eyes when they're out of sight. "Overprotective much?"

I laugh, then wince. "Guess they have a reason to be."

"I put them through the ringer."

"Yep."

"I did the same to you."

Darby's brow furrows. "Tell me about it."

I reach out to her. "Thank you."

She hesitates. "I'm so sorry. For ignoring you."

"It's okay. I'm sorry for scaring you."

She crosses her arms. "You don't have anything to apologize for. I was the one wigging out about you having Daniel's heart. It wasn't fair to you."

I lower my hand. "If it's any consolation. I was 'wigged out' too."

The corner of her mouth ticks up. "That's true."

"I have something to say."

She groans. "Don't tell me you've been thinking again."

I kiss her hand. "I hope you know I understand how precious life is. I want to respect your brother's gift. I want to live. But I need your help. Can you teach me?"

She stares at our entwined hands, then her gaze darts to mine. Her crystal eyes steal my breath away. "I do a lot of stupid things."

I scrunch down a bit so we're eye to eye. "That's part of life."

"I'll teach you how to live if you teach me how to think. I'm sure my parents will appreciate it. They may even be willing to pay you money for it." She shrugs a shoulder. "Shaw and I talked to Mom and Dad while you were resting, but we all still have a lot of work to do."

"It'll take time," I say.

"Yep."

I toggle my lip ring. "I have an idea right now."

She smiles. "Yeah?"

I press my forehead to hers. "Yeah."

She nuzzles me. "I think I know what you're thinking."

I trace my thumb along her jaw and across her bottom lip. "We can teach each other, then."

"Okay."

I kiss her, hard and deep until my breath leaves me, until my thoughts float away, and until all that's left is Darby and life.

ACKNOWLEDGEMENTS

It takes a lot of people to write a book and I struggle with acknowledgements because I fear I will forget to mention someone!

Here are the highlights of folks who helped me bring this book to life, whether they helped me keep plugging along early in my journey or they helped directly with making Adam and Darby's story shine.

First, I must thank my number one champion, Ronald Watson. Ron, you've kept me going even through the strongest temptations to quit. You helped ground me when I catastrophized. You always make me feel better about myself and my writing. And you always make me laugh. Thank you for your undying support; I really need it! PS: It's your turn now—get on it, manager! ;)

Momma, you're my *ultra* number one champion. You've always believed in me from day one. I know it's your job, but I also know it's genuine. So, THANK YOU for being the BEST MOM EVER. * hugs *

Thanks to Brenda Drake and #PitchWars. Without this, Adam and Darby would never have met the world. And thank you, Cole Gibsen, for taking me on as a mentee. I still feel SO blessed that you chose my book. WOOT! I learned a lot from you, lady.

I have long time friends/supports—too many to mention, really—but the folks who've stayed with me along the way since the beginning of my writing days include: Mary Lindsey, Lydia Kang, Sarah Fine, Jennifer

Armentrout, Vicki Tremper, Amie Borst, Karen Bynum, Brinda Berry, Theresa McClinton, Lisa Amowitz, Jennifer Nelson, and a whole bunch of others. (I'm sure I'll think of someone to add after this is published and I'll think myself a total heel for a long time …)

Here's a shout out for my work family. CIU, CIP, MCT, FS and Safety ROCKS! I'm a lucky gal to get to work with such talented, caring, devoted people. It really means a lot when you ask about my writing and when you show up to signings.

PS: High five Emily P. aka M. (or is it M aka P?)!!! #nerdsunite #youremindmeofthebabe

I'm extremely grateful for Georgia McBride who took a chance on Adam and Darby's story. I remember getting teary eyed on the phone when she explained just how much she "got" the characters. It's what every writer wants to hear. Thank you, Georgia.

Also thanks to the team at GMMG and Swoon Romance, for editing, proofreading, cover designing, etc.

Finally, thanks to my readers. This story is in your hands now. I hope you enjoy!

LAURA DIAMOND

Laura Diamond is a board certified psychiatrist currently specializing in emergency psychiatry. She is also an author of all things young adult—both contemporary and paranormal. An avid fan of sci-fi, fantasy, and anything magical, she thrives on quirk, her lucid dreams, and coffee. When she's not working or writing, she can be found sniffing books and drinking a latte at the bookstore or at home pondering renovations on her 225-year-old fixer-upper, all while obeying her feline overlords, of course.

OTHER SWOON ROMANCE TITLES YOU MIGHT LIKE

MY SENIOR YEAR OF AWESOME
EFFORTLESS WITH YOU
IN THE AFTER
RIVAL LOVE

Find more awesome teen romance books at http://www.myswoonromance.com/

Connect with Swoon Romance online:

Facebook: www.Facebook.com/swoonromance
Twitter: https://twitter.com/SwoonRomance
You Tube: https://www.youtube.com/swoonromance
Instagram: https://instagram.com/swoonromance/

MY
Senior Year
OF
AWESOME

JENNIFER DIGIOVANNI

EFFORTLESS *with* YOU

A NOVEL

LIZZY CHARLES

Swoon ROMANCE

IN
THE
AFTER

FIGHTING CHANCE
BOOK 1

elisa dane

Author of the DIAMOND GIRLS Series

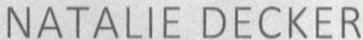

NATALIE DECKER

Rival Love

No Rules. Game On.

www.ingramcontent.com/pod-product-compliance
Lightning Source LLC
Chambersburg PA
CBHW021208250626
47155CB00008B/2723